Smart vs. Pretty

VALERIE FRANKEL

AVON BOOKS
An Imprint of HarperCollins*Publishers*

AVON BOOKS, INC.
An Imprint of HarperCollins*Publishers*
10 East 53rd Street
New York, New York 10022-5299

Copyright © 2000 by Valerie Frankel
Cover illustrations by Beth Adams
Inside back cover author photo by Michael Edwards
Interior design by Kellan Peck
Published by arrangement with the author
ISBN: 0-380-80542-1
www.harpercollins.com

Library of Congress Cataloging in Publication Data:

Frankel, Valerie.
  Smart vs. pretty / Valerie Frankel.
    p. cm.
  I. Title: Smart versus pretty. II. Title.
PS3556.R3358 S63 2000
813'.54—dc21   99-047068

First Avon Books Trade Paperback Printing: February 2000

AVON TRADEMARK REG. U.S. PAT. OFF. AND IN OTHER COUNTRIES, MARCA REGISTRADA, HECHO EN U.S.A.

Printed in the U.S.A.

03 04 05 06 RRD 10 9 8 7 6 5

○○○○○○

DEDICATED TO

Alison
Maggie and Lucy
Anna and Lily

ooooooo

Acknowledgments

Thanks go out to the following people: My editor, Carrie
Feron, and agent, Nancy Yost, were visionary and supportive over the many months we worked on the book. My
dad, Howard Frankel, the gentleman farmer of Vermont,
was invaluable as a reader and critic. My husband, Glenn,
schlepped the kids to Long Island on many weekends so I
could write—and he hardly complained at all.

Smart vs. Pretty

1

Ask any woman who has a sister: Are you the smart one or the pretty one? She'll have an answer. There may be fine distinctions, but eventually each sister knows well which role her parents assigned to her when she was too small to carve distinctions for herself. Of course, pretty implies not-smart—and vice versa—to a child. And some kids have a hard time swallowing compliments mixed with shortcomings. Especially the smart ones.

Sisters Amanda and Francesca Greenfield sat next to each other on bar stools inside their co-owned Brooklyn Heights café, sipping their drinks and staring at the busy city street. Which sister was pretty and which was smart would seem plainly obvious to any stranger, though both women shared a certain gray mood, despite the crisp mid-January brightness of New York.

"What about that one?" asked Amanda, pointing at a tall, thin man on the street, bundled tightly in a black coat and brown scarf. "No hat, advertising nonbaldness. Light-footed walk of a man without problems."

"Unless he's trying to disguise them," responded Francesca, known to everyone as Frank, her nickname since birth (not that the Greenfield parents wanted their oldest child to be a boy—a question that had been raised many times over the years). "His bounciness could be a cover for his disillusionment."

The man in question stumbled slightly as he walked past the coffee bar, his footing perhaps disturbed by the two women inside examining him like a moth on a pin.

Frank said, "Right there! Did you see that? Light-footed, my ass. He crumbles under scrutiny. A clear sign of something to hide." She paused to sip. "He's cheating on his wife."

Amanda shook her head slightly. "Unmarried. I can tell by the footwear. No woman would let her husband leave the house in those loafers. How he dresses is possibly the one thing you can change about a man."

"Look," Frank said, pointing at him openly now. "He's going into Moonburst." The man with bad shoes had to fight his way into Moonburst, the franchise coffee bar. It'd opened right next door to the sisters' café, Barney Greenfield's, two years ago. Frank swiveled on her bar stool away from the street to face inside her floundering place of business. Exposed brick, polished wood floors, ceiling molding. The street-level shop had once been the parlor floor of a Victorian brownstone. In its time as a coffee bar and before, the space had accommodated thousands of guests, the walls holding inside each brick the sounds of a hundred years of sitting and talking. That day only two customers were there. Just two. In the five seconds it took Frank to turn back around, ten customers had come and gone from Moonburst with a couple more waiting to enter. Frank sighed the dry exhale of radiator heat.

The younger sister, picking up on Frank's glumness, said, "Here's another one." She tilted her head out the window at another pedestrian. "Blond, small hands. Hard-set cast to his face shows determination, intense ambition. Red lips, passionate by nature, but reserved unless he's with a woman he truly loves."

"Can we stop?" asked Frank. "This game depresses me."

Neither sister was currently with a boyfriend or even casual fling. Hadn't been for a while. Frank's last boyfriend, Eric, the circulation manager at the magazine she used to work for, had left her abruptly after a three-year relationship, having woken up one beaming July morning with the sudden realization that Frank's "chronic mild discontentment" wouldn't be a healthy emotional environment for his future children. Frank suspected, after two years now of postrelationship hindsight, that any woman Eric dated would be left mildly discontented. Who wouldn't be with his dreary adherence to routine? Amanda, at the time, advised Frank that relationships between two people with similar characteristics tended to stall because they had nothing to learn from each other on their karmic quest.

Newly thirty-three, Frank saw her spinsterhood flung out before her like a worn black blanket. Amanda, twenty-nine, who'd never had a relationship that lasted longer than two months, couldn't understand her sister's preoccupation with the romance of loneliness. Amanda's remedy

refrain, "just go out and meet someone new," struck
Frank like a bitch slap, even though she knew her sister
meant no harm. Amanda never meant harm, though she
could dole it out unwittingly with ease—a veritable ven-
omous rose.

One of the customers, a cranky old woman the sisters
knew as Lucy, waved a liver-spotted hand in their direction. "Refill," she demanded. She'd had three cups already.
Frank hesitated. A couple of refills were expected. But a
bottomless pot—in their financial straits? The woman
pointed to a sign taped to the cash register. "That's what
the sign says," Lucy reminded them. Grudgingly, Frank
served the cup, placing it gently on the table, smiling a
plastic-fruit waxy grin. Lucy reached for her hot mug and
drank. Frank stepped back, watching her future flow down
the old lady's wrinkled throat.

From across the room, Amanda quivered slightly and
said, "I just got the strangest feeling, Frank. Like a wave
of negativity rolled all the way across the bar, from right
where you're standing to right here, by me." Amanda
curled her fingers over her curvy hip. "Whatever you've
done, apologize to Lucy," she said to Frank.

"I didn't do anything," protested Frank.

Amanda had long claimed she had unusually strong
intuitive powers. Frank dismissed Amanda's "cosmic sensitivity" as nothing more than finely honed observational
skills, which by themselves were impressive. Frank *did*
believe Amanda had other gifts, however. Long, wavy auburn hair. Flawless cream-and-petals skin. Grass green
eyes. Even a blind man could see that Amanda was gorgeous. Compared to that, Frank's smartness often felt like

birth's booby prize. The labeling hadn't been overt: Mom
had never once sat the girls down on her knee and said,
"Well, Frank, you're very clever and you learned letters
and numbers quickly, but you've got a flat face and stubby
feet. We'll call you 'the smart one.' As for you, Amanda,
your nose couldn't be teensier and your hair is a wonder,
but you show no interest in books. We'll call you 'the
pretty one.' " The message was more subtle than that:
Frank received praise for making As, and was punished
for Bs (though that happened rarely); Amanda got kudos
for her innate style and was criticized for gaining weight,
which she had a tendency to do (never a problem for
Frank).

Where Frank stood now, an adult who'd incorporated
her parents' appraisal into every decision she'd made for
thirty years, she knew that intelligence was more valuable.
For one thing, pretty was available to anyone who had the
time, energy, money, and will. And even without exercise,
makeup, and plastic surgery, Frank considered herself ser-
viceably attractive. She elicited grunts from workmen; bag-
gers at the supermarket, though, called her *ma'am*.

Amanda liked to use the suffix *-er*. She would tell
Frank that her hangup with pretty and smart wasn't con-
ducive to personal growth, that, perhaps, she, Amanda,
was pretti*er*, and that Frank might be smart*er*. But both
attractiveness and intelligence were culturally defined.
Who's to say that, in Tangiers, Amanda wouldn't be considered uglier and brainier than Frank? Whenever
Amanda presented her special brand of logic to her sister,
it made Frank's head hurt. Among other things, why
Tangiers?

Today Amanda was wearing a long, flowing peasant skirt (wholly inappropriate for the weather), a cashmere pullover, and thick-heeled black clogs. When she moved, the skirt dipped between her knees, making her legs seem even longer. She walked across the creaky planked floor to the cappuccino machine. It'd been dead for about a month. Amanda stroked its bronze casing as if her touch could ignite the fire of life. She said, "You know what would really cheer us up? Let's go shopping for a new one."

Frank couldn't help a tiny snicker. "Shopping?"

"What's with the snicker?"

"We don't have money to buy a cappuccino machine."

"Oh, let's just buy one of those cute little Krups ones. With the spout on the side."

"I don't think we can stave off ruin with a cappuccino machine that makes one beverage at a time," Frank said. "We can't afford a new café-caliber model. And we can't make much money without one." Not that having a working cappuccino machine would send the crowds at Moonburst back to Barney Greenfield's, where they belonged. Amanda and Frank had been minding the store since their parents' deaths almost a year ago. In less than fifty weeks, they'd minded it into the ground.

Amanda noted, "I'd say we're straddling the horns of a dilemma."

"You wish," Frank said.

Amanda laughed generously and twisted her hair into a knot at the top of her head in one fluttering motion.

"Unless something changes radically in the next, oh, ten minutes, this coffee bar is over," Frank said.

Amanda shook her head sadly, causing the soft auburn curls to tumble out of the topknot and tickle her cheeks. She kept her eyes on Frank while she rearranged her hair. "The tide can turn," she said.

"The tide can turn, but not the tidal wave," Frank said. "You know the kind of pessimist who digs deep and finds a reserve of optimism just when all seems lost?"

"And how you're not one of them?" Amanda responded.

"Exactly."

"Never heard of them." Amanda nibbled her manicure. "Okay, so I'm willing to admit that things have looked brighter. Yesterday things were brighter."

"It rained yesterday."

"I don't mean literally," she said.

Amanda hardly ever meant literally.

"Let's think about the good things in our lives," Amanda suggested. "Let's hang on to what we've got. Because . . . mystery lyric . . . we've got a lot." She sang, trying to cheer up her dour sister.

"We've got nothing," countered Frank.

"You're talking as if this is the end."

Frank sighed heavily. "This *is* the end." Frank knew a lot more about the family's finances than Amanda. For instance, Amanda was unaware (despite her powers) that Citibank was one mortgage payment away from foreclosing on the building. Since the sisters lived in the apartment above the store, a foreclosure would leave them homeless, too. Frank had heard rumblings that the manager at Moonburst was just dying to expand into Barney Greenfield's space. Frank could secure their apartment by renting the building's ground floor to her greatest enemy, probably at a screamingly outrageous price (plus the cost of their souls), but that'd be like spitting on the graves of her ancestors as well as admitting personal failure. Frank considered telling Amanda the true depth of their troubles. But why burden her with the horror, too? Frank thought it best to shield Amanda from reality, let her float along in the cushion of the cosmos.

"Just trust me," said Frank. "We're done."

The sisters stood together at the cookie case. The shop was filled with the gurgle of coffeepots. Amanda said, "I think we should hug."

She held out her arms to Frank and waved her in. The older sister, uncomfortable with nonsexual touching, felt something in her heart, some understanding that her little sister's compassion and love were sustaining and real, but Frank couldn't bring herself to get mushy. Instead of answering the call of Amanda's arms, Frank said, "I think we should consider our options."

"If you're rejecting my hug, you have to indulge me in a toss." Amanda jogged behind the cookie display case (Brooklyn's finest breadstuffs, delivered fresh three times a week) and opened the cash register. She removed six pennies from the till. Frank watched silently as Amanda shook the pennies in her hand like dice and tossed them onto the counter. The pennies spun and danced, eventually slowing and surrendering to gravity. Amanda arranged the pennies in a vertical row depending on where they fell. She studied the pattern of heads and tails. By doing so, Amanda believed she could see the future. The practice, known as the I Ching, had been a fixation of

Amanda's since . . . since the sisters stopped having regular conversations.

"I don't think your Chinese fortune-telling is going to drag paying customers in here," Frank said as her sister analyzed the toss.

"The idea is to see how our energy is flowing," explained Amanda. "Maybe we can get a clue about how to save ourselves." She examined the pennies carefully, gravely. "Sky over lake," she concluded. She reached for her handy I Ching translator under the bar. She dragged her finger along the laminated sheet until she found the right spot on the grid of sixty-four squares. She read, "Treading on the tiger's tail but the tiger does not bite." Amanda looked up at Frank with rods of hope shining from her eyes. She said, "Something's going to change, Frank. For the better."

Jingle. The door to the store jingled. The coproprietors turned to see a young woman—she couldn't have been more than twenty-three—in cigarette pants with a button- and eye-popping fitted black blazer. Her blond hair successfully achieved the high-maintenance, heavy-product, just-out-of-bed look. She walked straight up to the counter and asked for a tall, skinny cap, whip it (translation: a small cappuccino with skim milk and whipped cream). Knowing that a cappuccino wouldn't be possible, Amanda went behind the counter and, with a big smile, she pitched, "Nothing like a nice hot mug of good ol' Sumatran coffee, I always say."

Cigarette Pants frowned. "Cappuccino machine busted?"

"Actually, the whole store is busted," Amanda admitted. Cigarette Pants accepted brewed coffee and looked around the place. Besides the crone Lucy, the only other customer was reading a paperback romance novel while dipping her brownie. Lucy tapped frantically on the keyboard of her PowerBook, pausing momentarily to look around suspiciously from over the top of the monitor.

"The floor's sweet," said Cigarette Pants. "Venetian parquet. Giant storefront windows, antique panes. Steel counter—hygienic and aesthetic." The woman was sprinkling cinnamon powder on her Sumatran—something no connoisseur would ever do to a spicy Indonesian, thought Frank.

"Are you the owner?" asked the blonde. Frank nodded. The woman mirrored the nod and said, "You've got a really nice space here. But business doesn't look too good. You know anything about marketing? Public relations?"

Frank and Amanda had enough trouble with private relations. "We pass out fliers on the corner every day— dozens of them," Frank said, not sure why she was telling this woman anything about her business, but she was a real live customer, a break in the routine.

Frank was intrigued by the blonde. She'd never seen such self-assurance in a woman so young. Perhaps her confidence came from a strange place, a tiny world inhabited by a superior class of human—those with smarts and prettiness.

"Clarissa O'MacFlanahagan," the woman announced, her right hand stretched out, gold and jeweled rings on three of her fingers.

Frank shook. Her grasp was bony and dry, cool from

the January outside, but not cold. Frank worried that her own hand was clammy and distasteful. "Francesca Greenfield. This is my sister Amanda. We're co-owners."

"May I see your flier?" asked Clarissa. Amanda peeled a copy of the red page from the top of the stack behind the cookie counter. Frank picked out the color herself. She thought cherry was cheery.

"Gourmet coffees and cakes," Clarissa read. "Come for the hot coffee, stay for the warmth. Hmmm. It's sweet. But fliers . . . I don't know. They're soft sell. You need a pull."

Amanda asked, "What do you mean?"

Clarissa explained, "A pull is a marketing strategy. It's a tactic that yanks customers in to the store as if they had ropes around their waists."

"You mean belts?" Frank asked, wanting to sound wry.

"More like umbilical cords," responded Clarissa with a small smile. Frank couldn't help but smile back.

"How do we do it? What's a good pull?" asked Amanda.

Clarissa frowned. "It's kind of complicated; I'd have to explain the whole concept to you and then come up with a strategy."

"Can't you give us the Cliff's Notes version?" asked Amanda. It struck Frank that every aspect of Amanda's life read like the Cliff's Notes version—her relationships, her observations, the I Ching throwing. "Because, as you've noticed, we need help," said Amanda. "A lot of help. We can't do this by ourselves."

Clarissa looked around the café again. "I see potential.

I really do. But with school and . . ." She stopped suddenly and faced the sisters. "Actually, maybe I can do something for you. We may be able to help each other."

The sisters glanced at each other, Amanda's face full of hope, Frank's incredulous. "I'm not sure what we can do to help you," said Frank, certain that she had nothing this woman could use.

Clarissa took a long drink. "Great coffee," she said. To Frank, she continued, "I'm only credits away from completing business school—the Stern School of Business, NYU—major in marketing and public relations. I need a final project—a field thesis—to graduate with top honors. I'll save your business. No charge. And all you have to do is stand back and watch." She turned on the heel of her ankle boot and faced Amanda. "I can do it. I'm telling you. I feel it."

"Your confidence is catching, but I think you're a bit too late," said Frank. "The people have spoken, and they choose Moonburst. Quality isn't important. People want the chain-store brand. They want to dress in Banana Republic, have their living room outfitted by IKEA, brew their overroasted Moonburst coffee, and drink it out of a mug with a *People* magazine logo on it. Americans crave homogeneity. It relieves them from the mental work of having to make choices. By driving small businesses under, chain stores limit options. They're un-American, the very breeding grounds of evil. Except The Gap. I like The Gap."

That silenced the room. Even the coffee stopped gurgling. Amanda broke the quiet lull. "Please ignore everything Frank just said," Amanda pleaded. "We're not giving up and we'd love to hear your ideas."

Clarissa waited for a few beats. Finally Frank said, "Yes, of course. Please stay. I can't help myself sometimes. I tend to be defeatist."

"What next?" Amanda asked their new partner.

"We sit, drink and talk," she answered.

Frank said, "That's a real departure."

"Come on, Frank," admonished Amanda. "Give this ten minutes. We don't have anything to lose."

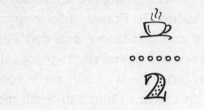

2

Amanda took one look at Clarissa and knew: she would be their savior. For starters, the blonde had the diamond-shaped face of a cat. Clarissa seemed to purr when she spoke. Amanda read once that cats served on Earth as conduits to the astral plane, that they connected people to forces from beyond this world and acted as guides. Of course, Clarissa was human. But her remarkable feline quality sent out waves of energy only Amanda (being sensitive) could properly appreciate.

Amanda asked Clarissa, "Have we met before?"

The cat woman said, "Not in this life." Perfect answer! Amanda turned a moony-eyed smile toward her sister. Frank had to feel it too—that Clarissa would change their lives forever.

Frank said to Clarissa, "It's obvious that you can build an outfit from the bottom up, but a business is far more complex. Even a small one."

Clarissa stretched her lustrous lips into a smile. She spoke, swiveling her head every several seconds to make eye contact with each sister in turn, playing into their vanities, holding both of their complete attention on the edge of her mascaraed lashes. To Frank: "I fully appreciate how hard it must be to run a business, and that's exactly what I need you for. I sense that you're the practical business brains in this enterprise. We can work together, shoulder to shoulder. You have so much to teach me, and I think I have a few ideas for you, too."

To Amanda: "And you're the heart, the furnace that keeps the café a warm, bright place. You're the shining face behind the register that makes it easy for people to hand over their money."

To Frank: "Of course, they're not handing over much money right now. That's going to change. First we have to get them inside those doors; then they'll know where to spend their coffee budget."

To Amanda: "It'll happen, if we believe in the spirit of reinvention. The soul of the place has to bloom."

To Frank: "We should start by coming up with a concrete plan."

To Amanda: "The first step of which is to reach out to the people. Who are you trying to reach? Who's your market?"

Amanda, watching Clarissa's head snap back and forth, was reminded of the time she went to the U.S. Open in Flushing, Queens.

Frank said, "Ideally, we'd like to reach coffee lovers. I spend so much time and energy pursuing the best beans in the world, I'd love to be surrounded by people who understand quality. Beyond that, I'd settle for just about anyone who can jingle a dollar in change in his pocket."

Amanda said, "Most of our customers are women who want a peaceful place to sit and meditate. It'd be lovely if they preferred our coffee to Moonburst's, but I'm not sure they have to."

"How could they not? Moonburst coffee is overroasted swill," said Frank.

"Coffee is coffee," said Clarissa.

Silence.

Amanda prayed Clarissa spoke out of ignorance rather than indifference. A coffee bean, however compact, was no small thing to a Greenfield. Coffee itself, the liquid finale of centuries of harvest and weather, was holy. Every family vacation they'd taken was to an equatorial coffee-producing country. Amanda's earliest childhood memory was of being chased by Frank through knotty coffee bushes in the sun-baked mountains of Guatemala. Her favorite childhood bedtime story was of Khaldi, the ancient Abyssinian goatherd, whose flock gorged itself on the red cherries of white-flowering hill trees. As legend had it, these fruit-stuffed, highly caffeinated goats got up on their hind legs and danced around the Arabian pasture. Soon after, every Arab goatherd who wanted a buzz was scarfing coffee cherries. The sisters never counted sheep; they counted dancing goats. Coffee ran through Greenfield veins. Frank was genius with it. She had the gift of a gourmet. Amanda was a well-educated gourmand.

"Coffee is coffee?" Frank blurted. Amanda felt her sister's restraint stretch like a rubber band. She waited, cringing, for the snap.

Clarissa said, "I want you to think of me as the typical consumer. I'm just like everyone else out there. Coffee is a caffeine-delivery system. If it tastes good, so much the better. I think Moonburst is great. It tastes better than Maxwell House. It blows Folgers out of the water. If you want to get more customers in here, you've got to cater to people like me. Quality doesn't mean all that much."

"Is that how you feel personally, or are we still in a marketing exercise?" Frank asked.

"For the sake of the exercise, yes, that is how I feel about coffee," said Clarissa. "Worshiping a beverage seems a bit precious to me."

"So why did you come in here in the first place?" asked Frank, both hurt and offended.

"The line was too long next door."

"We don't want to compete with Moonburst," Amanda said, trying to deflect the tension. "We just want to stay afloat."

"To stay afloat, you have to compete." Clarissa rose from her chair and began circling the table. Amanda noticed that her pants were expertly hemmed just below her ankle.

"You say most of your customers are women?" Clarissa asked, peeking over her shoulder at the two patrons. Strands of Clarissa's hair dragged across her lapels as she turned to look, leaving a few blond stragglers. Amanda held herself back from reaching out to pick them off her jacket. They weren't intimate enough for grooming gestures.

"Does that matter?" asked Frank.

Clarissa said, "Step one of any marketing plan is to identify your customer base. I'd do a poll but, no offense, it might not be statistically accurate, considering the size of our sample. So let's go with impressions. I'd say, from the look of things, your base is lonely, single women in Brooklyn Heights who have time to kill. They do it by drinking coffee, eating cakes, and conducting rich fantasy lives."

"You got all that from these two women?" Amanda asked, tilting her head at Lucy and the romance reader.

"Perception is everything in marketing," said Clarissa. "It's all about image, an idea. Once you figure out who you're selling to, and what they want, the next thing is to position your brand. All markets with homogeneous products—like coffee—have positions. For example, what do you think when you hear Ivory soap?"

"Coffee is not homogeneous," said Frank.

"Ivory soap is pure," Amanda said.

"Bounty?"

"Strong."

"Charmin?"

"Soft."

"Moonburst?"

"Poison." That was Frank.

Clarissa said, "Moonburst's position is quality. That they sell premium stuff—strong, serious coffee for adults. And, sorry to say, they've got the position locked."

"Sounds painful," Frank said. "Besides which, Moonburst isn't serious coffee. It's McCoffee. They uniformly burn their beans in giant factories with no regard to the quality of the individual crop, and then the beans sit in warehouses for God knows how long. They make such a big deal about using arabica beans. Every gourmet coffee bar in the world uses arabica beans. And their blends!

They'll wave a Hawaiian bean over a fifty-pound barrel of Colombian, and then call it a Kona blend! For Christ's sake, they permit hazelnut syrup!" Frank stopped to catch her breath.

"The McCoffee-drinking public doesn't know the difference. They just want their coffee strong, hot, and full of caffeine. Which Moonburst provides," said Clarissa.

"This is where any kind of education could be useful," Frank said. "The longer you roast a bean, the greater the reduction of caffeine. Moonburst coffee might taste strong, but it doesn't have the real kick of a milder arabica roast. In fact," Frank continued, "arabica beans don't have half the caffeine of robusta beans anyway. Supermarket blends like Maxwell House might taste like the shrubs they're grown on, but for pure caffeine, it's much better than Moonburst."

Clarissa nodded at Frank and said, "Okay. Good to know." To Amanda: "We still need a position."

"On top is good," said Amanda. "But it's been so long, I can hardly remember."

"Are you guys single?" Clarissa asked them.

"Not you," said Amanda.

"Can you believe?" said Clarissa.

Amanda was about to launch into a tirade about her sorry, single state (a sure way to insta-bond), but she could almost hear Frank blush with embarrassment. Frank hated to talk about dating, always waving off the subject by saying, "Not my area." For no reason Amanda could understand, Frank was incredibly sensitive about her desirability. An unfounded insecurity: Frank was completely adorable, always impossibly thin with dark, thick

hair as straight as a pin. Amanda couldn't remember
Frank ever breaking out or needing a facial. The younger
sister tried to send Frank a message telepathically—*Relax*.
Frank wouldn't fear harsh judgment if she weren't so
harsh and judgmental about herself.

"Am I interrupting something?" Clarissa asked, watching the two sisters lock eyes and then break apart nervously. "Am I prying?" she asked Amanda.

"Not at all. Frank's just a little jumpy about men,"
Amanda said. Frank looked a bit angry to be exposed, but
the chatty younger sister refused to feel guilt, saying, "We
need to talk about our fears, open them up, and air them
out. Don't you agree, Clarissa?"

"Of course," she said. "Free expression is the key to
happiness." Amanda wondered if Clarissa were even more
intuitive than herself. "If our position is also quality, we
need a gimmick," Clarissa said. "A reason besides the coffee to get business." She mused, "What do women want?"

"Long- or short-term?" asked Frank.

"We're not talking about an investment strategy,"
said Clarissa.

"We're not?" asked Amanda, making Clarissa laugh a
ringing, echoing sound, as if the blonde's insides were hollow. Amanda ventured, "Women want to be happy. Love,
security, passion, freedom. Spiritual enlightenment. To let
go of fears like death, disease, and poverty."

"Now you're talking."

"That's all she's doing," said Frank. "And this is the
last place someone should come to if they want to stop
thinking about poverty."

"I was intrigued by the love part," Clarissa said. She

pinched her cheeks rosy, deep in thought—so deep that Amanda wondered if Clarissa'd accidentally slipped into meditation mode. "A contest!" she shouted suddenly. "Most of your customers are women, right? And"—Clarissa leaned forward and whispered—"if they're as plain as these two, we can turn this dump into a gold mine."

All Amanda heard was the word *dump*. The brick might be crumbling, the gum under the tables might be thirty years old, nearly all the mugs were cracked, but it was not a dump. Barney Greenfield's was her heritage. Amanda felt anger rising in her throat, but she relaxed her muscles, did a few deep-breathing reps, and pictured waves breaking on the shore. At all costs Amanda avoided negative, soul-eradicating feelings. She calmed herself and waited for Frank to reclaim the family pride.

Frank said, "Gold mine, huh? Go on." Amanda turned toward her sister, stunned.

"Contests are one example of pull marketing," said Clarissa. "And the best part is, they don't cost much right out of pocket."

Frank said, "But I don't see how you get from *love* to *contest*. A contest offering the prize of love? That would be a 'pull,' all right. A pull of their legs."

"Just listen," said Clarissa. "What do women want? Men. To get more women, we have to get men in here. But not just any men. Superattractive, hair-on-head, washboard abs, tall, athletic men. If we can guarantee women that the café will be stocked with a constant supply of hot, young, *available* guys, the women will swarm in droves. And to get the men," Clarissa continued, "we need to offer them something *they* want."

"Sex!" Amanda said. That men wanted sex, she was certain.

Clarissa nodded. "Kind of illegal. Besides, the men we're after have plenty of access to sex already."

Frank said, "In my albeit limited experience, I've found that men love a woman's seeming disinterest, football, their 'space,' the Three Stooges, Laurel and Hardy, long, loud guitar solos, burping and farting at will, falling asleep with the TV on, their mothers, working on the weekends, complaining about working on the weekends, sex with more than one woman at a time and then lying about it."

Amanda said, "Men want mystery and intrigue. They want to be seduced with danger and the promise of something new and exciting. Then they want you to go out with them wearing short skirts and no underwear."

Clarissa said, "I was thinking more along the lines of complimentary coffee, combining two great male loves: hot beverages and anything that's free."

"Men also love to show off for each other," Amanda added. "So if a guy brings in a friend, he should get a free muffin as a bonus."

"I love that!" Clarissa said. "Brilliant!"

Amanda soaked up praise: "It's just a little something I thought up."

"Let's go all the way with it," Clarissa said. "Let's give the friend free coffee, too. Ten friends. The more guys, the better. To get it going, we'll pass out fliers—new fliers. We'll get an ad in the newspaper to solicit applicants."

"Applicants for what?" Frank asked, bewildered.

Clarissa explained, "We'll hold a contest to award one

handsome man each week with free coffee for himself and his equally hot and available friends. The applicants will have to have certain physical requirements. We can call the winner Mr. Barney Greenfield."

"Our grandfather?" asked Amanda.

"Hmm. Not very sexy. Mr. Coffee of the Week!" Clarissa declared. "While we're at it, we need to change the name of the place. Barney Greenfield's does not scream *sex*." Amanda had a sudden mental flash of her Grandfather having sex with Grandma, their bed rattling the tchotchkes on the night table.

"Barney Greenfield's has been the name of this shop for almost fifty years," said Frank.

Amanda said, "Change means growth."

Clarissa nodded encouragingly.

Frank leaned back defensively. "So you want it to scream *sex,* too?" she asked her sister. "Why do I feel ganged up against?"

"Let's just think of some possibilities before we decide against it," suggested Clarissa.

"The name has to scream sex?" asked Frank. "We might as well call the place Café au Lay."

"Or how about The Grind?" Amanda suggested.

"Maxwell Ho's?" Frank came back.

Amanda: "Javagina?

Frank: "Starfucks?"

The sisters tittered at their own cleverness. Clarissa laughed politely and held up her hand. "I was thinking the name should be more romantic. More poetic. Something that will lilt the customers into a feeling of misty, old-fashioned fantasy. How about Café Love?"

Amanda said, "Romancing the Bean?"

Everyone stopped talking. Romancing the Bean. Frank nodded amicably.

"That's it!" said Clarissa. "When you said that—Romancing the Bean—I got a chill. Have you even considered being a writer?"

"Frank's the writer," Amanda said, fanning away the idea like smoke, but loving the compliment. "What do you think, Frank? Romancing the Bean? Not too tawdry. Not too frilly."

Clarissa and Amanda watched Frank. She seemed to struggle with it at first. Frank wasn't—and probably would never be—a go-with-the-flow, adaptable type of person. Finally she said, "I like it."

Clarissa stood and said, "Does this mean I'm officially hired?"

Amanda nodded yes, but Frank said, "About your fee . . ."

Clarissa said, "I already told you I'll do it pro bono, with the understanding that I have complete control."

"I thought it'd be a team effort," said Frank. "You said 'shoulder to shoulder.' "

"Why don't we call it an informed collaboration?" Clarissa said.

"You can call it whatever you want," said Amanda. "I'm just so thrilled you're here!"

"Thrilled you're thrilled," Clarissa said, downing her Sumatran. "I've got to go. Class starts in a few. Don't worry about getting a new awning. I'll take care of it. You can repay me when business is booming—or should I say *brewing?*" She glanced at her watch. "In the meantime,

why don't you"— she pointed at Amanda—"write copy
for the fliers and the ad about the contest. We'll have to
convince the local paper to run the ad for free. And make
a poster to hang in the store window." Then Clarissa slung
her bag—Kate Spade—over her shoulder, and left without
a backward glance. Amanda almost called after her to ask
her phone number. She hadn't asked for theirs.

"She probably lives nearby. I guess she knows where
to find us," Frank said. "What was her last name?
O'McFlayertyO'Leary?"

Amanda couldn't remember either. But she was more
concerned with the tinny sound of discord still hanging in
the air. "You're not convinced," she said to her sister.

Frank said, "The contest seems pretty sensationalistic
and plebeian."

Amanda nodded. "I bet she's a Leo."

Frank said, "Javagina. That was a good one, Amanda."

"Maxwell Ho's—now that's inspired."

Frank absentmindedly wiped the table with a rag.
"Honestly—and spare me your rosy tint—do you think
this is worth a shot? Right now, we can go quietly into
that good night. Or do we go out with, potentially, the
greatest humiliation of our lives?"

"How can one fail if she's succeeded at trying her
best?" Amanda posed rhetorically.

"Fortune cookie?"

"Louise Hay."

"Hmmm." Frank said, "Let's throw some pennies."

Amanda was happy to, but surprised Frank suggested
it. Frank usually dismissed the I Ching. She grabbed the
six pennies she'd tossed before Clarissa came into their

lives. She cupped them gently and held out her hand. "You toss. If we see any yin come up, it has to be good."

"I always get yin," Frank said.

"You never get yin. You're confused. Yin is the tails side. Openness, flexibility. You're the queen of yang—rigidity, inflexibility. Most people have a healthy mix in their lives. You're all heads." Amanda tended to be all tails.

"Are you saying I'm unhealthy?" Frank asked.

"I'm saying you're unbalanced," said Amanda. "A coin with one side."

"Flat chested, but still top-heavy," said Frank.

"I never said flat chested," Amanda replied. "But now that you mention it . . ."

"Just give me the pennies." Frank took the coins and closed her eyes.

Amanda said, "Ask a question."

Frank said, "Will this be one more failure in a lifetime of bad calls? One more humiliation on top of all the others? Will this desperate act be redeeming—or mortifying?"

As Frank shook the coins in her cupped hands, Amanda chanted, "Breathe. In, out. See the waves on the beach. The rise and fall of the sun. The dark night, the bright morning. The moon. The stars."

"Will you shut up?" said Frank.

Amanda quietly stepped back. She breathed in, out, as Frank shook the pennies. The I Ching was Amanda's secret weapon, her way of testing her instincts or reinforcing her doubts. The practice sharpened her intuition, led her down one road or another. As a rule, Amanda didn't think it was possible to read the future—free will could trample on even the best psychic's predictions. But she did believe in a happy afterlife for good people. As the I Ching espoused, there was no death, only transformation of continuous and everlasting energy. Amanda kept these ideas to herself. She realized that most people would dismiss her worldview as flaky. Frank said her theories smacked of naïveté and wish fulfillment. Frank was certainly entitled to her opinion, however mildly discontented it might be.

Frank flipped the coins in her hands as if she were playing onesies in jacks. Then she flung them on the countertop. The coins rolled and spun and fell. Frank arranged them in a line. Amanda found her pocket I Ching chart. As usual, Frank's toss was nearly all heads, or yang. Only the coin at the bottom was tails. The trigrams—the top three and bottom three coins—read Sky over Tree. Amanda consulted her chart and then had to keep herself from gasping out loud. This configuration could be interpreted in dozens of ways, none of them good. Amanda's take: stable, solid trees will be disturbed by sweeping winds from any direction, and the skies will pummel the ground with storms.

Amanda struggled to flatten her forehead muscles. She didn't want to tell Frank the truth—her older sister didn't need any encouragement to be pessimistic. Amanda reminded herself that free will could override any toss. Frank stared at her sister expectantly, waiting for an explanation. Of the sixty-four possibilities, this configuration was one of the most ominous. Amanda smiled as bright as a bulb and lied to her sister, not wanting to burden her with the truth: "If this reading is any indication, we're going to be just fine."

Frank seemed satisfied with that, but she said, "It's bullshit anyway."

For the first time, Amanda hoped Frank was right.

REINVENTION CHECKLIST—ROMANCING THE BEAN

1. Menu (specials, sizes—Francesca)
2. Furniture (Claude)
3. Atmosphere (walls, fixtures, etc.—Claude and Mabel?)
4. Uniforms (all black—too slick or severe? I like.)
5. Help (preferably a sexy guy)
6. Contestant interviews (we do together)

The next afternoon, a Tuesday, Clarissa showed up with the plan. She spoke briefly to Amanda by the condiments stand (Frank thought it looked like whispery girl talk—were they excluding her?). Then Clarissa clickity-clicked in closed-toe heels over to Frank at the register, her smile growing as she got closer to the older sister. She handed Frank the Xeroxed sheet. "What about Amanda?" asked Frank while glancing at Clarissa's list. "Doesn't she get one?"

"She's composing the flier," said Clarissa.

Frank was annoyed that she hadn't been assigned to

the writing duties. "You know, Clarissa, I used to be on staff at a magazine. I wrote book reviews for a living."

"What magazine?" she asked.

"Bookmaker's Monthly."

"Gambling?"

"It's for the book-publishing industry, so I guess it is gambling, in a way."

"Really," said Clarissa, impressed. "Maybe I should have given the writing jobs to you, Francesca. But that stuff is really elementary. This"—she pointed at the Xerox of her schedule—"is a lot harder. I need your organizational skills desperately." The implication that she alone could handle the heavy lifting flattered Frank. Clarissa seemed to understand immediately each sister's true worth.

"Fixtures and furniture? It's all so superficial," Frank said.

"We're giving your store a facelift," Clarissa explained. "Not performing open-heart surgery. Everything else is fixed—rent, coffee prices, management. I could enlist an accounting major at school to go over your spread sheets. . . ."

"One step at a time," said Frank, hesitant (paranoid?) to show her Quicken files and bank records to a stranger. She held up her Xerox. "Where do I begin?" she asked.

"Start with the menu," Clarissa instructed. "We need daily specials, coffees of the day, cute names for the sizes. The names should make the customer feel like she's getting a bargain, like the tall, grande, supreme sizes at Moonburst."

"Something like big, bigger, biggest?" Frank suggested. Instantly self-doubting, she added, "Or not."

"Love. Write it down," Clarissa said. "Why don't you work on that while I take care of Claude."

Frank said, "Yes, I wanted to ask: Who is Claude and how much does he charge?"

"She."

"Claude's a woman?"

Clarissa said, "A friend from Stern. She's in the M.F.A. program. Fine Arts."

Frank knew what an MFA was. "Shall I assume, since she's a student, that her rates are reasonable?"

"Claude also needs a project for her program in interior design. She's working for free. We'll pay for materials."

Frank relaxed. "Is Mabel also working for free?"

"He is."

"He."

"Last name."

Frank nodded. "Another student?"

"Claude's boyfriend. A painter. He'll do the walls. Especially that one."

Clarissa pointed to the mural of a Brooklyn street scene that'd been on the exposed-brick east-facing wall of Barney Greenfield's since before Frank and Amanda were born. It'd been lovingly created by the best friend of Frank's grandfather, a blacklisted screenwriter who'd fled Hollywood in defeat. He returned to his native Brooklyn to start over. The mural looked like it'd been painted by a writer; the craftsmanship was poor, but the spirit of the work made up for it. Each detail—the orange cat in a boxed tree, the red flower on a woman's hat, the slick white splotches on the shiny black street—felt like a recalled, sweet memory. The mural was a homecoming, a clumsy work of heart. Frank, not much of an art lover, adored it.

"You can't paint over that wall," she said.

Clarissa sighed. She said, "To save the store, we have to make some wholesale changes, Francesca. You know that."

"Consider the mural retail."

Another sigh. Clarissa put her long, ringed fingers on Frank's shoulder. She said, "You really need that wall, don't you? It's holding you up in a way, isn't it?"

Frank felt vulnerable suddenly. "I wouldn't say that."

"It's a support for you. Load bearing."

"Not really," Frank said.

"That's good to know," said Clarissa. "Because if we don't completely change the atmosphere, you're sure to lose the store. That mural is too quaint. You know this. We have to get rid of it to breathe fresh air in here. Besides which, a new owner would paint it over anyway. Win or lose, the mural goes. So the question isn't whether or not to paint. It's what color."

Frank's resolve wilted. Clarissa was focused on the goal: solvency, ASAP. Frank admired Clarissa's determination. She would have to let go of any sentimentality and keep her own eyes fixed on saving her store, her legacy, her future. Her self-respect. Otherwise, for Frank, there wasn't much left to strive for. Finally, after a pause, she said, "Brown. Chocolate."

"I was thinking mauve," Clarissa said. "Lavender sconces."

"How much does a sconce go for these days?" asked Frank. "If it's more than thirty-nine cents, we can't swing it."

"I'll pay for them," said Clarissa. "I've got some money—dead aunt. You can pay me back when the shop is raking it in."

"Let's put a cap on my mounting debt," said Frank. "A few hundred dollars?"

Clarissa said, "I'll need at least three thousand for a respectable relaunch."

She might as well have said fifty thousand dollars. "What if we don't earn it back?" asked Frank.

"I will not fail."

Frank had read about this level of confidence, perhaps in a book she'd reviewed on some or other pathology. But Clarissa's faith was contagious. Everything about Clarissa made Frank believe. She said, "Mauve it is."

Barney Greenfield's was to close its doors during the renovations, scheduled to reopen as Romancing the Bean in three days' time. Clarissa wanted to hold the contest on Friday. The launch party/contest would publicize the new place. Clarissa was dead set on doing it Friday night. Only a few days away. Frank couldn't imagine doing so much in so little time, but if anyone could pull it off, Clarissa would. Frank dared to contemplate her future without wincing. Optimism was virgin ground for the older sister. Frank considered her positive outlook a major step toward her own reinvention; her fate, she knew, was linked inextricably to the café's.

Tuesday

Claude and Mabel showed up. Frank and Amanda introduced themselves to the couple. Mabel was the dark, strong, silent type. He bowed slightly to the sisters and immediately began unloading his brushes and tools. Frank held out a hand to the pigtailed, pudgy, twenty-fivish woman. She was dressed head to toe in purple (Amanda intoned, "aubergine").

"You must be Claudia," said Frank. The woman gave Frank's hand a crude pump.

"My name is Claude. Only my mother calls me Claudia. I hate my mother."

"Okay," said Frank. "I think I'll go work on the menu now."

Clarissa said, "Wait a second. Claude's come up with a few logo ideas."

The sisters perused the choices on Claude's colored printout. They picked a simple font of clean black letters, slanted to the right.

"Oblique," said Claude. "It's not slanted. It's oblique."

"It certainly is," said Clarissa, rubbing her M.F.A. friend on the back. Frank watched Clarissa's arm make the small, comforting circles with envy. She tried to guess how long it'd been since someone had touched her like that. Amanda frequently tried, but Frank couldn't accept affection from her sister. Amanda looked too much like Flo, their mother.

Amanda said, "Mom would like the logo. Don't you think, Frank?"

Wednesday

Amanda's fliers were everywhere: in storefront windows up and down Montague Street, in newspaper vending boxes, bulletin boards. Amanda crafted the text: "Who's got the hottest mug in Brooklyn? Find out at Romancing the Bean's first ever Mr. Coffee of the Week contest. We'll award the most handsome man in the neighborhood all the fresh, steamy coffee he can drink for an entire week. Friday at eight P.M. Help pick a winner. Contestants apply at Romancing the Bean, formerly Barney Greenfield's." Their address and phone number were printed at the bottom.

"Pithy," said Frank. "Does the job."

"Love!" said Clarissa. "Did you get the *Brooklyn Courier* guy to run the ad for free?"

Amanda grinned conspiratorially and said, "Of course."

"That's my girl," said Clarissa, giving the younger sister an impromptu hug. Frank watched the mushing of breast on breast and felt left out again. She'd been working, too.

"I placed the classified ad for a new hire," said Frank. "And I ordered new paper supplies. Extra Half and Half."

"That's great, Frank," said Clarissa. "It's all coming together."

The furniture arrived: bar stools and counters out; Formica tables and vinyl-covered chairs in.

"Vintage chic?" Frank asked Claude as she arranged the furniture. "Where'd you get this stuff?"

"It's all recycled," she said.

"You mean you pulled it off the street."

"And at rummage sales and flea markets," said Claude.

Frank picked at the torn vinyl on one mismatched chair. "Eclectic yet tattered?" she asked.

"Anything's better than those hackneyed bar stools," said Claude.

"Okay," said Frank. "I think I'll go work on those menus again."

Amanda and Clarissa were across the street at The Gap, buying black turtlenecks and boot-leg stretch pants. Amanda already had five of each in her wardrobe. When they got back with bags of clothes for Frank and their as-yet-unhired assistant, the older sister said, "No guy is going to wear flared pants."

"He'll wear these," said Amanda as she pulled out a new pair of straight-leg black jeans, thirty-two/thirty-six.

"What if that's not his size?" asked Frank.

"This is the ideal male size," said Amanda. "Any guy we hire has to fit the jeans."

The mural disappeared. Amanda cried gem-size tears. Frank's eyes, hands, and mouth were dry.

Thursday

Only one person responded to Frank's classified ad for an assistant. Name: Matt Schemerhorn. No permanent address.

"He's the one," announced Amanda.

"He's the only one," said Frank.

"No, I mean, he's come to us. It's his destiny and ours to work together. I can feel it."

"Convenience could be your middle name," said Frank.

"Clarissa thinks Matt Schemerhorn is our destiny, too."

"You and Clarissa are cozy," said Frank, surprised by the jealous tinge to her voice.

"She's pretty amazing, isn't she?" asked Amanda. "Truly amazing. It's like a fairy tale, her showing up. And we get to be Cinderellas, made over for the ball."

Frank said, "Why do I always feel like Drizella?"

Amanda said, "And that, right there, is your biggest problem."

Jingle. A guy ducked under the hanging paint tarp by the door and shuffled toward the sisters. He was skinny and wore scruffy jeans with holes and a too-tight black T-shirt with Timberland boots. His crew cut was so short, Frank wondered if he was shorn for lice.

Amanda said, "Matt Schemerhorn?"

"I'm early," he said.

"I have to ask why you have no permanent address." That was Frank. She noticed his small backpack—hardly enough room to carry a full wardrobe. "Are you a home-less person?" she asked.

"I have a home address," he said. "I just don't think it's important or necessary to share it with people I may or may not be working with. Do you give out your home address to strangers on the telephone? To, say, someone who takes your airplane reservation? I hope you don't. A lot of airlines and catalog companies employ prisoners to answer their phones and take orders. I don't know about you, but I don't want a murderer or rapist knowing where I live."

Frank blinked. "Do you have any references?"

"Aren't references subjective to the point of use- lessness? I could have worked as hard as anyone at my last job, but due to what's euphemistically known as a 'personality conflict' with the complete fascist asshole who ran the place—forgive me, but there's no other word for this man—my reference might be poor. You could call him and ask about me, ignorant of the depths of this man's assholeyness, and get the mistaken idea that I wouldn't do a good job for you. So no, I don't have any references."

Amanda tried, "Can you at least tell us what your last job was?"

"I was a barista at Moonburst. Midtown."

Frank asked, "How did you find that?"

He seemed puzzled. "I looked at the street signs."

"I meant, did you enjoy working there?"

Matt said, "I have complete contempt for the company and everything it stands for."

"Really?" Frank encouraged him to go on.

"Yeah," he said. "For one thing, they imported raw beans from all over the world, but they uniformly full-city roast, burning off the sugar and oil of each bean, killing its unique flavor. They turn everything from an Ethiopian Harrar to a Tanzanian peaberry into mud. Besides that, they pay shit."

Frank asked, "What were they paying you at Moonburst?"

"Six bucks an hour."

"Make it ten. And shower every morning before work."

"Message received," he said.

Frank added, "I don't ever want to hear the phrases 'grassy knoll' or 'book depository' exit your lips."

"Your loss," he said.

"What's your jean size?" That was Amanda.

"I have no idea."

Amanda walked behind him and folded down the waistband of his pants. "Thirty-two by thirty-six," she read off the label. "Congratulations, Matt Schemerhorn. You'll fit in perfectly."

4

Still Thursday

Pride swelled in Amanda's chakras. She had, after all, spent the last two days distributing fliers all over the neighborhood. She'd been Clarissa's "poster girl." Her efforts had obviously paid off. A couple dozen men had come to apply for the Mr. Coffee contest. The unspoken requirements—tall, athletic, under forty-five, hair on head but not on face, nice teeth, minimal intelligence—would mean instant elimination for at least half of the applicant pool.

Amanda sized up a few hopefuls. The contest was only a day away, and Clarissa wanted to decide on the five finalists in the next hour. They'd handed out numbers, pencils, and information cards and asked the men to wait their turn for an interview. Coffee and Danishes were on the house. The idea of interviewing and vetting twenty-odd men tweaked Amanda's senses. The aroma of romance, or the potential for it, commingled with Frank's new house blend and the tacky paint, making Amanda dizzy. How would she do it? Pick only five men from a crowd when she could find good qualities—physical, mental, emotional, and, certainly, financial—in any man?

Clarissa said, "As an owner, Amanda, you should avoid dating any of the contestants. These guys have to be available to the customers. It won't do if they follow you around all night."

"Business, not pleasure." For Amanda, there was no other business. "You and Frank are so committed to the cause," she said to Clarissa. Frank was . . . Amanda wasn't sure where Frank was. Doing something useful, no doubt.

"You're not?" Clarissa asked.

"I guess I don't have such clear-cut motivation," said Amanda. "Frank needs this place almost desperately, like it's her last surviving family member besides me. Actually, it is."

"Sorry again about your parents."

"I'm looking for my own family," Amanda went on. "I'm sure you think it's naive to believe in a soul mate. He could be here, right now. And maybe he's rich enough to pay off our debts. Then Frank could have her store. I could have my spiritual partner. Everyone would be happy."

Clarissa tallied the contestants. "Don't count on a man for anything, Amanda," she said. "I don't. Not that I'm cynical. I want love in my life. But I don't want to be disappointed, either. That's why I set realistic goals. I stick with the job in front of me."

"That's not cynical?" Amanda asked. "You're only twenty-four."

"I've lived in New York my entire life," she said. "So I'm older than that."

Amanda, also a lifetime resident of the five boroughs, laughed. She could learn a lot from Clarissa about one of her true failings: focus. She'd always been scattered, easily distracted, looking for the next love affair, job, or friendship. Amanda said, "Maybe I have ADD."

Clarissa said, "What are you talking about?"

"I really admire you, Clarissa."

"I like you, too."

"Is this a moment?" asked Amanda.

"Should we hug?" asked Clarissa.

Amanda was satisfied with the exchange of dopey grins. She felt excitement flutter in her chest. Would Clarissa—her equal in the attractiveness department—become a genuine friend? A female one, at that? The thought was almost as tantalizing as a new boyfriend. Speaking of which . . . "Number one!" Amanda called into the waiting crowd.

A man approached the two ladies as they sat behind one of the new Formica-topped tables. He was young—early twenties—with a goatee. Amanda whispered to Clarissa, "Long nose, sign of an honest and trusting nature. Curly hair, could be stubborn, but he'd back down without too much trouble."

Clarissa gave Amanda a fishy look. So not everyone appreciated her flash-appraisal game. Just do what Clarissa does, she told herself. Stick to the job at hand: scrutinizing contestants. Or potential soul mates. This is how lines get blurred, Amanda said to herself.

The man dropped his application card on the table and

introduced himself. He was cute, sweet. Amanda thought he'd make a cuddly little brother. After looking at his info, Clarissa said, "Pierrepont Street? That's a pretty ritzy block for a young guy like you."

"I still live with my parents," he said. "Mom thinks that in another year or two, I'll be ready to get a job and move out."

"Next!" said Clarissa.

Number two: "I'm just wondering if 'all the coffee you can drink' means you have to drink it here. Can I take some home with me? In a thermos? I've got a collection of thermoses. Five hundred of them from all over this great land of ours."

Number five: "I assume I don't have to do anything stupid like sing or dance for this contest. I'm not singing or dancing. No way. Because singing and dancing is for faggots. They can take their musical faggot shit and shove it up their asses."

Number nine: "The idea is to use me for chicks. I get it. I'm the whore and you're the pimp. Am I right? You're pimping me. Right? This whole thing is one big pimping operation. I'm right, aren't I? I can respect that. Where do I sign?"

After ninety minutes, sixteen men had been shown the door. Amanda asked, "Are we being too strict?"

Clarissa said, "If there are enough applicants, we might as well make it competitive. Number seventeen!"

Amanda's eyes rose to watch number seventeen slide up to the table. He was tall, with strong legs to carry him anywhere he'd want to go. He wore a heavy parka over a faded flannel shirt made soft by dozens of washes. His jeans were dark blue and stiff. Amanda found his green eyes glinty, twinkly. His lips were plump and red, a beacon on his diamond-shaped face. Amanda could hardly drag her gaze off those lips. She said, "Hello there."

He handed his info to Amanda and turned his lush lips into a pillow of smile. Transfixed, Amanda merely stared. Clarissa coughed politely and took the card out of Amanda's hand.

" 'Charles Peterson, nickname Chick. Environmental biology grad student at Columbia,' " she read. " 'World traveler, mountaineer, thirty-two years old.' Aren't you a bit old to be a grad student?"

"I took the summer after college to climb the three largest mountains in the Western Hemisphere," he said. "A monthlong summer trip turned into a decade. I'm only just back in America after a long stay in Jamaica." His voice was a bit high, an octave out of place, considering his height.

"No offense, but the contest is for straight guys only," Clarissa said.

"You think I'm gay?" he asked, turning a tomato hue. Amanda flinched, feeling his embarrassment.

Clarissa said, "If you're not gay, prove it."

Looking right at Amanda's button nose, he said, "If you weren't wearing that sweater, I'd be gone by now." He was referring to her baby pink mohair crewneck. It highlighted her rosy glow and auburn hair. When she wanted to be lethal, Amanda wore this sweater, the epitome of hyperfemininity made for women with large enough breasts and long enough hair. If she played her cards right, perhaps she'd be pulling off the sweater with

Chick Peterson later that night. *No, no,* she admonished herself. *Control, girl.*

He said, "When I go down on a woman, I never flick my tongue. The clitoris is very sensitive, especially right before orgasm—in fact, it pulls back into its hood as orgasm gets closer and closer. Long, flat tongue strokes, up and down, sometimes round and round, work well for me."

"Works well for me, too," said Amanda.

Clarissa said, "Be back here at seven o'clock tomorrow night. Congratulations, Charles. You're a finalist."

He left the store. Amanda wished his parka weren't long in back so she could have a peek at his ass. She instantly began fantasizing about when she'd see him again. What she'd say and wear. How he'd respond when she ran her finger up and down the length of his naked arm. The idea made her own arm hair stand on end.

"Earth to Amanda," Clarissa said, elbowing her in the ribs. "Remember what I said about not dating the contestants. Number eighteen!"

The next applicant was blandly handsome with a square jaw and shiny dark hair. The muttonchop sideburns saved him from being too conventional. He wore a suit and overcoat by Hugo Boss. Amanda touched it. "Cashmere," she said. A coat like that cost over two thousand dollars. "What's a natty guy like you doing at a coffee contest like this?" Amanda asked.

"This isn't the VH-1 Fashion Awards?" he asked. Clarissa chuckled. Amanda detected more than mirth in her response.

Clarissa read from his card, " 'Walter Robbins. Age: twenty-nine. Profession: Catalog model.' "

"Which catalogs?" asked Amanda.

"J.Crew mainly, but my agent is trying to get me into Eddie Bauer and L.L. Bean."

"You do look familiar."

"You've seen one guy in a nylon shell, you've seen them all."

"Seriously," said Amanda, "you don't seem like the daytime coffee bar type."

Walter Robbins flashed her a flawless grin. "I'm between jobs and, as a vain egotist, I'm in constant need of positive reinforcement."

"Can you wait over there for a second?" asked Amanda. She wanted a moment of privacy to confer with Clarissa. Once Walter was out of earshot, Amanda whispered, "He's a ringer."

Clarissa whispered back, "So what? The customers will love him."

"It's not fair to ask a quirky type like Chick Peterson to compete with a professional model."

"Amanda, they're not fighting to the death in a pit."

Clarissa motioned Walter back over. "Congratulations! You're a finalist. Be here tomorrow night at seven o'clock." He doffed an imaginary hat and left.

It took another hour to pick the last three contestants: an adorable twenty-four-year-old editorial assistant at a men's magazine; a forty-year-old, recently divorced construction worker who described his mental state as "very vulnerable right now"; and last, a nebbishy guy with a pointy chin and round glasses.

Amanda insisted the neb make the cut. It was an altruistic gesture, and payback for the man's politeness. Clarissa agreed, driven more by fatigue, Amanda thought, than bigheartedness.

In just over twenty-four hours, the coffee shop would reopen. The contest would begin. The place would be saved—or die. Either way, Amanda couldn't wait. She'd get to see Chick Peterson again.

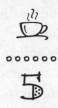

5

Frank watched the mass of customers from behind the
cash register on the big night. Four of the five Mr. Coffee
contestants were circulating through the crowd (the excep-
tion being the nebby guy, who hung in a corner, downing
mug after mug of French roast). Each guy was wearing a
Romancing the Bean T-shirt—designed and printed by
Claude as a parting gift. Frank had asked Clarissa repeatedly how much money had been spent during the renovations, but she never got a firm answer. This worried
Frank. Even the crush of paying customers in their re-
vamped space didn't completely calm her concerns. Optimism, apparently, was something to settle into slowly.

Amanda flitted by in her red scoop-necked dress,
shouting at Frank, "It's the best night in the history of
Romancing the Bean!" It was the only night in the history
of Romancing the Bean, but Frank didn't quibble. Amanda
was right—her parents had never seen such action in all
their years with Barney Greenfield's. Frank had personally
rung up orders for about thirty pounds of various varietals

for at least nine dollars per (wholesale prices were roughly
five dollars a pound, providing a profit of four dollars.
Depending on weather and availability, some beans were
much more expensive—Jamaica had a tiny, finicky crop,
so Blue Mountain cost as much as twenty-five dollars a
pound wholesale and up to forty dollars retail). But the
real profit was in individual mugs. The store made a profit
of $1.30 per $1.50 cup. Frank needed to sell four thousand
cups a month to cover overhead, or 133 cups of joe a day
(over the last year, the sisters averaged a dismal forty).
Frank had sold at least a hundred in the last hour. She'd
questioned whether a fresh coat of paint could increase
business by more than 300 percent. Now she had an
answer.

Frank tried to allow herself to enjoy (not quietly dis-
trust) the press of people crammed into the café (so
crammed that it was impossible for anyone to appreciate
the new tables and paint job). For once, she thought, she
was in the right place at the right time. The tinkle of
money on the counter was aural heroin. Frank took the
change with something close to a smile. The customers
seemed to enjoy her new house blend (a pinch of Guate-
malan, Costa Rican, and some Indonesian for kick).

Finally, at eight o'clock, Clarissa cleared a space in the
center of the room. Pockets of women at tables clapped
their hands. Frank wondered if they were applauding Clarissa's artful outfit—a lime green power suit emphasizing
her wasp waist with sheer tights and patent pumps—or
for the contest to begin.

Clarissa held a couple of index cards in one hand and
a Mr. Microphone (that's right) in the other. She an-

nounced, "Attention, ladies and gentlemen. On behalf of Romancing the Bean, I'd like to thank you for coming." The customers applauded demurely. "The rules of the contest are simple. One man will be crowned Mr. Coffee of the Week. He'll be awarded free drinks and muffins for himself and ten of his friends for the next seven days. Then, next Friday night, he'll turn over the crown to his successor."

At the counter, Frank—dressed in the all-black uniform of stretch pants and turtleneck—wondered how long this gimmick would work. She thought ahead a few weeks to the time when the Mr. Coffee contest was no longer novel. Then Moonburst would roll all over them again, like nothing had changed. Maybe she and Clarissa could put their heads together and come up with something else. They could brainstorm for ideas, like Frank used to do at the magazine. They could inspire each other to greater glory as a team. And maybe hit a movie together once in a while. Frank was snapped out of her reverie by a tap on her shoulder.

He wore a denim shirt tucked into green chinos with a brown leather belt. He was clean shaven, but his skin was chalky and blotchy, like that of most natural redheads. Signs of impending baldness were visible under his curly hair. He had a couple of extra pounds around the middle, but he dressed well to hide them. Like she cared. "Lonely tonight?" Frank asked the man.

"Hardly," he lied. The overcast gray of his eyes darkened.

"Poor Benji," she said. "For once I've got you beat. Ordinarily I'd be honorable about it, but not tonight. I'm going to be small and petty and gloat, gloat, gloat." She cocked her chin toward the crowd. "I've counted off at least two hundred heads." An exaggeration. "I'd watch my back if I were you. A chain store is only as strong as its weakest link." Benji Morton was the manager at Moonburst. When Amanda and Frank's parents had died last year, he sent flowers. Frank despised him.

He pursed his thin lips. "I'd mention something about a battle and a war, but I think that goes without saying. Mark my words, Francesca, in a couple of weeks, only one Montague Street coffee bar will remain standing or I'm a deluded asshole."

"I agree with everything you just said."

"I'm not going to be a small-business manager forever," he spit out. "I don't want to spend the rest of my life cleaning up coffee grinds and spilled milk. To be honest, I don't understand why you do. Why is this rivalry so personal for you? I'm not your enemy."

"Why are you here if you're not sizing up the competition?" she asked.

"I don't think of you that way," he said. "But I am sizing you up."

Was he flirting with her? A revolting thought. "By competition, I meant the contest."

"No, you didn't," he said. "But now that you mention it, I'd vote for the tall guy. He's a sure thing."

Frank hadn't realized that Clarissa was busy introducing the contestants and trotting them around the center of the room like ponies. Benji snickered behind her. Frank suddenly felt foolish, as though the whole contest idea was pathetic. She blamed Benji for blowing her mood.

Clarissa arranged the men in line. She said, "Okay, now that you've had a good look at all five contestants, it's time to vote for a winner." She held her Mr. Microphone over the head of the editorial assistant. The crowd applauded weakly. Too young. Next she held her hand over the construction worker. A more enthusiastic response. She moved to the tall, outdoorsy guy. Thunder. The model: tepid, despite encouragement from Clarissa— he was too polished. The neb registered nary a ripple of applause. So much for the drama of the voting process.

Clarissa waved for Amanda to give Charles "Chick" Peterson the scepter they'd made out of tinfoil. As she crowned him (headpiece also made of foil), Amanda stared into Chick's eyes. He stared right back. They took hands. Frank knew Amanda wouldn't be able to leave the contestants alone. In a mountain cave in the middle of the night, Amanda could zero in on the best-looking man in the room.

Frank turned around to invite Benji to leave, but he was already making his way out the door. Frank redirected her attention to the thirsty customers—there was a fresh demand for coffee. Amanda pushed her way over to the counter to help. The tinkle of coins in the register now sounded hollow to Frank. What was she doing with her life? Was clawing and scraping for her dead parents' business what she really wanted? At thirty-three, shouldn't she have her own plans and dreams? Shouldn't she be worried that she hadn't had sex since she and Eric broke up over two years ago?

Amanda said, "Is something wrong?"

Frank said, "What could be wrong?"

"The aura around you is positively black," Amanda observed. "What's wrong? You look deflated."

"Just count," Frank said, passing her a fistful of quarters.

Amanda insisted, "Tell me what's upsetting you."

Frank looked at her sister. Amanda was so pink and fresh and unlined. Frank knew her sister cared more than anyone else on earth. But she could never understand Frank's kind of loneliness, what it was like to feel misunderstood by every person in sight, even her own sister, despite trying, really trying, to connect—a condition that hadn't changed much for Frank since adolescence. Clarissa barely tolerated Frank compared to chummy Amanda. Who wouldn't? Amanda looked beautiful in that dress, her curly hair bouncing on her soft, white shoulders.

"How come you get to wear red?" asked Frank. "What about the uniform?"

"I figured for the launch, I'd dress for a party."

Frank raked her coarse black bangs off her forehead. "I have to go to the bathroom," she said. "Take over."

Frank pushed past Amanda, through the crowd, and out the door to the street. Sucking in the cold air, she felt somewhat better. A teenage girl walked by with a cigarette. Frank bummed one from her and sat on the bench in front of the shop, smoking, thinking, and shivering. She let her eyes wander toward the quiet Moonburst and imagined it blowing up in a fireball, chunks of glass and metal exploding into the air, Benji Morton's severed limbs raining down on the sidewalk. She took one last drag and put out the cigarette under her black boot.

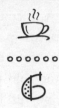

Chick's aura was purple. Whenever Amanda stood near him, she saw indigo flashes in her eyes. He made her feel small and helpless, intensely female. He smiled easily, sweetly, and naturally. When she placed the crown on his head, she felt his breath on her forehead. She couldn't stop staring at him, hoping he'd hit on her, sending him the telepathic message that she wouldn't say no. She took him for a risk taker, an adventurer, a selfless lover. And mountain climbers had such amazing thighs.

Amanda waited patiently for Chick to make his move. That was her style since college. She had a long list of one-night stands (along with awkward mornings after) to show for her juvenile rushings into bed. Since then, Amanda discovered she had more second and third dates by slowing down the seduction, luring men inch by inch into her soft, gooey center. The longer she waited, the deeper the men sank into her like quicksand. It wasn't a manipulation, nor was seduction a game to her. It was an art. She was determined to stick to her usual pace, no

matter how tempting it would have been to go up to Chick
and whisper nasty nothings in his ear.

Besides which, the wait could be exquisitely tense.
Amanda could taste her anticipation as she posed with
Chick, Frank, and Clarissa for the *Brooklyn Courier,* the
local paper. Chick did some solo poses drinking RTB coffee, displaying their logo on his (Amanda imagined hair-
less) chest. When the photographer finished, it was after
11:00 P.M. The crowd had thinned and everyone decided
it was time to close up. Clarissa wanted to go out and
celebrate. Frank wanted to stay in and count the money.
Amanda hoped Chick would invite her to a private party
in his pants.

She decided it wouldn't violate her code if she made
herself visible to him. So Amanda walked across the coffee
bar to where Chick was talking with Matt, the new hire.
She observed them from a comfortable distance of ten feet.
"Don't you get it, man?" Matt asked Chick. "If you don't
hop on the hamster wheel and run in tiny circles like the
rest of this fucking country, they're going to have to shoot
you or lock you up for being different. That's what they
do to artists in America. I like to make public art. Graffiti.
I could get thrown in jail for that."

Chick said, "Because you're defacing someone else's
property." Amanda loved his voice; it was neither brut-
ishly deep nor distractingly throaty. His words floated into
her ears.

"And why is it their property?" Matt asked Chick.
"Because they made a lot of money on the backs of the
black man and then signed a piece of paper saying, 'This

is mine'? That makes an entire building someone's personal property?"

"Possession is nine-tenths of the law," he said. Chick looked over the top of Matt's head and noticed Amanda.

Matt grabbed his arm. "That's bullshit, man. You've been to the mountaintop. I don't believe you go along with this ownership crap."

While she had his eye, Amanda raised a mug of coffee to her lips and gave him the vampish-innocent-takes-a-sip look. Then she shot him look number two: lower mug and offer the reluctant-yet-hopeful fluttering of the eyelids with an almost imperceptible brow furrow. Only to advance to look number three: the flicker of indecision (glance upward) followed by full-frontal eye contact. Hold for one, two, three, four. Then smile with just lips and look quickly to the left, as if she'd embarrassed herself with the very brazenness of her thoughts. A pretty blush punctuated the point, if she could manage it.

Chick responded predictably and ditched Matt. She kept up the full-frontal eye contact until he stood inches from her mug. To his back, Matt flipped Chick the bird.

She said, "Congratulations. You'll make an excellent Mr. Coffee. You have to remember to come often."

He said, "Go out with me. Tonight."

"Where are we going?" she asked.

"I guess it's too late for dinner."

It wasn't *that* late. She said, "I could eat. Are you hungry? And, more important, are you paying?"

He laughed and took her hand, which she thought was trampling slightly on their delicate flirtation. But she forgave him. She had a forgiving nature. "Heights Cafe?"

he asked. The bar/restaurant was a block away. It was called *cafe* (they'd forgotten the accent on the *e*), but their coffee was mediocre at best.

"I need to freshen up," Amanda said. "I'll meet you there in twenty minutes." She didn't intend to be there in less than an hour. She had too much to do: change clothes, reapply makeup, fluff hair, dab fragrance, and accessorize. Amanda knew that the pursuit of physical beauty chipped away at ideals of the soul. But a girl had to do what a girl had to do. Pretty could only help. She'd incorporated this belief into her system long before she'd ever tapped into her cosmic sensitivity. Since toddlerhood, Amanda knew the power of pretty. If she smiled and cocked her head just so, she always got more cookies from Daddy.

Amanda blew Chick a kiss as he headed outside, all bundled up in his parka. Amanda loved the sight of a man wrapped up like a present. Winter was the handsomest season.

"Where's he going?" asked Clarissa as the door jingled shut behind him.

"I don't know," Amanda said.

"Amanda, we talked about this. The contest isn't supposed to be your personal dating service."

Amanda nodded. "I could say the same thing to you, Clarissa. You think I didn't notice the way you and Walter Robbins were talking?"

Clarissa blinked. "I wasn't—"

"You were, too."

"It wasn't—"

"It was far from innocent," Amanda said. "He seems to really like you, too. Lots of forward leaning, arms relaxed at his sides, bent knee, sign of familiarity. And, of course, the triangle."

"The triangle?" Clarissa asked.

"When the path of his eyes makes a triangle on your face. Like this." Amanda demonstrated by looking at Clarissa's left eye, then her right eye, then her lips, and back to her left eye. "It's a triangular loop, you could say. A clear indication of interest, no less meaningful than if he'd licked his lips and drooled."

Clarissa said, "That's good to know." She sneaked a peek across the room, where Walter was talking to a customer. "Let's keep this a secret, okay? It might hurt Francesca's feelings if she knew we both hooked up."

Amanda hated deceiving her sister, but she had a new best friend's feelings to consider. "Good idea," Amanda said to Clarissa. "I love having secrets. It's like we're on a covert mission together."

"We're breaking our own rule," said Clarissa.

"How wanton," Amanda said, putting her arm around Clarissa's shoulders. The red in Amanda's dress clashed horribly with Clarissa's lime green jacket. "And when we go on our first double date, maybe we should talk beforehand about what to wear," she said. The idea made Amanda think of junior high. Secret pacts, color coordination, when friendships were the entire world.

"Maybe we can try on each other's clothes," Clarissa said.

"I could never fit into your clothes," said Amanda.

"Please."

"You know you're a pencil," said Amanda. Now she really felt thirteen. "I've got to go. I'm meeting Chick for dinner. Call you tomorrow? Maybe we can go shopping or something."

The two women parted. Clarissa went right over to Walter, and then they left together. Amanda liked Walter. He was a gracious loser. Matt stuck around to clean up. Frank would be hours counting the night's take of quarters and singles.

Amanda went outside and unlocked the street-side door to the apartment above the store. When their parents died and the sisters took over the business, Frank and Amanda gave up their Manhattan rentals. For Amanda, coming home had been nurturing and comfortable. Frank felt stifled by the closeness of all her mildly discontented memories. Despite Frank's lingering resentment for their parents' many failings (dying young among them), the older sister was adamant about staking out their old bedroom for her own (she got rid of their furniture and moved in her stuff). Frank said she wanted the room because it was the biggest in the apartment, and it had an attached bathroom. But Amanda theorized that, because Frank refused to talk about them now, insisting on living in their old room was her subconscious way of keeping Mom and Dad close.

Big closets. That was what Amanda's childhood bedroom had in abundance, and she'd been happy to reclaim them. She began to prepare for her date. Every girl should have preplanned ready-in-a-flash outfits that take into account three factors: season, situation, and intent. For example, the perfect all-season first-date outfit was black velvet jeans, a cashmere/angora/mohair twin set, Hush Puppies, diamond studs, a charm bracelet, and (for the long-haired) a velvet scrunchy. The current date climate called for a slightly higher-maintenance winter seduction ensemble. Ergo, Amanda wore a red ribbed turtleneck, black knee-length skirt, black tights, vinyl high-heeled ankle boots, silver hoop earrings, and hair down and curly (humidity was permitting).

Once dressed, she sprayed, slapped, polished, buffed, and adorned; Amanda loved being a girl. She ignored the fact that her skirt wasn't falling where it was supposed to fall, which meant she'd gained a few pounds. It still looked good. She felt confident when she sat down at the kitchen table for her usual predate I Ching toss. After some breathing—in, out—Amanda threw the coins. A lot of yin, as usual. But the alignment of the coins—from top to bottom: tails, tails, tails, heads, tails, heads—wasn't very auspicious. The upper trigram represented the earth. The lower trigram was fire. Her interpretations: (1) Her ground, her stability, was at risk of being burned; or (2) The light of knowledge—fire—was buried beneath the earth. The reading was a warning. It was telling her that she didn't know what she was getting into, and that she might find herself in a dangerous place when it was over. Amanda searched her intuition to see if the warning was for the date itself or for her choice of outfit.

Some *om*ing helped her understand the meaning of the toss. She quickly changed into an all-purpose gray cashmere minidress and was out the door, arriving at the Heights Cafe by midnight.

Chick was waiting at the horseshoe-shaped bar. Pink neon bounced off the mirror behind the bottles—highly flattering lighting. She pulled up a stool beside Chick and leaned over enough to breathe slightly on his neck. She could practically see his nerve endings salute.

"Sorry I'm late. Have you been waiting long?" she said sweetly. His answer would be a true test of his affections. She signaled the bartender for a drink.

"Not long at all," Chick replied. The bartender, her old friend Paul McCartney (no relation), heard Chick's response. He shook his head ever so slightly. Amanda nodded ever so slightly. Bartender Paul and Amanda had played this tape before—she'd had dozens of dates at the Heights Cafe. It was the only moderately priced, non-family-friendly restaurant in the neighborhood. The local singles depended on its low lighting, shiny black tabletops, piped-in smoky music, and strong drinks. Paul fixed Amanda a Kir Royale.

Chick asked, "Your usual?"

"You think this is a girly drink, don't you?" she asked. Amanda's on-a-date usual was a Kir Royale. Her off-a-date usual was a vodka tonic. On certain kinds of dates, however, she went with scotch, straight up (but not this one— he was a mountain climber, not a Wall Streeter).

Chick said, "I can honestly say that I've never given a moment's thought to the gender of a cocktail."

Good answer. This could be an ambience night. Amanda said, "So." She and Chick had spent maybe ten minutes together total. She knew him only from the contest, what he'd written on his entry card, his purple aura, and his generally friendly nature. And he'd said the thing about flicking. That was promising.

Amanda sipped and said, "So." She made it a policy to let the guy steer the conversation.

"This is awkward," Chick admitted. "Maybe we should chug a few drinks and relax."

Getting drunk as a conversational aid? Amanda hadn't heard that before. But if it was new, she'd try it at least once. Amanda clinked her glass against his and knocked back the Kir Royale in one shot. Chick was obviously impressed. He smiled and held up his hand for her to slap. She high-fived him. She didn't think anyone saw.

"Now you," Amanda instructed, pointing at his drink.

He swirled his Greyhound against the walls of his glass and then downed it. Amanda liked how his Adam's apple bobbed in his throat, sliding up and down under unmarked skin. She imagined kissing it. Chick really was a fine-looking man. He'd climbed all those mountains. He loved the great outdoors. Amanda was working on a nice little fantasy when he raised his arm again. He said, "One round down." He nodded at her. He expected her to high-five him again. She furtively reached up and tapped his palm. Paul rolled his eyes from across the bar.

Amanda said, "You know, I'm fascinated by mountain climbers. The danger. The adventure. The physical exertion. Rappelling. It's so adrenaline-based."

"I was more like a trekker than a climber," he said. "I set out to climb Everest, but I never went higher than five thousand feet."

"The ideal altitude for growing arabica coffee trees." Amanda threw that in. *What the hell.*

He smiled. "Is that a fact?"

"I've got a million of them."

"One at a time will be fine." He signaled Paul for another round.

The bartender brought the drinks. Amanda smiled and shooed Paul away. He had a tendency to hover. She detected a sudden bulletin from her intuition: *Get some privacy with Chick*. She didn't want Paul's smirks and eye rolling to distract her from the emerging warmth she felt in her pelvis. "Let's get a table," she said to Chick. Maybe if they were sitting across from each other instead of side by side, Chick wouldn't do . . . that hand thing.

Chick said, "A table sounds great, Amanda. In a nice, quiet corner." His eyes darkened sexily.

"Somewhere we can talk," she agreed.

"Somewhere private."

"A place where we can share our hopes and dreams," she said.

"Reveal our fears and fantasies."

They smiled at each other. "You're being ironic, right?" She had to ask. She knew she was. She honestly wasn't sure about him.

He laughed and tilted his head back, flashing her another nice clean shot of his lovely neck. He said, "You're hilarious. Ironic! I love that. Gimme five."

Oh, dear God. As he held his muscular arm aloft for the third time in as many minutes, Amanda suddenly understood why this gorgeous, intelligent man was single. She said, "I'm sorry, Chick. I can't do . . . that. I just can't."

"Do what?" he asked.

"That." She made a mini high-five motion.

"What's that?"

"The high-five thing," she whispered. "I'm not much of a sports fan."

His face turned to dust. He said, "Oh, Jesus. You think I'm a complete idiot, don't you? This is humiliating. Here I am, sitting with the most beautiful woman I've ever seen in my life, and I'm so nervous I'm reduced to ridiculous jerk-off behavior. Any excuse to touch you, I guess. This is too embarrassing. I've got to go." He leaped off his stool and threw a twenty on the bar.

Amanda, now mortified herself, said, "Please stay. I didn't mean to embarrass you." The most beautiful woman he'd ever seen? Any excuse to touch her? "You can touch me, Chick." She felt awful. You can teach a man to stop high-fiving, but you can't teach him to be gorgeous and adventurous. Why had she opened her mouth at all? She begged, "Really, Chick, please stay."

"Now I'm a pity case. I like you, Amanda. I really do. I think I love you. That sounds even more absurd than everything else I've said. I have to leave. Right away. I'll call you." And then he ran into the night, but not before accidentally kicking over his bar stool and disrupting a waitress's tray of drinks in the process.

Chase after him? Not in this dress, she thought. Amanda groaned. Paul brought her another Kir Royale. She asked the bartender, "Did you hear that?" The entire planet heard it. Paul just nodded. "I don't get it," Amanda complained. "He was so confident at Barney Gree . . . Romancing the Bean. He even held my hand. What happened?"

Paul said, "What you've witnessed tonight, my friend, was the difference between a man jacked on caffeine and a man tanked on vodka."

"Is this a pearl of bartender wisdom?" she asked.

Paul said, "He had three drinks before you showed up."

"Did you talk to him at all?"

Paul shrugged. "I listened to him babble."

"I shouldn't have made him wait," she whined. "It's my fault the date was ruined."

"Forget him, Amanda. He was just another loser with big plans and a light wallet—that twenty won't cover his drinks and yours."

"I'd do better with married fathers of two like you?" she asked, slightly annoyed with Paul's "you can do better" refrain. Paul seemed taken aback by her comment. She tried to laugh it off. "What's a girl with radiant beauty to do?" she asked him.

"Irony? You're hilarious. I love that. Gimme five." Paul raised his hand. She jabbed him in the ribs with a swizzle stick.

Amanda turned to face the windows. No sign of Chick outside. She drank her cocktail and thought about what could have been. Then she went home, determined to get in touch with Chick in the morning, apologize, and try again. She had to. If she'd scared him off, he'd never come into Romancing the Bean. And if he didn't bring his friends, the whole plan of using these men as bait would be botched. Amanda tried not to imagine Frank's reaction to the news of the date, Clarissa's disappointment in her. She'd have to tell her new friend she'd blown it with Chick. Clarissa probably never blew it. The whole double-date thing was out the window. Amanda couldn't believe she'd gone from new social circle to alone and miserable at a bar in five seconds flat.

If only she'd stuck with the skirt.

*   *   *

"He *what?*" demanded Frank. It was early the next morning. Amanda had had a terrible night's sleep. She was relieved in a way to tell her big sister what happened.

"I'm so sorry," she said. "Especially for Chick. You should have seen his face. He was so embarrassed. I hope he's not afraid of me."

Frank said, "It never stops with you. The innocent mistakes that I have to clean up or absorb. I'm tired of it, Amanda."

"I'm sorry, Frank. I didn't mean any harm."

"You never do. Get dressed," said Frank. "We're going to his place. Maybe if you beg him to forgive you, he'll come back to Romancing the Bean. His picture is going to be in the *Courier*. People will want to meet him." Frank paced. "I am furious about this, Amanda. Honestly, I'm surprised how angry I feel. If I were wavering about what I wanted out of life, at least now I know. We have to keep the store afloat. It's a noble thing to own a business, to work hard and provide a service to the community. Thanks to your bumbling, at least now I know for sure."

"You're welcome," Amanda said.

"Just get dressed," Frank said.

"Ten minutes." Amanda knew that not even the most potent chamomile tea could soothe Frank when she was in a righteous snit. So she got dressed (jeans and T-shirt, crewneck sweater, boots, and pea coat).

Frank's lecture about Amanda's recklessness continued as they walked the four blocks to Chick's apartment on Joralemon Street (they'd gotten his address from his entry card—the pile was still under the cash register).

Amanda half listened to her sister ("Actions have consequences," "You don't think before you act") while men-
tally preparing for her speech to Chick. She'd been mulling
about it all night: "Chick, I want to try again with you. I
sense real potential between us, not just sexual attraction.
Giving up on what could be something significant after
one weird date is like slamming the door on destiny. We
might be meant for each other. And the only way to find
out is to give us another try." Amanda believed every
word of it. She'd felt a real connection to him since the
minute they first met. Somehow she knew that their fates
were intertwined. He had to see her again.

As the sisters turned the corner onto Chick's block,
Frank spotted the flashing lights first. The ambulance was
parked in front of Chick's building. Amanda sucked in her
breath on reflex. Frank pulled her sister by the wrist as
she rushed toward the siren sound. They got to the police
blockade just in time to see Chick's stiff, blue body on a
stretcher being wheeled toward the ambulance. The cops
hadn't even covered his corpse. The indignity of it made
Amanda ache from sadness.

Frank called out to the EMS guy, "Suicide?"

As he loaded the stretcher into the back of the ambulance, he yelled back, "No." Amanda felt a rush of relief.
Not that her ego was so big. But the soul of a suicide was
doomed to be stuck between this world and the astral
plane until its natural life span was over—a horrible, tortured state of limbo.

Frank yelled again. "Accident?"

The EMS guy didn't answer her. He pulled the doors

closed and the ambulance sped off. The sisters watched it disappear down the block.

"I know what happened, Frank," Amanda said softly.

"I don't want to hear about your intuition right now," said Frank.

Amanda shut up as instructed. But she felt it in her heart. As soon as she saw his body, she knew.

Chick's death was no accident. His life had been taken, and not by God.

7

Dead bodies. Seeing one was enough for a lifetime. Frank had seen two before Chick's. She'd been the one to discover her parents' lifeless bodies in their apartment. Frank had described that wretched moment to Amanda as a giant squashing sensation. All the emotional security, warmth, and personal history she'd ever known shrank into a small, hard nub of bitterness—like a stale coffee bean—and implanted itself in her brain as a permanent reminder. When she was particularly lonely, Frank could feel the nub throbbing under her left eyebrow.

"You've never seen one before," Frank said to her sister.

"No," replied Amanda.

If there was a virginity for such things, Amanda's corpse cherry was now broken. On the night Frank had discovered Mom and Dad, Amanda was on a date. Frank called her number a hundred times until Amanda finally picked up the phone to receive the worst news of her life. Thank God Frank wouldn't have to make a call this time.

"It's bad luck," said Amanda.

"Yes, being dead is just about the worst luck you can have."

"Not being dead. Seeing the dead."

"Believe me," said Frank, "Chick's luck is a lot worse than ours."

The sisters beat a swift retreat to RTB. Amanda set herself up behind the counter to grind beans, pound after pound. Frank counted the money in the cash register five times, until she was convinced she'd added correctly. Anything to block out the sight of Chick, stiff and blue, rigored in a kneeling position on that stretcher. Gruesome.

"We have to open the store," said Frank.

"A man's dead," said Amanda.

"I'm very sorry about that. But we have to open the store. We can't afford to be closed for another three days. We can't afford to be closed for another three hours. I have no idea what we're going to say to people when they come in here." Frank felt slightly guilty for thinking only of herself and Romancing the Bean. Amanda was right: a man was dead. Should they sponsor a funeral service? With what money?

"We have to do something for him," said Amanda. "I could say a few words, like a eulogy." She cleared her throat. "Charles Peterson was a kind man, a humble man. He . . . uh, he had really long legs."

Frank shook her head. "You don't know a thing about him."

"I still feel for him. I still mourn his lost potential," said Amanda. "You can still care if you don't know someone well."

"I'm cursed, Amanda," said Frank. "Obviously cursed. Everything I try to do fails. And I let myself get hopeful. I let myself believe. Clarissa is going to be terribly upset. And it's all my fault."

Amanda said, "How is it your fault? Did you kill Chick?"

"It's my fault somehow," said Frank. "Just wait. Somehow it'll be revealed to be because of me."

The sisters opened late at seven-thirty. Customers streamed in all morning, asking about Mr. Coffee and when he would make his next appearance. Not wanting to explain what had happened, Frank lied. She promised the customers that the king himself should be walking in any minute. Amanda periodically excused herself to the bathroom for cry-and-dry cycles. In the meantime business was good—the storm before the calm, thought Frank. She tried to call Clarissa a few hundred times. No answer. Matt made his first appearance around noon. Frank told him that Chick was found dead at home.

Matt said, "What happened?"

"To be determined," Frank said. No one had any hard news about it.

Matt nodded and asked, "Where did you say he was found?"

Amanda and Frank looked at each other. "At his apartment on Joralemon Street. Why do you ask?" asked the red-eyed sister.

"Was he inside the building or outside?"

Frank had no idea. "I have no idea."

Amanda said, "Matt, had you ever met Chick before? The way you were talking last night, I got a strong feeling that you knew each other. Your body language said *familiarity* to me."

Frank rolled her eyes. She wondered if Amanda knew what Frank's body language was saying at that moment.

Matt said, "What the hell is this? Some kind of interrogation? If you ask too many questions in this country, you're thought to be either crazy or a criminal. I happen to be saner than anyone else here. And I follow my own rules, okay? I know the difference between right and wrong." Then he grabbed a broom and started sweeping frantically. The sisters thought it best to leave him alone and let him sweep.

The old lady, Lucy, she of the eternal refill, made her daily appearance just after lunch. She was carrying her PowerBook and seemed damned pissed off that she couldn't get a table to herself. She stormed up to the counter and said, "You are evidence enough that we live in a morally depraved society, where the responsibilities to family and home are ignored by greedy, virtueless people like you. Have you no dignity? That contest was deplorable! And now you're catering to the sex-obsessed rabble. God will punish you."

Amanda turned to Frank. "Is she right? Is Chick's death some kind of divine punishment?"

"Lucy," said Frank, "I appreciate that you've been a regular customer for years. But you can't expect us to hold a table for you. And we're not giving free refills anymore."

Lucy squinted. "Mistresses of Satan!" Then she left without even a cup to go.

Frank yelled after her, "You might find a free table at Moonburst."

On cue, Benji Morton walked in. He looked decent in jeans, a red barn jacket, and Timberland boots, a copy of the *New York Post* tucked under his arm. "Working on your day off?" Frank asked, trying hard to fake blitheness.

He said, "Killing off your best shot at survival? You might as well give the store away."

"News travels fast," Frank whispered. She didn't want the customers to know the truth.

"When it's on the cover of the paper, it does," he said, dropping the *Post* on the counter. "I'm happy to start talking about a lease arrangement for your space anytime."

Frank gasped. Amanda rushed over to take a look at the cover. The photo was just perfect: Amanda and Chick gazing dreamily at each other. The banner headline: DYING FOR COFFEE. The deck: "Coffee King Found Dead—Pretty Proprietress Prime Suspect."

"That photographer from the *Brooklyn Courier* must have sold the *Post* the pictures he took last night," said Frank.

Amanda held the paper in her trembling hands. " 'Pretty proprietress'? You'd never know it from that photo." Amanda's vanity proved to be deeper than her sorrow.

"It's a gorgeous shot, Amanda," oozed Benji. "You couldn't look more like yourself."

"My hair is frizzing. My skin looks blotchy. My chin— it's practically tripled. I wouldn't go higher than 'passable proprietress.' "

"You're worried about your hair?" Frank asked.

"Being called a murderer doesn't compare to your blotchiness? If you hadn't made that date with Chick, he would have been home watching TV like a normal person, not getting himself killed. And now it's all over the papers. Don't you get it? Who'd want to buy coffee from a murderer? You might pour arsenic in the decaf!"

Amanda stared. "Frank, calm down."

Frank said, "Just shut up about the picture, Amanda. You know you look fine. And even if you didn't, if you looked, say, puffy, no one would be so rude as to point that out." Frank snatched the paper and opened it up to read the story.

Amanda snatched it right back. "Vanity and grief exist on parallel planes. That's how a woman could be devastated by a breakup and still be pleased with the fact that she's lost ten pounds on the heartbreak diet. It's the reason Grandma always said, 'Put on some lipstick; you'll feel better.' And if I'm going to be on the cover of a major metropolitan newspaper, there's no crime in wanting to look good." Amanda, not a speechmaker, smiled when she finished. "And considering that the article is about me," she said, "I get to see it first."

"Fortunately for you, the *Post* is written on a third-grade reading level." Frank tore it out of her hands.

Suddenly the sisters were tearing the paper to pieces. Benji made a futile attempt to rescue his edition. "Hey, stop it," he yelled. "Someone owes me thirty-five cents." Customers watched in confusion.

The doors jingled open. Clarissa stumbled in, cradling about fifty copies of the *Post* in her arms. "Get ready, girls!" she bellowed. "Our ship has come in."

"The *Titanic?*" Frank asked.

"The *Bounty,*" she replied. The door jingled again, and in walked (catwalked?) the J.Crew model, also carting several dozen copies of the *Post.* "Just put those down in the corner," Clarissa told Walter. To the slightly askew sisters, she said, "Have you seen the story?"

Amanda said, "We were just ripping through it."

Benji relieved Clarissa of the pile and deposited all but one copy on the floor. He tucked it under his armpit, turned toward Frank, and said, "I'll leave you to your ruin." Which he did, with haste.

Frank grabbed the copy on top. Amanda snagged one, too. They read the story simultaneously. "How did the *Post* get photos so quickly?" Frank wondered.

Clarissa explained: "When I called the reporter to give him the story, I had the foresight to connect him with the *Brooklyn Courier* photographer. You need good art these days to sell newspapers. No photos, no story. I learned that in my media-relations class."

The sisters barely heard Clarissa's self-congratulations as they read. Amanda, aloud: " 'According to Paul McCartney, bartender at the Heights Cafe, the couple sat together for only fifteen minutes. Then Mr. Peterson ran out of the restaurant. McCartney told a *Post* reporter that the couple had had a terrible argument. Once Mr. Peterson was gone, Ms. Greenfield swore she'd get her revenge on him for deserting her.'

"This is completely untrue!" Amanda couldn't believe Paul McCartney would say those things to a reporter.

Frank read: "The cause of death was a blow to the head. Mr. Peterson's skull was fractured. The medical examiner had also requested blood tests for a toxicology report."

"I never swore revenge," Amanda pleaded to the room, still incredulous. "This is libel, right? Slander? Which is it? The entire article is a lie. Poor Paul. He must feel terrible to be misquoted like this. I can sense his pain from here."

"It's an exaggeration, of course," Clarissa said to Amanda. "We needed the sensationalism factor. The story you told me on the phone wasn't very juicy, so I told the reporter he could embellish."

Frank was now completely confused. She turned toward Amanda. "I've been trying to reach Clarissa all morning."

"I called her cell phone," said Amanda.

"You have her cell number?" asked Frank.

"And her pager."

"I don't have her pager number."

Amanda smiled. "Maybe that's because Clarissa doesn't want you to page her."

That hurt, thought Frank. "I don't get it."

"Clarissa doesn't want to hear from you," repeated Amanda.

"I meant, why is this good? Why is this the *Bounty?* Are we going to mutiny? Who's the captain? You planted the story?" Yet again, Amanda won the popularity contest. And Frank thought Clarissa really liked her.

Before Clarissa could speak, Walter J.Crew said, "The best publicity is for the press to rave. The second best is to have them roar. You'll see, Francesca. The people will come." To Clarissa he said, "Where should I sit? In the window? And I'll need some coffee and cookies."

"Sit at a central table," Clarissa instructed him. To the sisters she said, "Since Chick is dead, I appointed Walter, our runner-up, to take over as Mr. Coffee. And he's exactly right. All press is good. The cover of the *New York Post!* It's massive! That's why I arranged for the photos; that's why I convinced the reporter to do the story. And, just for the record, Francesca, Amanda didn't know what I'd do with the information she gave me. And I gave my cell and pager numbers to her last night for both of you."

Frank watched Clarissa and Amanda make eye contact. Was it a lie? Why wasn't she the one trading secret glances with Clarissa? Frank couldn't keep the horrible feeling of rejection from flooding her. "What happens when the police come here to arrest Amanda?" she asked.

"It'll never happen," Clarissa assured them both. "The police spokesperson is quoted in the story as saying they have no evidence linking Amanda to the murder. In fact"—she approached Frank and pointed to a line of type at the very end of the article—"it says right here that the police are more seriously considering several other suspects. I have no idea who they might be. I don't really care. Who knows what kind of muck Chick was into? What do any of us know about him? That he was out of the country for the last ten years? Climbing mountains? He could have gotten himself into all kinds of trouble abroad. I'm sorry that Chick is dead. He was a nice man. But the rest of us have to go on living, and that means making a splash for the sake of the store. I'm sure Amanda agrees with me."

Clarissa was standing close to Frank. The overwhelming scent of vanilla reminded the older sister of her mom baking Santa cookies for the customers at Christmastime. She asked Clarissa, "What reporter would knowingly print a nonstory like this? Isn't that completely unethical?"

Clarissa smiled, catlike and mischievous. "That depends what your definition of unethical is. Now, Francesca, how about a cup for our new Mr. Coffee?" Clarissa approached a tableful of customers. She said, "Ladies, you don't mind if our Mr. Coffee of the Week sits with you?" They didn't. He sat down between two eager patrons. They giggled when he took off his overcoat, revealing a nice set of arms under a starched royal blue button-down shirt.

Clarissa buzzed around the customers, handing out copies of the *Post.* They would gasp, look up at Amanda, and order another mug of coffee. Frank, dumbfounded, asked, "Is this really happening?"

Amanda nodded. "I wonder what we can do to help."

Clarissa slunk back over. She was wearing a silk seashell-colored shirt. Frank could swear she saw the outline of her nipple. Clarissa said, "This is so, so great! I can see it all unfolding, just like I imagined. There must be forty people here! That's quite a few more than when I first walked in last week—but I'm sure I don't need to remind you of the way things were." She gazed over at Walter. He was doing a fine job of entertaining his female tablemates. "And Walter—he's a sweetheart. He has some great ideas about the contest. We were up all night talking about what we should do during his tenure as Mr. Coffee. We agreed that if he and some of his model friends come in regularly, they're worth more than just free coffee and cakes. I told him we'd pay them thirty dollars an hour. I think that's fair, considering how much more coffee we'll move and how much publicity we'll get. Just think: we could do a Romancing the Bean calendar. Mugs. Coaster sets. We'll make a fortune."

"Incredible," said Amanda, apparently settled into her role as house slaughterer.

"This is going too fast for me," said Frank. Her control over her own store was slipping away. When she allowed herself to envision their great revival, this wasn't how she pictured it.

"Think of the buckets of money," said Clarissa. "I'm seeing expansion. Opening a site in Park Slope."

"Hold on," Frank said, her hands raised. "I'm still confused about a couple of things."

Clarissa and Amanda again looked at each other sympathetically, as if they were united in their tolerance of Frank. Clarissa said, "What don't you understand?"

"Why would you be up all night talking to Walter about his reign as Mr. Coffee?" asked Frank. "Chick's body wasn't found until morning."

Clarissa seemed momentarily flustered. She said, "Excuse me?"

Frank asked again, "What made you think that Walter would be Mr. Coffee before you knew that Chick was dead?"

Amanda watched her sister and her new friend square off. The confrontation disturbed her. Amanda hated tension of any kind, except sexual. And even that wore on her nerves before long. She said, "I called Clarissa when I got home late last night. I wanted to prepare her for the possibility of finding a new guy. I didn't know if Chick would ever talk to me again."

Frank nodded. "I see. Well. Then all this makes perfect sense, of course."

The blond woman settled her blue cut-glass eyes on Frank. Amanda watched her sister squirm a bit. Clarissa said, "I'm glad you asked, Francesca. It's good to ask questions. That's how we learn in life. And I wasn't offended in the least." To show her continuing support, Clarissa mussed Frank's black hair. It fell back into shape immediately.

"So you and Walter spent the night together?" asked Frank.

Clarissa said, "I guess we did." So much for Amanda and Clarissa's little secret pact. "Just talking. Nothing happened, if you want the truth," Clarissa continued. "You seem disappointed, Francesca. You were hoping for something more exciting?"

Frank said, "Actually, I was hoping for something incredibly dull, like running a coffee bar. Love affairs are not my area."

Amanda attempted to make peace. "Come on, you guys. We all want the same thing. And we're succeeding. Look at Walter. Look at all the customers. We're making it."

"I'm still not sure why it was necessary to portray Amanda as a murderer," said Frank to Clarissa.

"Please, Frank," Amanda pleaded. "Can you let someone else be right? Can't someone else make a few hard decisions? Clarissa knows what she's doing. I trust her completely."

Amanda knew that her defense of Clarissa would antagonize Frank, but she felt she had to do it. Otherwise the two women might lose sight of what was really important. Amanda was the victim, if there was one, of Clarissa's plan. Her picture was on the cover of the paper. If she wasn't mad, why should Frank be? Maybe Amanda should be pissed off. No, she swatted that idea out of her mind. She couldn't manufacture anger if she didn't feel any. And why would she want to? Hatred, even justified, only corrupted the soul. That included contempt for something as inert as broccoli.

Frank said, "One day of good business is not a turn-around. But it is progress." She paused, wrestling with a decision. "No more contests for a while. Let's see how things unfold over the next couple of weeks without one. Doing one every Friday is too much anyway. People will get bored."

"It's probably a good idea to wait," said Clarissa, ever the diplomat. "My plan has always been about buzz. The opposite of bored."

On that, Frank and Clarissa took to opposite corners of the shop: Frank went to help Matt brew fresh pots (she hated letting coffee sit for longer than half an hour); Claris-sa circled the tables and made all the customers feel wel-come. Her beauty, Amanda observed, wasn't the kind that made other women envious. With her grace and style, Clarissa drew admiration, not criticism. She moved as flu-idly and softly as her flannel pants.

Amanda didn't know who to talk to next. If she went to help Frank, Clarissa might feel betrayed. But if she fol-lowed after Clarissa, Frank would feel conspired against. She wished she could turn back the clock: only twenty-four hours ago, Frank and Clarissa had had a nice, budding professional relationship and Amanda had found a man with real potential. Now her two allies had built a wall between them, and she was as alone—romantically speak-ing—as ever. The sudden crush of desperation weighed on Amanda's soft shoulders.

To everyone, Amanda said, "I'm going out for a little while." She collected good-byes, slipped her tightish pea coat over her black turtleneck and boot-cut black trousers (miracle pants, she called them), and went outside. For the first time in years, Amanda decided she could use a midafternoon cocktail. Her bartender friend, Paul McCartney, would make her feel better. He had the knack. And she could assure him that she didn't blame him for fabricated quotes in the paper.

Amanda headed for the Heights Cafe. On the way, she was gawked at by people on the street. A couple of old ladies nearly stumbled on the pavement as they swerved out of her path. At first she thought the avoidance was in her imagination. But everywhere she looked, strangers pointed and scrambled away from her. She cut a wide swath on the Montague sidewalk. Amanda subconsciously wiped at her face and clothes. One thing she hadn't anticipated about the exposure in the *Post*—it left her exposed.

She breathed deeply, in, out, in, out. Only two blocks separated her and a friendly face. Amanda wondered what Paul had really told the reporter. She waited for the light at Hicks Street. The woman standing next to her screamed suddenly and ran to the other side of the street. A man bumped into her shoulder a bit too aggressively. She felt under attack and started to run into the street against the light. A couple hissed at her as she raced by.

Using both hands, she slammed through the Heights Cafe's double doors. The familiar surroundings filled Amanda with relief. Todd Phearson, the shrimpy, fifty-something owner/maître d', rushed to meet her at the door. Amanda expected him to encircle her in a teddy-bearish, supportive hug (he was an old friend of her parents' from the neighborhood). Instead he put his hands in the upright "halt" position.

He said, "I'm sorry, Amanda, but I think we should keep our distance until this whole thing blows over."

Was he kicking her out? She couldn't believe what she was hearing. "You don't think I could kill someone?" she asked. Of every person he knew, Amanda had to be the last one to fit the role of killer. She wouldn't harm a fly. She'd caught flies to set them free. Amanda had caught mosquitoes to set them free. It was no simple trick to catch a mosquito in a Dixie cup.

"Amanda, you know I'd never suspect you of such a thing," he whispered as his needle gaze never left her face. Amanda recognized this as a sign that he was lying: Honest people look you in the eye. Dishonest people stare you in the eye.

"I want to talk to Paul," she said, backing away from Todd. Her stomach lurched. This shunned feeling was ghastly. It was as if she'd entered a parallel universe where everyone hated her.

"Paul isn't here," said Todd quietly. "I told him to stay home today. I don't want any more trouble to come to my restaurant. Your presence might be disturbing to the rest of the staff—and the customers. I can't risk it. I've got a business to run."

Amanda couldn't believe the betrayal. She'd known Todd for a dozen years. To be treated this way over nothing, a publicity stunt—it was ridiculous and hurtful. With great restraint, she said, "I've got a business to run, too, Todd. That's what this is all about."

Todd sighed and pushed her toward the door. "You

handle your business and I'll handle mine. I'm very sorry
this is happening to you, but I'm also angry you've involved my restaurant in this mess. Once it's resolved, come
in anytime."

He might as well have said, "Your parents meant nothing to me." Amanda struggled with the bubbling volcano
of anger in her chest. She'd been fighting to maintain her
sense of self. Everyone assumed she was a killer; she knew
she wasn't. Amanda knew she was a good person. She had
a river of love in her heart. She believed in God. She gave
to charity. But this ejection. This turning out. This was
over the line.

As she looked at Todd's pinched face, she saw him
clearly for the first time. He was a spiteful, unkind man.
"Dad was right about you," she said, tears spilling out of
her green eyes. "He always suspected you were an anti-
Semite."

Todd's face twisted even more. "Just get out,
Amanda," he said.

She took one, two, three, four deep, cleansing breaths
(the sun, the moon, the waves, the sand) and tried to
control herself. Didn't work. The hurt and anger were
now unstoppable forces of nature. She said, "You're very,
very abnormally short." Then she ran out.

Short taunts. Was this what she'd been reduced to?
Insulting a man about his physical limitations, as if his
stature had anything to do with the content of his soul?
Amanda huffed and puffed down Hicks Street, wondering
how she could sink so low. Poor Paul must have received
a tongue-lashing from Todd, too. All because of her.
Amanda let the guilt gather in her gut. It was one thing

to be used for her own sake, but Paul had been taken advantage of by that reporter.

Amanda knew Paul lived on Grace Court Alley in one of the few apartment complexes in Brooklyn Heights (pre-war brownstones or townhouses were the norm). His 1950s deco sprawl was the last structure on the cul-de-sac. He'd told her that his apartment had a view of the East River, the murky body of water that separated Brooklyn and Manhattan island. The building was square, about five stories high, with a courtyard in the middle. Amanda had walked past the structure before, but she'd never been inside. She wasn't sure which floor he lived on, or even which wing, but she resolved to find out what happened between Paul and Todd. If his job was endangered, she would do whatever she could for him. Paul's marriage wasn't on such solid ground. Being out of work could do more damage.

She was thankful she wasn't tormented by anyone as she made the short walk to Grace Court Alley. At the entrance to Paul's building, Amanda approached an old woman in ermine with a pit bull on a leather leash. Amanda said, "Excuse me, ma'am. I'm looking for Paul McCartney."

"Try Liverpool," she said.

Amanda followed her into the main lobby. No door-man on duty. No directory of apartments. She closed her eyes and tried to picture a door with a number on it. The door to Paul's place. Where he lived. With his wife. And two daughters. The door. It was red. With a gold handle. And the number on the door was . . . This was ridiculous. Amanda wasn't getting anywhere. How she wished she had some tangible psychic abilities. Instinct was good. But if she could see visions, the future . . . that would really be something. Of course, Amanda would use her powers for good. She'd help people. She'd— An *ahem* behind her drew her attention back to sad reality.

Spinning around, Amanda found herself face-to-face with a nice-looking dirty-blonde in an overstuffed goose-down coat, a purple ribbed turtleneck, and black leggings. Amanda hadn't seen a woman wear leggings in earnest since 1997, the year of the trouser. Two little girls and one Jack Russell terrier stood at the woman's side. The older girl—maybe five—glared at Amanda as she clasped her mother's hand. She seemed so serious. She must have an old soul in her new small body. The way she held her head and looked up at Amanda from under half-closed lids made the girl seem wiser and wearier than her years.

"You look just like your picture," said the woman. Her voice was sticky, as if she'd just eaten a fistful of honey.

"You must be Sylvia," Amanda said to Paul's wife. "I've heard so much about you. It's great to meet, finally." Amanda leaned down to acknowledge the girls. The younger girl—about three—had golden ringlets around her face.

The toddler giggled and said, "You're pretty."

Amanda said, "So are you." Turning toward her older, more serious sister, Amanda started to say "You, too," but the girl interrupted.

"Let's go, Mommy," she whined. Not in the mood for chitchat. Neither was Mommy.

"I've got to go," said Sylvia, pulling on the leash.

Amanda hadn't been invited up. She quickly said, "I

came by to see Paul. I need to talk to him." Amanda paused as Sylvia examined her pea coat, or what was underneath it. "Do you think I could come up for a minute?" she asked.

"Girls, why don't you push the elevator button for Mommy," she instructed her children. The three-year-old ran off immediately, taking the dog with her. The older child refused to let go of her mother's hand. Sylvia had to insist. Once the women were alone, Sylvia said, "I don't want you to see Paul. Ever again. Stay away from my husband. You're the reason my marriage is in trouble."

"I beg your pardon?" Amanda asked, shocked.

"That article. He read it and nearly passed out at work," she said. "Todd sent him home. Paul was a complete mess. I'd never seen him such a wreck. And then he told me everything. How he's been in love with you for years. That he works such horrible hours because he's hoping you'll come in for a drink. How he tries to make fun of the men you bring to the restaurant so you lose interest in them. How he gives you free drinks and rushes your dinner orders. I had to get the girls out of the house. I didn't want them to see their father like that."

Amanda was speechless. "I didn't . . . I wasn't . . . You don't think . . ."

"He told me that you've never . . . that nothing's happened," she said. "That you see him as a friend. But when Todd told him to stay away from the bar for a few days, Paul broke down at the thought of not seeing you. In my seven years of marriage, I've never seen Paul cry. I can't believe I'm not up there crying myself." Amanda had never picked up on Paul's secret love. Strange. Perceiving male attraction was her specialty.

"You poor woman!" was all Amanda could blurt out.

Sylvia continued, "I don't really know how I'm supposed to react. He doesn't want to leave me. He says he loves me. Paul's been so absent in the last few years, I've come to expect little from him emotionally. I've got my own life, my own ambition, the girls. I've been fine with the aloneness. But now—maybe it's you—I really feel like talking. You don't have a few minutes to grab a cup of coffee, do you?"

Amanda shrugged, still mute with shock. Sylvia took that as a *yes* to chat. She said she was going to let the girls into the apartment and she'd come right back down. Amanda was supposed to wait for her. Outside, the night had turned black already. It was only around 5:00 P.M. Amanda watched Sylvia walk toward the elevators. She stood stony as a statue, paralyzed by the cumulative events of the day. The planets had to be in kooky alignment. In a few moments Amanda snapped out of her stupor. Without a glance over her shoulder, she ran out of the lobby, up the street, and around the corner. She would have kept running, but it was cold and she wasn't in the best of shape. So she slowed to a stroll and did some more cleansing breaths. In, out, repeat. A few cycles of this led to a stark realization: breathing was like aspirin; what she needed was a scotch.

Instead she kept walking. It felt good to be out in the open air, however nippy. Night fell early in winter, and the dark saved her from menacing looks. She kept her head down and watched her loafers take one step, and then another. She didn't know how long she'd been walking when she felt a shudder. She looked up and found herself at the top of Joralemon Street—Chick's block. Visions of the scene that morning popped into her head. She ventured down the block and stood in front of Chick's brownstone. Yellow police tape blocked the gated area by the stoop. The garbage cans were, apparently, off-limits. Amanda checked to see if anyone was watching and stepped under the tape. In the dark it was hard to make out any sign of blood. She'd just assumed Chick died in his apartment, but from the look of things, his body had been found outside, practically on the street.

Amanda heard the sound of clicking metal and ducked into the hollow underneath the building's stoop. One of Chick's neighbors was leaving. She didn't want to be seen inside the police-protected area (in fact, she thought to herself, it had been stupid to go in there, leaving fibers and hair and evidence of herself all over the crime scene— too late now). She cursed herself silently and waited for the resident to pass. She was leaning as far into the hollow as she could when she saw the decidedly male figure descend the stairs and proceed up the street. She watched his back. The barn jacket was familiar. So was his walk. And his red hair. He was in the middle of the block, standing under a streetlight, when she heard a loud bang. The man's head snapped in the direction of the sound. Amanda caught his profile.

Benji Morton. As she lived and breathed deeply in and out.

Amanda waited for him to go far enough up the street before she scrambled away from the building. She sat on a neighboring stoop and waited for her heart to beat at a normal rate. Benji and Chick lived in the same building. Maybe they'd met, been friendly? It seemed odd—they couldn't be more different.

After a few minutes her pulse returned to normal and the cold started to harden her muscles. Amanda needed to go somewhere quiet to process all this information. And she was desperate to do an I Ching toss. Deciding there was no place like home, she headed back toward Montague Street.

That was when she heard the police siren.

The loud pop sounded enough like the report of a handgun to send the customers under the tables. Frank wasn't fooled. Having lived in Brooklyn her whole life, only a mile from the neighborhood of Cobble Hill (the Italian enclave infamous for setting off mountains of Roman candles on the Fourth of July—resulting in the highest per capita lost-finger rate in the city), Frank knew a firecracker when she heard one. As the powder sticks exploded on the sidewalk outside, everyone but Frank and Matt took a dive. Frank was proud to see that there wasn't an empty square foot of floor real estate to be had.

There was a time in her life—about five minutes once, in college—when she could have tried to understand the pent-up aggression that resulted in random crimes of mischief (vandalism, fireworks, and phony phone calls). But any residual sense of recklessness in her had died with her parents. Or maybe it had died with her virginity. That scene was tragic and chaotic and dismal enough to crush reckless abandon forever.

Matt snapped Frank back to the present. "People! People! Everything is okay! No one is trying to bomb the café!"

A woman in overalls and a cable-knit cardigan rose to her feet. "What was it?" she asked nervously.

"Just some firecrackers," Matt assured the room. "Nothing to fear!" To Frank, he asked, "Free coffee for the crouched masses?"

"Good idea," she said. "But give them the Colombian." Who would do that? Someone could have been hurt, thought Frank. She assumed the prankster was some idiot kid.

"It was probably Benji Morton from Moonburst, jealous of our taking his customers," said Clarissa as she dusted off her pants. She, too, had hit the dirt when the firecrackers went off.

Matt shook his head. "It wasn't Benji Morton."

"How do you know?" asked Frank.

"He'd never have the guts to light the string," he said.

"Setting off tiny firecrackers isn't exactly a courageous act," Frank said.

Matt shook his head. "Not setting them off. He'd be too scared to break the rules, to get caught. He's got a spine of butter, not a risk-taking bone in his whole pudgy body. How do I know? He's the manager at Moonburst, isn't he? That's about the lowest-risk job in the world right now, isn't it? That man will live his life in quiet safety, wake up one morning at ninety, and wonder how he could have wasted all those years as a do-nothing, try-nothing, be-nothing."

"Okay," said Frank. "I think I'll serve some coffee now."

Clarissa said, "Good to know, Matt. Thanks. Oh, Francesca, can I have a word?"

"Sure, take any word you want," said Frank, then instantly regretted her sarcasm. "I'm sorry, Clarissa. What's on your mind?" She was afraid to hear what the blonde had to say. After all, they'd practically come to blows. Well, maybe not blows, but hard words had been exchanged. Well, maybe not hard. Medium words, tough enough to make Frank feel as if she'd destroyed any chance of a friendship with the superior human.

Clarissa cleared her throat. "Listen, I feel terrible about what happened before. I should have made my goals clearer to you. I was just doing what I thought would help. I admit that my methods can be extreme. But I guess I'm the opposite of Benji Morton: I'm good at taking risks. But I need your approval, Francesca. You're so quick and smart. You're the kind of person who plays chess five moves ahead. I get the feeling you think I'm frivolous. I hope you don't. I want to impress you." Clarissa looked at the older sister with big, moist blue eyes.

Frank's chest swelled and her heart caved at the same time. "I've been trying to impress you," she said. "You're everything. The complete package." *And I'm nothing*, thought Frank. *Small breasts and stringy hair. How could this Valkyrie be seeking my approval?* she wondered with awe. It was like the most popular girl in school begging for the bookworm's vetting. "You're doing a great job," Frank said. "I hope my hesitancy hasn't made you rethink your plans."

"What a relief," said Clarissa with a winning smile. "I thought I'd blown it with you."

Not knowing what to do next, Frank put her hand on Clarissa's shoulder. She actually reached out and touched her. Frank couldn't believe her forwardness, but the praise had a narcotic effect. She gave Clarissa an unsteady pat and said, "I think we need to calm the customers. They still seem a bit shaken."

Clarissa put her cool, dry hand over Frank's and said, "You're right, of course." Frank wondered if Clarissa respected Amanda. That was the most important thing, thought Frank. Amanda might appeal to Clarissa's juvenile girly side, but Frank could be a friend of true substance. She smiled at Clarissa, trying to let her know that she understood: Amanda was just a plaything.

Calm now herself, Frank served fresh coffee. Clarissa soothed the customers. Matt mopped up small rivers of spilled joe. Walter cleared some tables and even refilled the napkin containers. When the crowd had settled down, Frank thanked Matt and Clarissa. Walter joined Frank behind the cookie case with some coffee-soaked washcloths. She pointed him toward the small sink next to the brewing pots and said, "Cleaning up exceeds your Mr. Coffee duties."

"It's nothing." He smiled bashfully.

"No, really. I want to thank you," she said, still on a Clarissa high.

"You don't have to insist, Francesca."

Frank had to ask: "Besides your thing with Clarissa, and your supposed bottomless craving for positive reinforcement, why are you doing this?"

He wrung out a rag. "Doing what?"

"If you're a big J.Crew model, why do you care about free coffee? Don't you have bookings, or sittings, or go-sees? Whatever it is you models do, how come you're not doing it?"

"Let's just say that I'm no fan of the homogenization of America, which Moonburst has made a huge contribution to."

"Unlike J.Crew?" she asked.

He laughed. "It could be worse. It could be The Gap. Besides, J.Crew is mainly a mail-order business."

"They won't open up on my block," she said, nodding. "But every year twenty million trees will give their lives for that catalog. And why do I have to get one in the mail every single day?"

Walter laughed—again. *He thinks I'm funny,* Frank thought. *Yeah, funny looking.* She hadn't been paid this much attention by a handsome man in . . . could she even remember when? Maybe Clarissa's tacit acceptance made Frank irresistible to others of her kind.

Walter said, "I said I had a problem with homogenization, not deforestation."

"So thousands of spotted owls can come live at your place?"

"Honestly, I don't give a hoot." He paused, as if waiting for her to laugh. She resisted. He said, "I've never seen a spotted owl up close, but I'm sure their feathers would make a great stuffing for a quilted jacket." Another pause. "Man, you're tough. If you don't at least smile at my jokes, I'm going to start crying."

"I'll smile when you say something funny," she said.

As he rinsed his hands, Frank studied his profile. His nose was pug. She hated that in a man. But she did admire his tiny pores and his sideburns—they nearly touched his sharp jaw. Most important, he didn't have that block-headed, macho-feminized, cock-forward posture of most male models.

He grabbed the soap when he said, "The truth is, I got involved with the contest because I saw someone in trouble, and I wanted to help her out."

"Helpless wasn't my initial impression of Clarissa," said Frank.

Walter leaned forward and grabbed a dry towel off the rack. Walter said, "I wanted to help you, Francesca. I like you. I liked you on that first day I walked in here to apply for the contest. You pushed past me like you didn't even see me. I vowed that I'd get you to notice me, like I noticed you." As he stroked his forearms dry, he looked down at Frank. She felt a sudden undeniable rise in the temperature of her skin.

Walter said, "God, you're so intense. Your features seem locked together, like they're holding each other in place. I bet if you smiled, your whole face would change completely. Do it, Francesca. Let me see."

Sirens blared, lights blazed.

Frank turned toward the storefront windows. A police cruiser had pulled up on the street outside. The uniforms ran inside, guns drawn, prepared for action, ready to take the place *down*. They quickly realized that forty-odd ruffled women, already flying from free caffeine and adrenaline, weren't in need of another boost. Before the two cops could saddle their weapons, a rumpled man in a dirty brown unbelted trench scuttled into the store. He quickly snapped some photos of the cops with his thirty-five-milli-meter camera. Frank was caught in the background of a few of the frames.

Frank stepped forward. "This is my coffee bar. I'm not sure why you're here," Frank said to the men in blue. Out of the corner of her eye, she spotted Matt scowling at the cops, distrustful of authority figures as a rule.

"This way, Officers!" said the trench-coat guy. Frank and the cops looked in his direction instinctively. He snapped their picture.

Cop number one, the shorter one at six-foot-five, said, "We got a report of shots fired outside."

"Gunshots?" asked Frank. "No, no. Some idiot set off a string of cheap firecrackers on the street. No one was hurt." Trench Coat stared at Frank as she spoke to the cops. Frank felt his eyes on her back as she led the cops outside to show them the remains of the fireworks. Cop number two, a towering six-foot-seven, took a clipboard off the dash of the cruiser and asked her to sign a piece of paper.

Amanda came running up the street. She was breath-ing hard, as though she'd sprinted in from New Jersey. Frank told her everything was okay, to relax. Cop number one recognized Amanda from the newspaper. He asked her for her autograph in a flirty way that meant he'd rather have her phone number. He wasn't wearing a wed-ding ring, but one could never tell with cops.

Resigned to a talk with Amanda later about the dan-gers of dating a cop, Frank left them alone. She noticed that Trench Coat was still staring at her, camera ready to shoot. She stepped back inside, bracing herself against the dry rush of radiator heat.

Frank marched right up to Trench Coat and said, "You've got black smudges on your hands—gunpowder black."

"Very observant, Nancy Drew." The gnomish rumpled man actually sniveled at her before—*whap!*—he took her picture.

Frank was astonished by his rudeness. She said, "I'd like you to leave." She reconsidered. "Who are you?"

"The name is Piper Zorn," he announced. Frank was certain she'd never laid eyes on him in her life. And her memory was keen.

"Doesn't that name mean anything to you?" he asked impatiently.

"You're the *Post* reporter who wrote that fabrication about my sister," Frank stated. "I can't say I admire your work."

"Piper!" sang Clarissa, sliding over to Frank and Trench. "I wasn't expecting to see you tonight." Clarissa and Piper Zorn hugged. His hand brushed over her butt. She pushed it away. Her eyes traveled toward Walter, who was taking orders and making change.

Piper said, "Just doing some follow-up. I wouldn't want this to be a one-day story."

"You're so good to me," Clarissa purred. Frank marveled at how she had this man eating out of her hand. Even though she'd agreed to let Clarissa do what she thought was right, Frank was still uneasy about Romancing the Bean's coverage in the city tabloid.

"Perhaps in tomorrow's story, you can report what

actually happened instead of sensationalizing it," said Frank.

"Francesca," Clarissa started, "I thought we worked this out."

Piper Zorn interrupted her by saying, "You of all people are preaching to me about journalistic standards?" He snorted. "I need some pictures. If you'll get out of my way?" He pushed Frank to the side and walked toward a semicircle of recapping customers. She considered stopping him, but her instincts told her that would make things worse.

The two women watched Piper in action. Frank said, "When you said you had a reporter in your hip pocket, I had no idea he could really fit in your hip pocket."

"Diminutive only in stature," Clarissa assured her. "Piper is a veteran reporter and author. I think he's won some awards."

"He set off fireworks outside the store and called the cops," said Frank. "Are you sure he's trustworthy?"

"He'd never do anything to compromise my plans," said Clarissa. "I have complete control."

Frank doubted that, but she didn't want to spoil the new understanding between them. It occurred to Frank that complete control was probably an illusion for everyone who sought it, including herself. "Piper acts as though he has a personal problem with me," said Frank.

"That's ridiculous," said Clarissa. "I know he's a bit odd, but think of his value. An A-list reporter from the city's biggest daily. He's taking it upon himself to cover your store. Each paragraph in the paper is like paid advertising. This is golden, Francesca."

Frank nodded. "I know all that, and I appreciate it. But he seems so hostile."

"You're paranoid."

"It's not paranoia if someone really is out to get you," Frank explained. One of Frank's pet fears was typical for New Yorkers: She'd be walking by herself late at night, going home from the subway. On a deserted street she'd hear footsteps behind her. Before she could run or call for help, the rapist/murderer/cannibal would attack. It wouldn't be a random act of violence. No. The maniac had picked her out months earlier. Maybe it was the color of her shirt (perhaps this was why 95 percent of New York women wore all black, all the time). Maybe it was an expression on her face, one that said "I'm mildly discontent"—psychopath translation for "kill me now." Frank wasn't inclined to trust strangers. Especially twitchy, antagonistic men in trench coats.

Out of habit, Frank counted heads. The police excitement drew some passersby off the street. The crowd around Piper was animated. By morning, the nonstory of the fireworks exploding would probably be reported as a full-scale race riot. Frank watched as a handful of ladies picked mugs and coffee presses off the products display. She walked behind the register to take their money, not sure why the items that had sat dusty on the shelves for so long were now hot. Then she got it: these people wanted souvenirs, mementos of their big night on the front line. Maybe there was something to this coffee-house-as-spectacle thing.

Amanda was nowhere to be found. The cops were inside, lapping up some complimentary brew (show of support for the police presence). Amanda had probably slipped upstairs for the night. It wasn't like her to miss out on hubbub, but Frank assumed she was worn out from the long day, especially considering that it'd kicked off with her dead date on a gurney.

"Do you have wrapping paper?" asked Walter at Frank's side. "This woman wants to gift wrap her French press."

"No, sorry," Frank said to the customer, who bought the press anyway and slipped the box into her purse. Frank had to admit that, with Walter at her side, she was glad her sister had disappeared. Amanda never meant to take male attention away from Frank. But she did, starting with their father, continuing with boys in school, and finishing with Eric, Frank's ex-fiancé, who came to life at Greenfield family gatherings.

Frank wondered why Walter paid any attention to her with Clarissa in the room. But hadn't she said they spent the night talking? That nothing happened? Was it even remotely possible Walter was interested in her, not Clarissa? Frank let a small fantasy surface. She imagined herself in a gown, Walter in a tux. They were dancing somewhere elegant, a ballroom with heavy curtains, a long spiral staircase and a balcony. Yes, a balcony with a view of a fabulous garden, the air heavy with pine and roses.

"Francesca." He said her name like a song as they dipped to violins. She was draped in backless satin.

"Uh, Francesca." His voice again. Soft and heavy at the same time. They kissed by moonlight. Walter touching Frank's face gently with his hands. Then touching her shoulder. Then shaking her gently, then a bit more firmly.

"Earth to Francesca," Walter said.

Frank descended back to reality. "Yeah," she sputtered. "I'm here. What? Walter, what?"

"This lady would like her change," Walter said evenly.

"Here you go." She passed some quarters to the customer. Frank's face had to be poker red.

Walter said, "Where were you?"

"Forget it."

He said, "I'd like to go there with you sometime."

"You just can't be for real," she said dismissively. He couldn't be.

A flash went off. Piper Zorn had taken their picture. Clarissa was standing next to Zorn, smiling slyly.

"It's nice to see you two are getting along. Looks like the start of a beautiful friendship," said Clarissa, emphasizing the word *friend*. Clarissa turned to Piper and pecked him on the cheek. "Thanks so much for coming out. I'll call you tomorrow."

She waited for Piper to clear the door. Then, to Walter, Clarissa said, "If we leave now, we can still catch the show."

Walter said, "That's right. I completely forgot." To Frank he said, "We have concert tickets. I'm sorry, Francesca. I'll come in again soon. And I'll bring in all my friends. We'll suck in every woman within a fifty-mile radius. Your café is safe with me."

"But you're not safe with me," Clarissa said. She took his arm and led him out the door into the cold night.

The fantasy over, Frank reminded herself that Walter would never prefer her to Clarissa. Any hopes or expectations were bound to leave Frank disappointed. Besides, if

he were interested, Frank would never betray her friendship with Clarissa. That had to have more value than any
man. Frank resolved to eject Walter from her mind and
go about her lonely, spinsterlike business as usual.

Even if it killed her.

10

The cop was cute. He was rugged and tall and furry and unquestionably Italian. Jewish girls were drawn to Italian men. They seemed to respect women, love children, and value family. Amanda had to crane her neck to look at his dark face. She fantasized briefly about sex with him, his largeness, how he could probably pick her up and spin her around like a pliant rag doll. She would be physically powerless under his massive maleness. Amanda smiled at the police officer, wondering if he had any clue about the picture she painted of the two of them. He asked for her phone number. She wasn't surprised. But she took his instead. Amanda would never out-and-out refuse attention from a desirable man, but right now she couldn't imagine falling for anyone while she was still mourning Chick, her latest great hope for a soul mate.

She said good-bye to the cop with a pretty smile and went upstairs to her apartment. Sleep would be her bedroom activity of choice tonight. Frank was downstairs with all those people. She could handle it. Amanda, usually a reliable squeeze of social ointment, just couldn't make small talk after her daylong bombardment of negativity. She didn't even bother applying her replenishing overnight creme before she undressed and slipped into her four-poster fluffy, ruffly bed in the pink-wallpapered room. She couldn't shake the sight of Paul and Sylvia's daughter, yanking her mother's sleeve, saying, "Let's go, Mom." Guilt, guilt and more guilt. Amanda searched her memory for overlooked signs of Paul's secret love. He smiled at her a lot. And offered her free drinks. Paul did roll his eyes a lot around her dates. He doled out unsolicited advice. But most men treated Amanda that way. Was every guy she knew hiding a secret passion for her? How completely horrible. And absurd. Amanda knew pretty was a tool, but it wasn't *always* a hammer. She imagined Chick being battered on the head and cried a bit in the dark.

"Everything has gone downhill," she said to herself. And it all started when Clarissa had walked in the door. No, it wasn't possible. A person wasn't a bad-luck charm. Amanda thought of that ominous I Ching toss of Frank's. She closed her eyes and tried to sleep.

Amanda must have dozed for a little while; she didn't remember hearing Frank come in. The digital clock by her bed blinked 4:39 the last time she checked. Only an hour and a half before six o'clock. She'd be a zombie all day.

Whenever she had trouble sleeping, Amanda thought about her past loves. That morning she thought about an affair she almost had in college with one of her professors, a man she'd had a crush on for semesters. One night this professor got drunk with a handful of students while watching a basketball game at the local bar. At halftime, he put his arm around Amanda's shoulder and said, "My wife is having a troubled pregnancy. She's refused sex for months. I think about you often, Amanda. And not in the way I should." The invitation to sleep with him was embossed, with gold trim and red letters.

Amanda, twenty-one at the time, agreed to leave the bar and go to a local off-campus inn with him. They didn't speak on the drive over. Once in their room, they fell on the creaky bed, kissing. After about ten minutes of rolling and making out (Amanda never detected much life in his slacks), the professor started to sob. He sat up, threw his legs over the side of the bed, put his elbows on his knees and his face in his hands. He cried like the baby on the way.

In her room, Amanda threw aside her comforter and got out of bed. No use lying there, recalling other aborted love affairs. Chick's dying was a sign, she decided. She'd never find her romantic ideal. She was cursed—pretty enough to attract hordes of men, but none she really wanted. She might as well be like Frank and give up, she thought bitterly. Her soul mate existed only in her dreams.

Amanda's pink flannel nightshirt wasn't warm enough, so she slipped on her chenille bathrobe and slid in her slippers to the living room. She sat down at the window seat and looked outside at empty, deserted Montague Street. The predawn hours in Brooklyn were peaceful. The sidewalks were empty, the streetlights glowing yellow-pink. Amanda imagined how romantic and tragic a figure she made, sitting alone in that light in the window. A few pigeons loitered on the curb in front next to a tree planted in a cutout square of dirt on the sidewalk. Someone must have thrown some bread down for them. Frank always complained about the pigeons—her big urban-renewal idea was to catch them, cook them, and serve them in homeless shelters as squab. Amanda loved all creatures and wished harm on none. Pigeons would have to be slow-roasted for hours to kill all the germs. God knows what kind of—

Crash.

The pigeons flew to the bottom tree branches. The sound seemed to come from underneath her, inside the coffee bar. Amanda looked for signs of activity, but she couldn't see anything from her perch directly on top of the store. She should go down there. Investigate. Or she could wake up Frank and go down together. But that wouldn't be fair. Frank needed her beauty sleep, Amanda thought jokingly. She quickly admonished herself. Just because she was feeling like a failure was no reason to poke at her sister's insecurity, even in her own mind. The pigeons drifted back down to the curb. Amanda's heart slowed in her chest. There had been no crash. It was all in her imagination. Frank hadn't seemed to hear anything, but then again, she slept like the dead.

Crash.

The pigeons flew away for good this time, heading west toward New Jersey. Amanda decided that, since she felt so inept at her prime directive of finding true love, she might as well seek purpose as it presented itself. She went into her room and dressed in cat-girl clothes—black wool drawstring palazzo pants, a black long-sleeved Lycra T-shirt, a black leather car coat, and black Adidas (black cashmere socks, of course). She put her hair up in a ponytail. Since it was so dark, she didn't bother with makeup. On her way out she touched the knob on Frank's door. She'd be proud of me for handling this on my own, Amanda thought, smiling to herself. Since their mom and dad had died, Amanda sought the equivalent of parental approval from her big sister, even though Frank rarely supplied it.

The morning cold bit into Amanda's naked neck. Outside at street level, all was still. No sign of activity. No nothing. Amanda rattled the storefront's folding metal gate to make sure it was secure. The bars were like icicles. The front window was intact. She unlocked the gate and let herself in the front door of the café. All the lights were out except for the neon in the display cases. She checked the bathrooms and behind the counter. No one, nowhere. Relief warmed her. She'd set a goal and completed it. Wouldn't Frank be impressed?

Creak. Not a crash this time, but the sound of tired wood weeping. Amanda nearly jumped out of her skin at the noise. It was clearly coming from the basement. She picked up the phone to call the cops. No dial tone. The line was dead. She big-gulped fear. What now? she wondered. Amanda breathed in, out. She closed her eyes and summoned courage from previous lives, grabbed a bread knife, and walked toward the basement stairs. She opened the door as silently as possible and peered into the cellar. A dim light was on somewhere down there. She listened and heard muffled sounds, like sneakers on cement.

She could turn back now, give up. Get Frank, not finish the job by herself. But Amanda resolved to press on, to do something all the way through. Small steps toward self-improvement, she thought. As she crept down the stairs, Amanda was glad she'd chosen sneakers—actual gumshoes, a smart choice. She edged along with one hand on the railing. In the dim light, she couldn't see much. When she hit the bottom step, a swell of pride filled her body. She'd achieved another goal. Maybe sticking to the matter at hand wasn't so hard, she thought. Clarissa would give her an A+ for this effort. Should she venture into the basement? Amanda paused for breath, listening to the air whooshing in and out of her nostrils. She looked around. No signs, no shadows.

She peered ahead into the L-shaped space. Not two steps forward, Amanda felt a cold, dead hand fall heavily on her shoulder. Her skin icing over, she shut her eyes and shrieked. Her feet lifted off the dirty floor and dangled. She was being held aloft, a thick arm encircling her waist. She shrieked anew. A large hand covered her mouth, nose, and eyes. She struggled and kicked backward, trying to hit her captor in the knee. In the struggle, she barely heard the ringing clang of metal landing cleanly on skull.

Suddenly airborne, Amanda landed on the floor. She scrambled to her feet and turned to see Matt, the anarchist barista, broken cappuccino machine in his arms, leaning over the motionless body of a giant dough man in an apron. The man's bloodied head was resting on the bottom step of the basement stairs.

Amanda exhaled. "Matt, you saved me!"

Matt blushed. "Just doing what I can to protect the oppressed," he said, shuffling his feet.

Amanda looked at the unconscious human mound. His

apron read, *Patsie's Breadstuffs*. She said, "He could have killed me."

"No chance," Matt said. "Not with me around." Matt dropped the cappuccino machine and took a small steno pad out of the back pocket of his jeans. He read, " 'At four-fifty-seven, *X* opened the street-side basement hatch door with his own key. He walked down the hatch door steps, carrying three gray cardboard boxes. He closed door behind him. He put down boxes' "—Matt pointed to the stack—" 'and checked their contents. Weapons cache? Explosives? Bombs? He exited hatch, returning moments later with more boxes.' " Matt looked up at Amanda. "Then you came down. I'm not sure what this is about, but it smells like a conspiracy to me."

Amanda approached the alleged weapons cache. "Smells like cookies to me," she said, opening the lid of one of the boxes.

Matt screamed, "Nooooooo!" and dove behind the basement steps.

"Mmm. Chocolate chip," she said. The box was filled with cookies. The next one had muffins. The one beneath that had croissants. "You didn't notice the smell?" Amanda asked Matt. The aroma was heavenly.

Matt peeked out from under the steps. Convinced that an explosion was not forthcoming, he came over to Amanda. "Born without a sense of smell," he said. "But I still know when something stinks."

Amanda picked up a cookie and bit. "What are you doing down here, anyway?" she asked.

Matt fumbled with his steno pad. "I've been kind of camping out for the last couple days. Hope you don't mind." His eyebrows went up like a white flag of surrender.

"This is why you wouldn't give us an address. You *are* homeless," Amanda said.

"Don't look at me like that," Matt protested. "I'm between addresses."

"That's why you keep a notebook?" she asked. "You're not some kind of undercover restaurant inspector looking for rats and bugs, are you?"

"You think I'm an undercover anything? I pride myself on being the opposite: one man's honesty—and poverty—against the money machine of lies and deception. And occasionally I like to take notes. Literary types might even call it a journal."

Amanda reached out. "Can I see?"

"It's not ready."

"Just a peek?"

"I'll show you mine if you show me yours," he said.

Amanda groaned. "Not another one. Please, Matt. Keep your secret passion to yourself."

Matt seemed puzzled. "Didn't I just say that I hide nothing? If I have passion for you, it's not a secret. Not that I do. I'm considering my passion for you. Once I make a decision, you'll be the first to know."

"I can hardly wait," she said. "Meanwhile, what do we do about the muffin man?" Amanda had the vague recollection that the muffins were delivered on Mondays, Wednesdays, and Saturday mornings (it was Sunday). She never gave much thought to who made the deliveries or what the procedure was. Frank dealt with all of the suppliers. She now remembered seeing the Patsie's Breadstuffs van parked on the street out front. From the living room window where she'd been sitting when she heard the crash, the street hatch door wasn't visible.

"Do you think he's all right? Should we call an ambulance?" she asked. "What did you do to my phone?"

Matt said, "I unplugged it so the ringing wouldn't wake me up."

"We don't usually expect calls to the store in the middle of the night."

He said, "You could get a wrong number. Look, I always unplug the phone before bed. It's a habit."

Matt did whatever he could to disconnect himself, Amanda thought. She did whatever she could to connect. He was her opposite. "Can you please replug the phone? And get a wet rag. Let's try to revive this man," she said.

Matt tucked his notepad into his back pocket and went upstairs. Amanda hoped Frank wouldn't fire Matt for this. He meant no harm. She kneeled over Patsie Strombo and slapped the muffin man gently across the cheeks. They jiggled and wiggled. His skin was flaky and white, like flour, and his chins were multiple. His eyes fluttered.

Amanda said, "Hello? Are you terribly hurt? Are you in pain?"

The muffin man shook his head. A drop of blood rolled into his ear. "What happened?" he asked.

Matt came down the steps and handed Amanda a rag. He said, "Hey, man, I'm sorry I hit you. I thought you were going to do something unspeakable."

Patsie rolled to the left and then to the right. He rested in the middle.

"Do you need help getting up?" asked Amanda. The

muffin man was too big and rattled to get on his feet. Matt got behind his shoulders and helped him sit up.

The man dabbed at his head wound with the towel. "I heard someone coming down the stairs," he blubbered. "I didn't want to frighten you, so I put my hand on your shoulder. And then you screamed and scared me."

"Why didn't you say something?" Amanda asked.

"My mouth was full," said Patsie.

Matt and Amanda looked at each other. "Pardon?" she asked.

"My mouth was full. I was eating a corn muffin. That's why I didn't say anything when you came down the stairs."

The blood on Patsie's head wound had already begun to congeal. He struggled to his (incredibly tiny) feet. "I've got other deliveries to make. I'm okay; don't worry. I won't sue." Patsie climbed the hatch steps, opened the door, and left. Matt and Amanda followed him out. They watched as his van pulled up the street, stopping in front of the Heights Cafe.

Amanda said, "I have some special powers, Matt. I don't know if you're aware of them. And I'm getting a clear message that you're holding something back." Amanda had felt a tweak in the force, but besides that, she noticed several huge footprints in the dirt on the floor: oversize shoes that weren't Matt's boots, Patsie's tiny slippers, Frank's narrow loafers, or Clarissa's spiked heels. "You've harbored someone down here, haven't you?" she asked. "Who was it? A friend? Another homeless person?"

Matt's brow knit like a sweater. "I was planning on telling you. I just hadn't compiled my notes."

Amanda was suddenly uncomfortable, as though all her clothes had shrunk a size. "Who was it, Matt?"

He lowered his eyes. "It was Chick. Peterson. The dead guy."

11

Frank's eyelids snapped open—a grueling way to start the day. "What time is it?" she asked the blurry blob hovering above her head.

"It's about five," said the voice she knew to be her sister's. "Sorry to wake you."

"Yeah, you sound real sorry," Frank said. She blinked a few times and her eyes focused. Even predawn, Amanda looked like Miss America. If she weren't her sister, Frank would swear she was Stepford.

Frank groaned and sat up in her maple sleigh bed. "What? Had a bad dream?" She noticed her sister's outfit. "Dressed already? Am I missing something?"

"We need to talk. Matt's waiting in the living room," said Amanda.

"Matt who?" asked Frank.

"You know. Matt Schemerhorn. Our new hire. He's been sleeping in our basement."

Frank rubbed her forehead. "You woke me up for this?"

"There's more," said Amanda. "Chick Peterson was sleeping down there, too."

"Maybe we should be charging rent—that'd be one way to make some money." Frank kicked off her covers. She grabbed her baggy pants off the bedroom floor and put them on. "Okay, okay. I'm up."

Amanda said, "You should buy jeans that fit, Frank."

"I need a French roast," said the older sister.

"I could eat," said Amanda.

"Diner?"

"Let's go."

Matt, Frank, and Amanda left soon after, walking the six blocks to the diner in silence, respecting the quiet of the early hour. The bustle of the city picked up as they got closer to the restaurant. It was located across the street from Cadman Plaza, a little patch of green off the exit ramp of the Brooklyn Bridge that the city had classified as a "park."

The Park Plaza Diner had been a supermarket before it became a restaurant. The produce shelves were still used to stock supplies in the kitchen. The walls were covered with beveled mirrors, the carpet (not common to diners this far from Long Island), was maroon with an orange swoosh pattern. The tables were so thickly coated in lacquer that you could scratch the surface with your fork for hours without hitting real wood. The red vinyl on the chair seats was secured with tacks. And the booths: red vinyl with lacquered tabletops again, and each one had a minijukebox nailed into the wall. You got two songs for a dollar. The selections ranged from early Whitney Houston to the late Doobie Brothers. The volume knobs didn't work. If someone across the football field–length restaurant had a hankering to hear "The Greatest Love of All," every other patron would share the pleasure in decibels that would rival an airplane hangar. Despite the wealth of restaurants in the neighborhood, Amanda and Frank ate at the Park Plaza at least once or twice a week. Eating together was their time of truce, the diner their neutral ground.

The owner's son, Harry, wasn't in yet. A man they'd never seen before ushered them to a booth facing Court Street. Even at that hour on a Sunday, the traffic toward the bridge was heavy. The twenty-four-hour diner was a quarter full with maybe thirty early risers. Frank couldn't believe so many people were functional at that hour. Their regular waitress wasn't in yet either. A tired-looking woman with a puff of dyed black hair handed out menus.

Amanda said, "It's such a different world at five-thirty. Kind of makes you wonder what you've been missing."

Frank said, "Maybe it makes *you* wonder what you've been missing."

"That's what I said."

"You said, 'It makes you wonder,' presumably speaking about me. If you were speaking for yourself, you would have said, 'It makes *me* wonder.' "

"I was speaking for the collective 'you.' "

"Count me out of the collective." Frank grunted.

"With pleasure," said Amanda. "You're an incredible bitch before you've had coffee."

Matt said, "Man, is this what sisters do? You say the

most bile-filled, mean things with no holding back, and still expect the other to love unconditionally?"

Amanda and Frank looked at each other. The younger sister said, "Pretty much."

"Cool," he observed.

"So you've been camping out," said Frank to Matt. "I hate not knowing what's going on in my store. Say you got hurt down there, Matt. We don't have insurance for squatters. You could sue us and we'd lose everything. Not that we have much left to lose."

"This might be a good time to tell you about Patsie Strombo," said Amanda. "The baker kind of got hit on the head down there this morning." Amanda filled in the details.

The nub of tension throbbed under Frank's left eyebrow. "Great. Now we *will* be sued. Just when things seem to be getting better, something happens. Have I said that ten times in the last few days? I feel like Sisyphus with this café."

"Who?" asked Amanda.

"The guy with the rock, right?" asked Matt.

Frank turned from Mutt to Jeff. "Did Patsie say he was going to sue?" she asked.

"He very pointedly said he wasn't." That was Amanda.

Frank nodded. "Matt, you've got to get out of the basement. I'm sorry, but you have to find another place to stay. You can"—Frank paused, not sure why she was being so generous—"you can stay on our couch if you're desperate."

"You're not firing me?" he asked.

"Not yet," Frank said.

The waitress returned and they all ordered the $2.50 Breakfast Special #1: two eggs any style, home fries, toast, juice, coffee.

"Why would Chick be hiding out in the basement when he had his own apartment?" asked Frank.

Amanda pressed her butter knife into the napkin, making little hash marks. "I don't think Chick really had an apartment," she said. "I think he was staying with Benji Morton."

"Benji?" asked Frank.

Amanda said, "I saw Benji coming out of Chick's building last night. Chick's alleged building."

Matt said, "You're an observant person, Amanda. Maybe we should hang out sometime. You know, away from work. Not a date. Dating is just another of society's enforced rituals by which people judge each other on superficial terms of questionable value, such as the media-imposed definition of physical attractiveness and the ability to communicate using easy-to-digest platitudes that have nothing to do with what a person is really thinking and feeling."

Frank said, "Am I crazy, or is he starting to make sense?" Of course, any chain of events led directly to a date for Amanda. Visions of Walter flashed before Frank's eyes.

Matt said, "A lot of people are surprised by it, but the truth does make sense. More often than not, the truth also hurts."

"Oh, God." Frank groaned.

"Groan all you want. But you know exactly what I

mean. It's hard to trust anything these days. You can barely trust what you see right in front of your eyes. I suspect everything and everyone. Because we're all guilty of something."

"Everyone is guilty?" Frank asked. If Clarissa thought Frank was paranoid, she should get a load of Matt.

"That's right," he said. "I'm guilty of helping myself to your hospitality. And I'm prepared to face the consequences. But there don't seem to be any."

"Not yet," Frank repeated.

"What am I guilty of?" asked Amanda.

Matt smiled. "Not a thing. You, Amanda, are pure."

Frank said, "You, Matt, are pure. Pure bullshit." She could think of a million things Amanda was guilty of: impulsiveness, selfishness, vanity, grabbiness, to mention a few.

"What are you guilty of, Frank?" asked Matt. "I have an idea."

"What?"

"Backing down from your own judgment to let Clarissa walk all over you just so she'll be your friend. Self-annihilation."

Frank gasped. Was that how it looked? "Clarissa wants to be *my* friend. And I'm not backing down. I'm deferring to her professional opinion." How humiliating that anyone would view her as rolling over for Clarissa. It was outrageous. She refused to accept Matt's interpretation. Frank examined the scruffy barista. She didn't feel self-conscious at all around Matt. Strange; he was a man. A young man, though.

"I can see you have a lot of faith in Clarissa," said

Matt. "But until you have faith in yourself, you'll never get what you really want. You'll never even know what you really want."

Make that a very young man, thought Frank.

Amanda continued playing with her utensils. "I'd like to hear about Chick. You spent more time with him than anyone else, Matt. What was he like?"

"He was a nomad," Matt said. "No roots. No ties. He told me he had no close family or friends. I think he grew up in California."

"Did he talk about me at all?" asked Amanda.

"Oh, yeah. He said how beautiful you are."

It always had to come back to how beautiful Amanda was. Frank watched her sister glow with the compliment. How many times could she hear the same thing?

Frank said, "Yes, so Chick responded predictably, anthropologically, to Amanda's symmetrical features and her appetizing waist-to-hip ratio. Did he say anything about why he might have gotten himself killed?"

The food came. The trio ate and reflected. Amanda asked, "How many nights was Chick in the basement?"

"Just Thursday, the night before the contest," said Matt.

Frank couldn't believe it'd taken this long to find him out. Anyone could have gotten down there at any time and hidden for days, robbed them, hurt them. "Why didn't you ask us first?" she said to Matt.

"You might have said yes. There's no thrill in having permission."

"I think I may fire you now."

Amanda asked, "Had Chick stayed with Benji at all?"

Matt nodded. "Morton was the reason Chick came to Brooklyn from Vietnam in the first place. That's what he told me, anyway."

"Vietnam?" asked Amanda. "He was in Jamaica."

"No, definitely Vietnam. That's where he met Benji Morton's former college friend. That guy set up Chick with Morton."

"Chick told me he didn't have any local friends," Amanda said.

"Morton wasn't his friend," Matt explained. "They had a *mutual* friend. A guy like Chick would never consider a guy like Morton a friend."

Frank said, "Okay, then who's the mutual friend?"

Matt flipped through his steno book. "Fortunately for you, I've taken copious notes. And I'll assume that I won't be fired?" He waited for Frank to nod. "Good. This mutual friend was an American in Vietnam." Matt paged back a few sheets and read, " 'Bert Tierney.' He's an entrepreneur, trying to set up a vacation resort on a South Vietnamese beach."

Frank noticed that Amanda had barely touched her breakfast. It'd been two solid days of stress. Was her sister falling apart? wondered Frank. "Are you okay?" she asked Amanda.

"Just thinking about Chick," she responded. "How little we knew of him. You should be with people who know you and love you in the days before death, don't you think? Doesn't it seem wrong that he was surrounded by virtual strangers?"

"So now we're going in search of Chick?" asked Frank. "I thought we were hot on the trail of a livelihood."

"That's not very generous of you," said Amanda.

Matt said, "I can tell you one thing: Chick was a coffee man."

Frank turned to Matt. "You say that as if you're a coffee man."

Shaking his head, Matt said, "I have no sense of smell, so I'll never come close to you. But coffee has texture, a weight on my tongue. I don't have too many complex beverage experiences."

"What makes you think that of Chick?" asked Amanda.

"Chick had a bagfull of coffee beans. He constantly popped them into his mouth raw," Matt said.

Beans as food? thought Frank. In Yemen and Ethiopia, the only countries on Earth where coffee trees were indigenous, the natives had long eaten the cherries and leaves as a narcotic. In some parts of Turkey, coffee beans were used in soups.

"The beans were green?" Frank asked.

"Blue. Dark blue. Almost purple."

Amanda said, "Purple beans?" She looked at Frank. "Kona?"

The older sister and true connoisseur shook her head. Hawaii's volcanic soil produced a blue bean, but she'd never seen a purple Kona bean. "Maybe," said Frank.

Matt read from his notepad. "Chick originally came into Romancing the Bean because he saw Amanda. He asked me what I knew about you. I didn't know anything. And that was pretty much it for conversation." He went back to his home fries.

Frank asked, "How'd you sneak into the basement? You hid in the bathroom? You'd wait for us to leave. . . ."

"Better that than picking the hatch door lock, like Chick," he said. "The night Morton threw him out. That's how he got in."

Amanda said, "I need to lie down." She did. Right there in the booth. Typical histrionics, thought Frank. She moved across to Matt's side of the booth to give Amanda more room.

Frank said, "Amanda, if you and Chick were meant to be together, he wouldn't be dead. And I mean that in the nicest possible way." Thank God Chick hadn't died in their basement. "I would have loved to see one of those beans," Frank said to herself out loud.

"You paying for breakfast?" asked Matt.

"Sure," she said.

"For your kindness," he said. Matt reached inside his jeans pocket and pulled out a paper napkin. He carefully unfolded the napkin, revealing seven dark blue, almost periwinkle, peaberry coffee beans. Peaberries are small round beans. They occur (rarely) in nature when a cherry contains only one seed, as opposed to the usual two flat-sided seeds. For some reason, the Tanzanian crop of robusta trees grown at the base of Mount Kilimanjaro yields a lot of peaberries, but those raw seeds are green. The aroma in these blue beans was nearly gone, which meant that the flavor was, too. She'd never seen anything like them before.

"Amanda, have you ever heard of Vietnamese coffee?" asked Frank.

Amanda's voice rose weakly from under the table. "No."

Frank hadn't either. She tried to picture the topography of Vietnam. She knew the country had jungles and beaches, but she wasn't sure it had mountains high enough to grow arabica trees. The only Pacific coffee regions Frank was familiar with were China, Indonesia, and Hawaii. "Chick gave these to you?" she asked Matt.

"He left them in the basement."

Frank smelled the beans again. "Most curious." She folded up the napkin and slipped it into her own jeans pocket.

"I don't think those beans are good luck," said Matt. That made Amanda stir.

"You're superstitious, too?" asked Frank. An ambush, she thought.

"They sure weren't good luck for Chick. But maybe his bad luck came from you two," said Matt. "Maybe it's not the beans. Maybe you girls are the trouble. There's a dark cloud sitting on your heads. It's practically visible." After that gloomy pronouncement, Matt looked gravely at each sister in turn. Then he stared straight into Frank's eyes and asked, "You going to eat those potatoes?" Frank pushed her plate in his direction.

It was around six-thirty when they paid the bill. Amanda wanted to use the change to throw the I Ching. Matt and Frank watched. The pattern: heads, tails, tails, tails, tails, and tails on the bottom.

Amanda sighed. "Mountains over earth. The mountain topples and crushes a solid foundation."

"Good thing the I Ching is meaningless, or I'd be more worried than usual," said Frank.

At that moment, Harry, Park Plaza's owner's son, entered the diner to begin his shift. He was wearing a heavy snow parka and carrying a copy of the *Post*. As soon as he saw Frank and Amanda, he approached their table. He wasn't smiling.

Frank said, "Coffee tastes better today."

Harry nodded. "We upgraded to Excelso." Colombian Excelso. That's an upgrade? thought Frank. It wasn't a particularly high-grade coffee by any standard. "I'm really sorry," Harry said. Then he handed Frank his Sunday *Post*. The cover copy: GUNSHOTS AT CAFÉ MURDER. She quickly scanned the story—written by Piper Zorn with photos from last night—which compared Frank and Amanda to the Borgia sisters (he made one reference to "possibly poisonous caffeinated potions"). The story implied that a visit to Romancing the Bean would put one's life at risk. The photo of Amanda and Chick was reprinted, and Zorn included a new one of Frank looking extremely angry. Pissed proprietress? Piqued proprietress? Purple-faced proprietress?

Frank said, "Can I keep this?"

"It's yours. And breakfast is on the house," said Harry.

"We already paid," said Frank.

The three walked out into the cold Brooklyn morning. The wind had needles in it. Matt pointed at the air over Frank's head. He said, "You see?"

She looked up, and there it was. A small black cloud, hovering five feet above her. She reached up to touch it, and in that instant it disappeared.

12

Amanda couldn't stop thinking about Chick. What exactly did she owe him? If his involvement with her had anything to do with his death . . . she couldn't even contemplate the meaning of that. Her karma would never recover. She attempted to clear her mind with some meditation. In, out, the sun, the moon, the waves, the rocks, the beach, the sand, the sandbox, the dirt, the bugs, the decay, the death. Not working. An image sprang to her mind: a drunk and wobbly Chick, cornered against the brownstone wall, trying to defend himself against the Shadow Murderer. A caveman club (her spontaneous vision of a blunt object) cutting through the dark night, landing with a barbaric thud on Chick's lovely cranium, the sound of skull collapsing into squishy brain matter, like the splat of rocks on mud.

"Your face is turning green," Matt said to Amanda as they stood outside the Park Plaza, deciding what to do next.

"I want to have a talk with Piper Zorn," said Frank.

"I doubt he's a reasonable man, but if I explain to him that we already have a long list of problems without his assistance, he might stop writing about us."

Amanda shook her head. "Clarissa won't like that."

Frank looked directly at Matt. "I'm not sure I agree with Clarissa's strategy in this regard—only in this regard. Otherwise she's doing an incredible job for us, which I appreciate from the top of my head to the bottom of my feet. And"—she turned toward Amanda—"you'll be sure to tell her I said that when she finds out I went to visit Zorn at the *Post*. I hope he works on Sundays."

Amanda clutched her churning gut and said, "I guess I'll go back to the café and open up."

Frank said, "Matt, you think you can open the store for us today?" He nodded. Frank continued, "Amanda, why don't you go to Moonburst and talk to Benji? He knew Chick the best of anyone around here. Maybe talking about him would make you feel better."

The younger sister was genuinely touched. "I'm sure it would," said Amanda. "I have to admit, I'm surprised."

"Didn't think I had an ounce of compassion in me?" Frank asked.

"Not compassion," said Amanda. "Patience."

"I don't have time for your many chakra blockages?"

"You don't seem to, no. And since we're on the subject, it's always hurt my feelings that you dismiss me so easily." Amanda's stomach tension loosened with the admission.

Frank said, "Now I'm surprised."

Amanda asked, "What?"

"I'm surprised to have had such an effect on you."

The sisters stood silently, looking at each other, arms hanging at their sides, their white frosty exhales meeting in the space between them and dissolving in the air. Amanda itched for a hug. This was clearly a moment, a cracking of the surface of their Frank-enforced (Amanda thought) cordial-but-strained relationship, revealing the hint of something honest and durable underneath. Amanda knew that if she reached out and tried to widen the crack, Frank might pull away and seal it right back up.

Matt said, "Now that I'm officially staying at your apartment, can I do my laundry?"

Frank said, "Please do."

"You can borrow some clean socks in the meantime," offered Amanda.

"Message received," said Matt.

Frank headed for the Clark Street entrance to the numbers two and three trains. Amanda and Matt bundled themselves as best they could and headed back toward Romancing the Bean.

Amanda shivered slightly as they walked and wrapped her pea coat closer to her chest. "Chilly today," she said.

Matt said, "I don't small-talk."

"Talking about the weather isn't small talk." Moods shifted with the wind, the heat, and the dampness of the air. The brightness of the sky. How many times had a sunny morning lifted her whole being to a higher level? "Farmers happen to take the weather very seriously," said Amanda.

"I meant what I said inside about the two of us hanging out sometime."

Amanda tried to change the subject. "Didn't Patsie

smell a bit like reefer this morning? I detected a definite pot scent."

Matt said curtly, "I don't smoke. Or smell."

That was it for conversation. They walked in silence, which, Amanda had to admit, was more comfortable than trying to put him off. It wasn't that she found Matt repellent. She just couldn't consider dating until she'd cleared her mind of Chick. Besides, they worked together. And Matt had no money at all. For all her spirituality and sensitivity and seeing the good in anyone, Amanda had dating standards. She didn't need a man to be rich. She didn't even need him to be employed. But if he couldn't pay for dinner, she wouldn't pay attention.

Once they'd arrived at the café, Amanda gave Matt her keys to the gate and the front door of Romancing the Bean. She peered into the window at Moonburst next door. The gate was up, but Amanda couldn't see anyone inside. She knocked on the window and waited. After what seemed like ten frozen minutes of waiting, she spotted Benji Morton plowing up the street, a ring of keys in his hand. He didn't even look at her as he unlocked Moonburst's front door. He opened it, stepped in, and then held the door open for her. Like a proper lady (and adhering to her men-must-make-the-first-move rule), Amanda wouldn't enter until she'd had a verbal invitation.

"Are you coming in or not?" Benji asked. Amanda smiled sweetly, counted one, two, three, and entered wordlessly. He closed the door behind her.

He shrugged off his barn jacket. He wore his regular work uniform of khakis, a denim shirt, and a tie. Amanda had to admit that she was drawn to his red-haired, fresh-scrubbed burly looks, but she'd never acted on her attraction—Frank would never stand for her dating the enemy. Amanda wasn't convinced that Benji himself was truly evil. But Frank's hatred of all things Moonburst kept Amanda from getting to know him better. This estrangement didn't make it easy for Amanda to walk in and strike up a personal conversation about a hurtful subject (it was for her, anyway; she wouldn't guess yet how Benji felt about Chick's death).

Benji draped his coat across the counter. Amanda registered his tubular middle. He could use some exercise, but who was she to judge? Saying nothing, Benji strode past Amanda to his computerized cash register and started tapping buttons. She cleared her throat. He didn't look up. He seemed to want nothing to do with her. *The rudeness.* Frank might treat him rudely, but Amanda had never been impolite to Benji. And she wasn't used to such disregard from men.

His insolence provoked her. She looked at the menu on the wall behind Benji and said, "Arabian Mocha-Java. A classic blend. The world's oldest. One part mocha beans from the Red Sea region of Yemen. Two parts Java arabica beans from Indonesia."

"What of it?" he asked.

Not to be undone by his surliness, Amanda batted her lashes and said innocently, "Java hasn't produced quality arabica beans in decades."

"Point?" he snapped.

"It's just that I thought Moonburst sold only top-grade arabica beans," she said softly. "That's what it says in your brochure." Amanda plucked a Moonburst pamphlet out of the bin in front of the register and held it aloft.

"No one cares, Amanda." Benji slammed the register closed. "Does any schmuck on the street give two shits what's in the coffee? Our customers just want it hot and strong. And that's what we give them. Moonburst could put out a Malibu Beach blend and people would buy it. That's what you and your sister fail to understand. The customers don't want to be connoisseurs. That takes time. Work. Thought. At Moonburst, we do the thinking for the customer."

He was so angry. At me? she wondered. Amanda said, "All that negative energy is terrible for your health."

Benji didn't even look up. He made some scribbles on an order form. "I'm sure my health isn't what brings you here at this hour," he said. "What do you want? I'm busy." He put down his clipboard and started emptying five-pound bags of beans into the store's giant burr grinder.

Amanda was now beyond hope of connecting with Benji. And his open, hot hostility was hard to steel herself against. She said, "You're being really mean to me, Benji."

"You started in on me," he said. "You may act like a flake, like you're some kind of magic princess who's too delicate for this world, but the truth is, you're as obnoxious as your sister."

An impromptu personal critique—completely untrue—was not what she'd come in for. When the tears gathered in her eyes, Amanda let them come. And they came in streams. She sobbed heaves from deep in her belly. She covered her face with her hands, sank to the floor, and let it pour.

Benji sighed. "Oh, great. She's hysterical. This is just fucking great."

Amanda cried even harder. Benji grunted and then knelt down by her. He said softly, "Stop crying. You've got to stop. The sound of a woman crying is like an ice pick in the eye to me. I'm sorry. I didn't mean it. You're a very nice person. You're not a flake. Look, I'm having some personal problems. I shouldn't have taken them out on you. Please stop crying. I can't stand it. I'll do anything. What can I do? Just tell me."

Amanda hiccuped and gulped for air. "Anything?"

"That's what I said."

"Tell me about Chick."

Benji's muscles stiffened. Amanda could see his thighs bunch up under his khakis. He said, "Chick who?"

"Benji, I know he was your friend. I just want to learn more about him. What was he like? Did he take long, hot showers or short, cool ones? What kind of food did he eat? Did he laugh a lot? Just tell me what you know. I feel like there's a hole in my heart that can only be filled with information about Chick. I need to get to know him, like I would have if he hadn't been murdered."

Benji scrambled to his feet, leaving Amanda alone on the floor. "I didn't get to know him either."

"Then can I have a phone number for Bert Tierney in Vietnam?" she asked. Their mutual friend might talk to her.

Benji said, "Bert who? I don't know anyone in Vietnam."

Why was he lying? "Why are you lying?" she asked.

Moonburst's doors flew open. From her position on

the floor, Amanda looked up to see two men in polyester-blend three-button suits with their wallets in their hands. Police. The one with the mustache said, "Benjamin Morton?" Benji nodded. The one with the beard (but, strangely, no mustache), grabbed Benji under his arm and handcuffed him on the spot.

Mustache asked Amanda, "Who are you? And why are you crying? Did this bastard hurt you?"

She said, "Dust in the eye."

Mustache said, "Name."

"Amanda Greenfield."

"The pretty proprietress."

She blushed. "I wouldn't say pretty."

The bearded cop said, "I would."

Mustache followed up with, "Well, Amanda Greenfield, you're officially off the hook for Peterson's murder."

"Was I ever officially on the hook?" she asked.

"Only to the press," Beard said. "Come on, Morton." He yanked Benji toward the door.

Completely unsatisfied, Amanda lifted herself to her feet and said, "Where are you taking him?"

"Are you involved with this man?" asked Beard.

"Are you asking as part of your investigation, or out of personal curiosity?" asked Amanda.

"Enough, Pastelli," said the mustachioed cop to his partner. To Amanda, he said, "We're taking Mr. Morton to the precinct. A witness came forward and we need to put him in a lineup."

"A witness to what?" she asked.

The cops looked at each other as if Amanda were incredibly thick. The bearded one finally said, "He's been accused of murdering Charles Peterson."

Exactly what Amanda was afraid to hear. Her mind refused to compute the idea: Benji, the arrogant guy next door, couldn't have committed a vicious act of violence against a gentle soul like Chick. Benji's face was white. He looked like he was about to faint. The cops led him outside with a few well-placed shoves. Amanda followed them, not sure what else to do.

The cops forced Benji's head down to get him into the police car. It was right around six-thirty. Despite the hour, a crowd of a few dozen watched Benji's mortification in the clutches of the law. Montague Street was suddenly congested with spectators, all eyes on Benji, the accused.

Once seated, Benji screamed, "Amanda, if our friendship means anything to you"—she was sure it meant nothing to him—"stay inside and wait for my staff to show up so they can open the store."

"Where are the keys?" Amanda asked.

The cops slammed the car door. Benji mouthed through the soundproof window, "On the counter." Amanda nodded and the car sped off.

Amanda went back into the empty Moonburst. She locked the front door from the inside. She was still in shock that Benji had been taken off by the police. But even as reality settled in, her all-seeing, all-knowing third eye refused to believe that Benji was guilty. She wasn't sure where this intuition was coming from, but she trusted it. Despite her certainty, Amanda's stomach had returned to full churn about the mystery of Chick. If Benji couldn't help her contact Bert Tierney in Vietnam, she'd have to help herself.

At best, she figured she had about fifteen minutes before EBAT (estimated barista arrival time). She started rummaging under the counter (poor Benji left his coat behind). Finding nothing, she went toward the back of the store to Benji's office. She tried the keys on Benji's ring, fumbling and dropping the set over and over, wasting precious time. Her heart was ricocheting off her ribs. Finally she got the door open. Inside was a space no bigger than a closet. But this windowless hole had a desk, computer, phone, and file cabinet. And a Rolodex.

Amanda flipped to the Ts. Tierney, right in front. She quickly scrawled the number on a Post-it note and stuffed the yellow square in her jacket pocket. She checked her watch. EBAT: eight minutes. A call to Vietnam would probably cost a fortune. She sat down in Benji's chair and dialed the international operator. He helped her place the call.

On the first ring, a man answered. He said, "Silver Coast Resorts." Amanda was relieved to hear English.

She said, "Bert Tierney, please."

"Speaking."

Amanda squirmed in the chair. "Hello, Mr. Tierney. My name's Amanda Greenfield. I'm calling about Chick Peterson."

"Yeah?" he prompted.

Amanda realized suddenly that she'd have to do the ugly business of telling this man that his friend had been killed—and that his other friend, Benji Morton, was the accused killer.

The phone said, "Hello? Are you still there?"

"I'm calling from Benji Morton's office," she said, not knowing how to start this terrible conversation.

"Patch him through, will you, honey?" asked Tierney.

Patch him through? "He's not here right now; he's—"

"They probably keep him in meetings all day long. Just between you and me, I never thought Benji Morton would be vice president of global sales for Moonburst. Unbelievable. He wasn't exactly the most likely to succeed in college."

What on earth was this man talking about? "I'm sorry; I'm not sure how to say this."

"You want a reference for Chick? I know, it's awkward to ask if someone's full of shit or not. Just tell Benji that Chick is okay. We've got the real thing down here. A whole new concept. And be sure to give Benji the message that there's more where that came from."

The front door rattled. At the sound, Amanda threw the phone receiver across the room. She scrambled to pick it up, saying, "Got to go," before hanging up.

She took a few in-outs, deep ones, and got up. As soon as she stepped out of the office, Amanda saw a young woman in jeans and a down jacket peering into the storefront window. She relocked the office door despite her shaking hands and walked toward the front. She unlocked the door and exited Moonburst.

The girl barista on the street couldn't have been more than eighteen. She said, "Don't you work next door?"

Amanda ignored the question. She relocked Moonburst's front door from the outside—her forehead veins nearly popping from the force of her blood pressure—and said, "Benji had an emergency. He asked me to make sure his staff got the message."

"What message?" the girl asked skeptically.

Amanda calculated the karmic weight of what she was about to do, and decided to go ahead anyway. She said, "Tell them Moonburst is closed until further notice."

Then Amanda took three big steps to the curb and chucked Benji's keys down the sewer.

13

Less than a year ago, Frank had taken the number two train from her Greenwich Village studio apartment to and from her midtown office building every workday. Now she was a B-and-Ter, someone who had to cross a bridge or tunnel to get to Manhattan. Frank never really thought Brooklynites counted as B-and-Ters, despite their technical qualification. But all her former New York City colleagues and acquaintances had acted as if she were heading for the farm whenever she mentioned a trip to the largest of the five boroughs.

Nowadays Frank rarely ventured into Manhattan. The ride on the number two from Borough Hall in Brooklyn to Times Square brought back memories, not all of them unpleasant. It was almost 7:00 A.M., and the car was nearly empty. Frank stood, gripping the aluminum pole above her head, staring numbly at the MTA advertisements on the car wall. Go to the Bronx Zoo, visit the Children's Science Museum, take the whole family to the Hayden Planetarium. None of those destinations had anything to do with

Frank's life. Probably never would. She could see herself
marrying and having kids as easily as she could picture
herself performing the tightrope walk in the circus. Actually, the tightrope wasn't as far a stretch, as it were. Frank
shuffled her feet, knocking into someone's feet. She muttered an apology. The woman sitting in front of her
sneered.

Frank decided to prepare a speech. "Clarissa, I know
we discussed Piper Zorn's role in Romancing the Bean's
comeback. But I can't shake the idea that it's a big mistake
that could destroy my life." Too paranoid. "Clarissa, I
know you don't approve, but I had to made a judgment
call—it is my business, after all, and I have the right to
veto strategy." Too polemic. How about: "I was so tickled
by Zorn's writing that I wanted to congratulate him personally on his coverage of our little café. I hope you don't
mind that I didn't clear the visit with you first. I was
feeling, I don't know, *dangerous* for the first time in my
life, and thought I'd go with it." Forget that one. Clarissa
would never buy it.

It frustrated Frank that she had to justify a difference
of opinion with Clarissa. In the past Frank had always
been able to stick with her opinions, however bleak they
might be. What was it about Clarissa that filled Frank with
doubts? Personal involvement, of course. If she didn't care
about the friendship, working with Clarissa would be
easier.

No need to prepare for the talk with Piper. Having
nothing at stake emotionally, she knew she'd be sharp and
swift as a knife. The *New York Post*'s offices were in Times
Square—Frank got off the train at the Broadway/Forty-

second Street stop. The paper used to be located on South
Street on the lower tip of Manhattan, but the press moved
uptown and now resided next door to the *New York Times*
and Condé Nast Publishing (*Vogue, Vanity Fair,* and *Mademoiselle,* among others). Times Square itself had been
through a complete transformation in the last few years.
Seeing it now, in the glow of early morning, Frank was
both awed and troubled by the change. All the nudie the-
aters were gone, replaced by Broadway musical produc-
tions *The Lion King* and *Grease* (although both of those
names would make great porno titles). Not a single piece
of trash, literal or figurative, rolled down the street. A
dozen tourist-friendly restaurants had replaced fast-food
joints and bodegas. Playland—New York's longtime red-
hot center of teen prostitution—had turned into a Disney
gift shop. Of course, any sane person would prefer the
selling of stuffed animals to the pimping of kids. But
Goofy's rubber face plastered on a Broadway billboard
frightened Frank the way a benign, well-meaning clown
could terrify a toddler. The rank consumerism could only
result in trouble. Now that Times Square had been sani-
tized, where would deviance go? Into homes and schools.

Across the street, Frank beheld the behemoth Virgin
Megastore. Next to that, the All-Star Café (some café—
she wondered if they even knew what a varietal was). A
Moonburst on the corner completed the picture, nearly
puncturing Frank's already thinly stretched membrane of
hope for Romancing the Bean. If she couldn't hold on to
the store, what did she really have? What could she hold
up to the light and claim as her own? She would be lost
without her café, her anchor. It occurred to Frank that

life would be safer if she diversified. What could her Plan B be? An image flashed before eyes: Frank crying on Clarissa's shoulder when Romancing the Bean went down the tubes, the blonde stroking her black hair, saying, "Don't worry, Francesca. I'm here for you all the way."

The bittersweet daydream carried her inside the tabloid's office building. In the lobby, a newsstand carried every paper and magazine in existence, but prominently displayed stacks of the home team's product. She checked the directory for Zorn. Sixteenth floor. Finding no elevator security, she took the next car up without hassle.

The doors opened right onto the editorial offices. Compared to the relative quiet of the lobby, the newsroom was chaos (the city paper never slept). Men and women of all ages scurried around like wired mice in suits. Frank took them to be the editors. Men and women of all ages lazed at their desks, looking like relaxed mice in jeans. She took them to be the reporters who'd just finished stories. She was impressed by the diversity of the staff—not just their clothes and ages, but their ethnicity as well. In the magazine world, the vast majority of writers and editors were white women between twenty-five and fifty. That'd been Frank's experience, anyway, but she'd worked at two women's-service glossies before going to *Bookmaker's Monthly*. Generally, the staff of a magazine tended to reflect its niche readership. Newspapers, especially daily tabloids, had to have a more diverse staff to appeal to a wider audience. This seemed healthier, less insular. Frank liked it, and let herself soak up the kinetic air.

A young man bumped into her by the elevator doors. Frank asked him to point her in the direction of Piper

Zorn's desk. He seemed extremely put out by having to jerk his thumb to the left. Frank thanked him overly nicely just to be annoying. She needed to ask the same question a few more times before finding Piper's desk in a maze of computer terminals. It was in the corner of the newsroom. Not in a corner office. Just stuck in the corner like it was almost, but not completely, forgotten. She sat down in his swivel chair to wait for him. Clarissa on her mind, Frank wondered if she'd be stopping by to see Zorn, too. She hoped not. That would be a run-in Frank wasn't up for.

Frank checked her watch. She'd been waiting for fifteen minutes. Maybe Zorn wasn't planning on coming to work that day. She'd give him another half hour. Frank poked around on Zorn's desk to kill time. She picked up some of his notes, but his scrawl was illegible. She used his desk phone and called her home number to check for messages. The first one: "Clarissa here. See the *Post* this morning? Isn't it great? I'll see you both tonight around six." By then Clarissa would know about her confrontation with Zorn. Frank was torn between looking forward to seeing Clarissa and fearing her scorn. Frank was so distracted by her feelings that she almost missed message number two: "Hi, Francesca. This is Walter. I can't stop thinking about you. I have to see you again as soon as possible. I'll come to Romancing the Bean this evening. Maybe we can have dinner together? See you then."

Just as the machine was telling her there were no more messages, Frank's eyes trailed across the newsroom and settled on the back of a man at a Xerox machine. He had a long, straight back and even longer legs. His hair was the same color as Walter's. He turned in profile. He had plunging sideburns. Frank closed her eyes. When she opened them the man was gone. It was incredible what the mind could do, she thought. Hearing Walter's voice must have made her project his likeness on a man with similar looks.

Piper's phone rang. On reflex Frank picked it up and almost said, "Barney Greenfield's." But before she could say anything, a woman's voice squawked, "Okay, Zorn. You owe me big-time. I want flowers. Candy. A hotel room. I want romance. Compliments. You have to tell me I look beautiful every fifteen seconds. I want you to keep your eyes open when you kiss me and to do it with the lights on. And say my name, over and over. Clear?"

Frank said, huskily, "I'm sorry—"

The woman cut her off. "You're not sorry and you can't worm out of this. The toxicology reports on Charles Peterson are being reanalyzed for confirmation, but the preliminary results show that the cause of death was a blow to the head. But even without the head trauma, he would have died within the hour of a caffeine overdose. According to the report, to get a caffeine level as high as his was, he'd have had to drink a hundred cups of coffee in one hour or taken three bottles of NoDoz. The overdose resulted in complete paralysis of the body—a rare reaction to unusually high levels of caffeine in the blood. Once Peterson had crossed the line, his muscles froze completely and, if he hadn't been killed, he'd have gone into cardiac arrest." Frank heard the clicking of a keyboard. "And that's about it. I'll expect you to pick me up tonight, at my place, at eight. If you stand me up, I'm telling the police you stole hospital records. And don't forget the flowers. Nice ones. You show up with carnations, you're dead."

The woman hung up. Frank looked around to make sure no one was watching her and dialed *69. She had to explain to the caller what'd happened, if she could squeeze a word in. Someone answered on the first ring. A man. He said, "Morgue." Frank hung up.

Zorn dated his sources. What would Clarissa say if she knew he was swapping sex for information? What kind of woman was the morgue attendant to want Zorn so badly? Chick Peterson OD'ed on caffeine? Frank had never heard of such a thing. Could it have been from any of the beans in her shop? She remembered the purple peaberries in her pocket, the ones Matt had given her. They could be lethal. She'd have to figure all this out, maybe take them to the police. Chick's final moments must have been ghastly: being bludgeoned without the power to defend himself. Frank's mind spun like a computer hard drive, processing and downloading. This would have to be another secret to keep from Amanda, thought Frank. Her sister was distraught already. What would the real details of Chick's demise do to her? Frank would have to bear this burden, like so many others, herself. The resentment crept up, but Frank, as always, swallowed twice.

Once he got the correct report on Chick's death, Zorn could step up his attack on Romancing the Bean, really playing up the Borgia sisters/poison coffee thing. An interview with Frank at this point would only turn into fodder. She had to go (Frank was partially relieved—now she wouldn't have to face off with Clarissa again). As she stood up to go, Frank noticed a small bookshelf next to

Piper's desk. The first shelf seemed to contain a matched
set of dozens of volumes. She took a closer look. All the
black-jacketed hardcovers were the same book, a novel
called *The Dock Side of Murder*. It was published by one of
the lowest-rent operations in New York—Shotgun Press.
Author's name: P. E. Zorn.

Well, how about that? thought Frank. Piper had written himself what appeared to be a mystery novel. Frank
pulled a book off the shelf. Thick at 450 pages. The back-
jacket copy described the work as "a hard-boiled noir
flashback to the gritty days of New York City's great
butcher era." Great butcher era? When was that? The back
cover also reprinted a blurb review from *Bookmaker's
Monthly*. It read, "A . . . novel of intense . . . integrity.
The book is full of . . . vivid . . . characters and . . .
shocking . . . violence." The ellipses said it all, thought
Frank. If a reviewer wrote, "An incredibly lousy read,"
the blurb on the book jacket would state, "An
incredibl[e] . . . read." Frank could only imagine what the
review had really said. She never recognized her own reviews on covers.

She glanced around—no one was watching—and
flipped the book open to the first page: "Chapter One: The
Bloody Docks at Dawn. The meat packers hacked away at
the giant pig. He was still alive for God knows what un-
godly reason. Once dead, this porker will fill a freezer but
good, thought Sammy, the one-armed ax-swinger who had
a bone to pick with the unions—and the mob. Finally, the
great bloated beast's fatty heart pumped gallons of lumpy
blood out of the gashes in his neck and into the gutter.
Paulie wiped his brow with his sweat-, blood-, and viscera-

drenched bandanna and said to Sammy, 'It doesn't get better than this.' "

Frank dropped the book in her lap. "Oh. My. God." She'd read those words before. She looked again at the title. "Holy shit."

A couple days after her parents died, Frank gave notice at *Bookmaker's Monthly*. Her boss asked her to do just a few short reviews before she officially quit. He needed the eyes, and he also thought that reading a few upcoming novels would help get her mind off the tragedy. The reviews she wrote for him that week were some of Frank's best writing. She felt freer that she'd ever been before, reviewing books as if she were in a vacuum, as if her criticisms would never be read, especially by the authors. When she'd seen Piper's book at that time, the title was *Meathouse Murder*. The story contained images of butchery so graphic, grotesque, and stomach-turning that she'd actually vomited after reading a passage about the exsanguination of a cow. Meat grinders, hooks, sides of human beef. Human meat sausages. The entire book was so demented and repugnant that the only reason she could imagine anyone publishing it was for pure shock value. But there was no value in the book, shock or otherwise.

Frank wrote a scathing review that practically called for the author's imprisonment. That was the last she'd heard of it. The book was published—she held a copy in her hand—but it never made any major lists. Then again, most books didn't.

Frank replaced the volume. She wanted to run and never stop. The Meathouse Man was Piper Zorn. That oozing pustule of a book was a product of his twisted mind. At least now she knew why he had it in for her. A bad review in *Bookmaker's Monthly* wasn't the kiss of death, but it could hurt, especially to a writer's self-esteem. Had all the evil forces in the world conspired in the last two weeks to get her? Would her pathetic life never turn around? Frank had to get out of there. She darted toward the elevator. Once out on the street, she bolted for the subway. Zorn would be a dangerous enemy—all the more reason to avoid him. Frank prayed no one would tell him that one of his Borgia sisters had sat at his desk for nearly half an hour and had answered his phone.

Frank made it to the subway in seconds. She had to get out of Manhattan and back to the safety and sanity of Brooklyn. She would have run up and down the track had the train not come immediately. She would have run up and down the train car had it not been crowded. Not knowing where to go, or what to do with her nervous energy, Frank got a bright idea. When the train stopped at Fourteenth Street, Union Square, she got off, loped up the steps, and proceeded to race east across town. Frank turned south a few blocks down Broadway, and then jogged east for a few more.

She was out of breath. The urge for speed had run itself out around First Avenue. Porto Rico, a coffee and tea import retail store, wasn't open yet. Frank banged on the door until Brant appeared on the other side. He squinted through his round John Lennon glasses at her. Brant had long hair tied up in the back with a scrap of leather. He had lots of crocheted bracelets on his wrist. His clothes might date back to the late sixties, but Frank suspected he carefully and painstakingly shopped for new stuff that just looked authentic. He was from Seattle, the national home of gourmet coffee. A decade earlier, Brant had tried to open a café to compete with Peet's and Starbucks. It was a dismal failure. He closed his doors and decided to come to New York, where the locals would do or buy anything that was considered cool. He'd lost all his money in the Seattle flop, so Brant got a job at Porto Rico with the hope of one day opening his own coffee bar.

Never happened. Not that Brant was bitter. He seemed content sitting in a small store, buying gourmet beans from all over the world, and selling them to people who had knowledge and taste. Brant let Frank in and locked the door behind her.

He said, "Coffee emergency?"

As always, Frank was bowled over by the aroma of the tiny shop. Dozens of twenty-pound burlap bags of coffee cluttered the floor. It was nearly impossible to walk between them, they were so tightly arranged. Her nostrils drank in the smell, and all her anxiety vaporized. Coffee was Frank's opiate; Porto Rico was her opium den. She stuck out her tongue to taste the scent, rolling it around her mouth.

"I needed that," she said. "What's steeping?"

He smiled. "Ahh, something that might stump even you, Francesca." He poured her a cup from the French press by the register.

She inhaled. The aroma was so delicious, tears nearly came to her eyes. Lovingly she sipped. Heavy on the tongue, smooth down the throat, sharp aftertaste. "Costa Rica," she said, inhaling again. "Tazzura region." She sipped. "Estate of Tres Rios."

Brant shook his head, but admiringly. He said, "So close."

Frank couldn't be wrong. She said, "Dota?" Another Tazzura estate.

"Precisely."

"Fresh?"

"Couldn't be fresher."

"I'll take five pounds." Brant found the appropriate burlap bag on the floor (Frank had always wondered why he stored his beans in nonairtight bags—they were plastic-lined, but hardly sealed—since coffee goes stale so quickly) and he scooped the order. While he measured, Frank said, "If I can stump you, oh coffee master, how's about you give me the Costa Rican for a discount."

He said, "If you can stump me, you can have it for free."

"You're full of cock."

He laughed. "Whatever you've heard—it's all true."

She took the purple Vietnamese beans out of her pocket. Brant sealed up the five-pound bag of Costa Rican before examining Frank's stash. "A raw seed?" he asked. "If this was smuggled in illegally, I'll have to report you to customs." He was kidding. The customs officials at Kennedy were no friends of his. Brant picked up one of the beans. He smelled it. "May I?" he asked. She nodded. He popped it into his mouth.

"Phew," he said while chewing. "Not a quality bean by any standard. Definitely robusta or liberica. Peaberry. High acidity. Hardly any aroma, but that just means it's stale." Frank could see his tongue moving in his mouth. "That color. I've never seen anything like it. And I've seen just about everything." He looked at her strangely. "Where did you get this?"

"No clues."

"This is not my official guess, but I have to assume this seed comes from a hybrid plant and was harvested in a controlled environment." He swallowed.

Frank shook her head. "Mountain-grown. I think."

He smacked his lips, taking in the aftertaste. "Regardless of where it was grown, the tree was not cultivated to produce a tasty bean. The bean is far, far from tasty."

"What other reason is there?" Frank asked. Flavor was everything to her.

"Coffee beans are a wonderful, natural source of caffeine. And this bean has some kick." He picked up another one of the purple seeds. "I'm not stumped yet. But you're sure this wasn't harvested in a greenhouse?"

"I'm not sure of anything," she said. "Except that it's imported." Smuggled, whatever.

Brant replaced the bean in the napkin. She folded it up and put it in her pocket. The bag of Costa Rican sat by the register, unclaimed. Frank reached for it. "Not so fast, Francesca," he said. "I haven't guessed yet."

"No rush."

"This is a toughie. But by a process of elimination based on its flavor and color, and the fact that it's a hybrid, I'm going to have to guess . . ."

She tapped her foot. "I'm waiting."

"Vietnam," he said finally.

Frank's eyes must have bugged. Brant laughed and said, "From your expression, I'll assume I can ring up this purchase?" She nodded numbly. He went behind his butcher block table/counter and punched some buttons. "I'll give you ten percent off if you tell me how the hell you got those beans," he prompted.

"I'll take five percent if you tell me how you guessed."

Brant smiled smugly. "Like I said, a process of elimination. They are like no beans I've ever seen, and I've never seen a Vietnamese bean."

"I didn't even know there was such a thing."

"Whole new experiment in coffee," he said. "South Vietnam has the climate and a high enough elevation for robusta trees. Some industrious Vietnamese decided to force a crop in the foothills of the Buon Mathot region. I read an article about it in *Bean Counters*." A trade newsletter for wholesalers. "I figured that the beans weren't worth importing—I don't deal in robusta beans and it takes at least a few dozen years to make a good crop. The Vietnamese produce around sixty-five thousand tons of beans a year—hardly anything. And hardly any of it is exported."

Clearly Chick's caffeine overdose was the result of popping these raw beans. Hadn't Matt said he ate them one after the other? Frank didn't think one would hurt Brant. She hoped it wouldn't.

"How'd you get those beans?" he asked again. Frank shook her head. She must have seemed nervous. He said, "It's a secret. I won't ask again. But just tell me this: Does it have anything to do with all this coffee-killer nonsense in the *Post*?"

"Can the short answer be 'not really'?" she asked. Frank didn't want to get into it. She was still overwhelmed by the events of the past few days. She needed to sit down and sort it all out. That was when it occurred to her for

the first time that figuring all this out might be the only
way to save the store and herself. That this mess was a test
of her worthiness—for happiness or security or something.

Brant said, "If there's anything I can do, even if you
just need someone to talk to . . ."

She said, "The truth is, Brant, I'm not really sure what
I'd have to say. I know that I'm in pretty bad shape. But
I feel overwhelmed by threats and information. I don't
know what to do, or whom to trust. This sounds paranoid,
I realize. But I've been so scattered lately, jerked from one
emotional moment to the next. I feel like . . . well, I suppose I feel the way Amanda does normally." Frank had to
admit, a frenzied emotional life was exhausting.

"You know, Francesca, I've just assumed that everything printed in that newspaper is bullshit," said Brant.
"In fact, I think that every article in every newspaper is
bullshit. Consider the sources. Who's feeding the journal-
ists their stories? Publicists? Politicians? The authorities?"
He made quote marks in the air when he said *authorities*.
"As far as I'm concerned, there isn't a single sentence
published in the media that hasn't been tainted by someone's bias, either the journalist's, the paper's, or the
source's. And, if it means anything, I'm telling the same
thing to everyone who comes in here and asks about you."
Brant smiled. He said, "Take the coffee. On the house."

"Thank you, Brant." Frank was embarrassed by her
own gratitude.

"You're welcome." He handed over the bag. "And
next time you have a coffee emergency, wait until business hours."

14

Meanwhile, back on Montague Street, Amanda faced off with the girl barista. "What the hell are you doing?" asked the coffee teen, a smirk on her lipsticked mouth.

Amanda said, "This has nothing to do with you."

"I'm calling the cops."

Amanda loved the way the girl said it. It sounded more like a dare than a threat. Amanda gazed into her fresh face with its freckles and pimples. The still-emerging cheekbones. She was so spirited, like a spunky little lamb. Amanda would have liked to sit her down and tell her all about men and dating and college. Instead Amanda said, "Go ahead. Kiss my ass while you're at it."

The phrase had never passed between Amanda's lips before, despite her Brooklyn upbringing. Her fluttering fingers flew to cover her mouth, as if to corral any additional rudeness. She had no idea what had come over her. Amanda wondered if the stress of the last few days was to blame. But a part of her—somewhere low, around the ninth chakra—had relished the crass epithet. It had tasted like cream over her tongue.

Amanda had never been satisfied by one taste of anything. "What's more," she added, "screw you."

"Screw you right back," said the teenager. The girl mugged royally and then huffed down the street to, Amanda assumed, call the police. That wouldn't do her much good, since they'd only just left.

Although Amanda was a student of the ever-changing flow of cosmic energy, fluctuations of her own psyche rattled her. Should she now expect to insult strangers regularly? *Not good*. Amanda saw herself as someone who radiated sunshine and light, not emitted harmful negativity. Had she picked this up from Frank? Were the yang forces in her soul screaming to get out? Amanda searched for the answer in her heart. She closed her eyes (she looked a bit odd standing there at the curb in her pea coat, meditating), and concentrated on her most vital organ, listening carefully for it to beat out a message to her in code. After a few minutes of *thud-thud, thud-thud,* she felt sleepy and decided her intuitive powers would be more precise after a nap.

Instead of going to Romancing the Bean, Amanda went upstairs to her apartment and flopped onto her fluffy bed. She'd gotten only a few hours of sleep the night before, and the day's events had already worn her out. She closed her eyes and began to drift.

Ring. Phone. *Ring*. One more and the machine in the kitchen would get it. She half listened to the clicks and the sound of rewinding tape. Then the machine started to play the new messages. It had to be Frank checking in.

Amanda kicked her bedroom door closed. She didn't want to hear who'd called. Sleep was more important. More pressing. Nothing else mattered. Not breathing. In or out. Or waves. Crashing. On . . . the . . . beach.

A broom handle banged on the floor beneath her. Matt must have seen her sneak upstairs. He shouldn't be expected to run the store alone, Amanda thought guiltily. Slowly she got up, acknowledging that it wasn't her destiny to rest right now. She redressed in clean jeans, a soft red mohair sweater, and brown loafers (screw the uniform, she thought). Twisting her auburn hair into a loose ponytail, Amanda pulled out some tendrils to swirl (as if by happy accident) down her back. She slapped on some makeup and spritzed on some perfume. She decided that she looked decent, considering how little sleep she'd had. Making change with her foggy brain could be a problem, but at least she'd be pleasant to look at.

When she got downstairs, Romancing the Bean was exploding with customers. It was eightish. She watched a couple of people try the door at Moonburst, find it locked, and then shoehorn themselves into Romancing the Bean. Amanda elbowed her way through the throng of people, pushing aside impatient men and women who were waving dollar bills and demanding their morning caffeine. From behind the counter, Matt was screaming above the crowd, "No cappuccinos or espressos!"

Amanda yelled, "Matt! I'm here." Poor Matt. He looked crazed, pouring with one hand, making change with the other. Trying to keep fresh pots brewing. Dozens of people were calling out their orders at once. It was chaos. Matt wasn't even ringing up charges on the register.

He was just taking the money and throwing it in the till. Dollar bills and quarters spotted the floor at his feet.

Immediately jumping in and filling orders, Amanda felt her adrenaline kick in. She became a whirling coffee dervish, pouring, grinding, brewing. If she was too far from the till, she dropped the money on the floor behind the counter and stooped to make change (the best exercise she'd had in months). Matt and Amanda chugged at full steam like this for two solid hours. Once the massive influx slowed, they started scooping coins off the floor in great shiny handfuls. Amanda counted over four hundred singles and at least another hundred in quarters—the most lucrative morning ever. So much for bad publicity (closing Moonburst hadn't hurt either). Amanda wondered if anything could or would keep Americans from their 450 million cups of fresh-brewed coffee a day.

Matt was lying on his back behind the cookie display with his hands over his face. He was moaning softly. Amanda said, "Matt, you were wonderful. I'm so proud of the work we did. I'd love to take you to lunch later. Not like a date. But I thought it'd be nice to hang out." She smiled broadly. "But if you're too tired, I understand."

Matt slowly climbed to his feet. "Tired? I'm way past tired. I think I'm in a walking coma. But," he said, "even in my weakened state, I could get in to hanging out with you."

Amanda grinned from tendril to tendril. "That's great, Matt!" She hugged him. "Just a few things before we go. The cookies and muffins need to be restocked. The garbage has to be emptied. The napkins and milk containers have to be refilled. The counters and tables have to be wiped off, and the floor needs to be mopped." Amanda gave him a big, platonic kiss on the lips. "You're really just the best."

Shaking his head from side to side, Matt said, "I'm not some drooling kid with a hard-on. I'm fully aware that you're asking me to do all this work in exchange for some of your full attention."

"And?" Amanda asked.

"And . . ." He paused. "And I'll get right to it." He grumbled and picked up the mop.

Amanda, the energized, successful café owner, busied herself counting the money, cleaning the coffee machines, brewing fresh pots, and singing in her crackling, tuneless voice.

The old woman, Lucy, their loyal customer, showed up for her 10:00 A.M. mug. Amanda was glad to see that she wasn't too angry to come in again after Frank had taunted her the other day. Lucy arranged herself at a freshly cleaned table and removed a legal pad and a few pens from her massive shoulder bag. Amanda walked over with a cup of Brazilian and a bran muffin. Lucy barely glanced at her. Wanting to be hostesslike, Amanda joined the crone at her table. She said, "What happened to your PowerBook?"

She said, "Broke it over someone's head."

Lucy was such a kidder. "What are you writing about today?" Amanda asked.

Lucy's faded eyes flitted over the pretty proprietress. She must have decided Amanda wasn't making fun of her. Lucy answered, "Same as usual. Decay of values in American society, in particular the breakdown of the family. Working mothers, absent fathers."

"Have any of your letters to the editor been published?" Amanda asked politely.

"You think I would spend hours and hours writing them if no one ever read them? You think I'm some kind of lunatic old lady?" was Lucy's retort.

"So you've had some success."

"You've got your father's brains." Amanda and Frank's father was the emotional, if not intellectual, center of their family.

"Where, if you don't mind my asking, have you been published?" Amanda asked.

Lucy seemed puzzled by the question. Amanda wondered how often anyone gave her a second glance, or asked her to do anything besides get out of the way. Lucy reached in her shoulder duffel and took out a small photo album. She dropped it splat on the table. Amanda opened it up. On each page she'd pasted a reduced Xerox of a newspaper or magazine letters page. Each miniature sheet fit perfectly in the photo album, but it was impossible to read any of the text. Amanda squinted and held the album a couple inches from her face. Somewhere on each page, she could make out a tiny byline with the first name Lucy. The last name was a long blur. Looked like it started with a *P*.

Amanda said, *"The Iowa Register. Plains News. The Podunkian. Jacksonville Monitor.* Impressive." Lucy must have reached dozens, Amanda thought.

Lucy snatched the album out of her hands. "Impressive, huh? I hear the mocking tone in your voice. I don't come in here to be insulted by a harlot like you. You've turned this place into a brothel, with these vulgar pink walls."

"That's not vulgar pink. It's strawberry chiffon," Amanda said.

Lucy said, "Call it what you want; I know what it is."

Amanda felt a few choice words filling the inside of her cheek. But she kept her mouth closed. Rudeness to teens was one thing. But Amanda could never flagrantly insult an old woman like Lucy. That would be cruel. Amanda left Lucy to her notepad and coffee. Matt was nearly finished with his mopping.

Frank came in, bringing a gust of cold air with her. Amanda watched as she unzipped her puffy Michelin Man jacket and sat down with a harrumph at the table in the window. Things hadn't gone well with Zorn, thought Amanda. She fixed a cup of Oaxoxoa for her sister and brought it over.

"Have a seat," said Frank.

"Was it awful?" asked Amanda, pulling up a chair.

"He never showed."

"You seem upset."

"I wasted the morning."

Amanda knew Frank wasn't telling her everything. "I saw Benji. He was just about to open up to me when the police came and arrested him."

That got Frank's attention. "For what? Is smug obnoxiousness a crime?"

"A witness has accused him of killing Chick," said Amanda.

Frank crunched her forehead muscles. "Does this help or hurt your healing process?"

Amanda wasn't sure if Frank asked out of genuine concern or her own smug obnoxiousness. "Neither," said Amanda. "Now I feel sorry for Benji *and* Chick." Amanda thought of the way Benji had portrayed himself to his friend in Vietnam, as some honcho in the Moonburst organization. "I don't believe for a second that Benji could kill a man. He's really kind of sad, don't you think?" asked Amanda.

The older sister blew the steam off the top of her Oaxoxoa. "The depth of your compassion is bottomless."

From across the room Matt yelled, "A little help!" He was standing on a chair, holding five single-pound bags of whole beans in his arms, attempting to get them down from a high shelf.

Amanda chimed, "One second." She picked up the bag of Costa Rican that Frank had brought back with her. "You went to Porto Rico?" she asked her sister.

"Brant confirmed that the beans are from Vietnam."

Now Amanda couldn't deny the facts. "You know what this means," said Amanda. "Chick lied to me." In Amanda's book, a lie, any lie, was a stomp on the neck of love. And so early in their relationship. Practically from the moment they met. The worst part was that the lie seemed to do no service. He said he'd last been in Jamaica, but he'd really been in Vietnam? Who cared? Why would he lie about something as insignificant as that?

From his teeter across the room, Matt yelled, "A little *more* help!"

Frank got up and took the bag of Costa Rican with

her. She relieved Matt of his bundles and lined up the fresh bags of whole beans on the counter. Amanda watched as Frank smelled each bag separately to judge its freshness and snap.

Matt jumped down off the chair, wiped his hands on his shirt, and said, "I'd like a lunch break."

Frank said, "Go."

Matt smiled. "Amanda, you coming?"

Frank raised her eyebrows at that, which made Amanda feel a twinge of embarrassment. Frank said, "I'll woman the fort."

Amanda said to Matt, "Give me ten minutes." Amanda needed to refresh her makeup. "Meet me out front."

By the time she finished her application, Matt had been to the supermarket and back. He held a bag of groceries under his arm.

He said, "Follow me."

The two walked out into the January midmorning. Only a couple passersby recognized her. No one pointed or ran screaming to the other side of the street, to her great relief. They walked straight down Montague Street, all the way to the East River.

"Where are we going?" Amanda was stone cold. Her pea coat wasn't nearly warm enough for the weather, but it looked cute.

Matt said, "Here we are."

They stood at the entrance of the Brooklyn Heights Promenade in front of the George Washington/Battle of Long Island memorial plaque. "I thought it'd be nice to eat outside," Matt said.

"Al fresco?" she asked. "How romantic."

"Are you making fun of me?" he asked.

Amanda thought she might have really hurt his feelings. "The ships look nice," she said. A few cargo ships
floated down the East River, right under the beautiful
crisscrossed steel-cable lattice of the Brooklyn Bridge. The
sun was out, bouncing off the water and the fifty-story-
high glass and iron buildings across the river on Wall
Street. The promenade in winter. No noise. No smelly,
overflowing garbage cans. No Apple Tours buses blowing
fumes and discharging short-panted German tourists. Just
crisp air, a breathtaking view, and peace. Amanda said,
"If we sit in the sun, it'll be okay."

"We can huddle together for body heat."

"Don't even think," she warned.

"Amanda, why do you assume that any man who
wants to spend time with you is plotting to get you
naked?" he asked.

"Aren't you?"

"No. I'm not."

"Good." This was the kind of lie Amanda tolerated.
It wasn't like Matt was making up a whole phony history
for himself, as Chick had. Amanda watched the sun on
the water and reconsidered her debt to Chick. Did she still
need to learn more about the man who'd intentionally
tried to keep her from knowing him? Should she respect
his living wish to be mysterious or continue trying to un-
bury the truth?

"Can we sit down and eat?" Matt asked. "I'm
starving."

They picked a bench in direct sunlight midway down

the promenade. Amanda faced west toward New Jersey to look at the Statue of Liberty. "Avocado," Matt said, taking a green oval from his shopping bag and placing the fatty fruit on the bench between them. He removed each item from the bag. "Italian bread. Brie. Plastic knife. Brooklyn Lager. Mustard. Tiny pickles. Lemon juice. Mint Milanos."

His selection was charming. "Vegan?"

"No," he said as he sliced into the cheese. "I'm more into textures than flavors—the no-sense-of-smell thing— and the texture of meat is kind of disgusting. Have you ever bitten into a big Texas rib, with the slimy fat and the grease? Revolting."

Amanda watched him. Matt wouldn't have made the Mr. Coffee competition cut. He was cute and scrappy, she guessed, like a dog with short, scruffy hair and wide eyes. She was only five years older than he was, but his antigovernment rants made him seem even younger.

"What's with your whole anarchist-nomad thing?" Amanda asked as Matt sliced into a pickle.

He handed Amanda a piece of bread with a schmear of Brie on one side, a mushed slice of avocado on the other. "Mustard and pickles with the cheese, lemon juice with avocado," he instructed. "I can see life going two ways: toeing someone else's line, or toeing my own. I choose to do my own thing."

Amanda bit into the Brie side. She felt her body react instantly to the food—she must have been hungrier than she thought. Between bites, she said, "Even if that means sleeping on a dirty floor in the basement?"

"Especially that."

"I don't get it."

"You do, Amanda," he said. "I know the idea of roughing it isn't for you, but you follow your own heart no matter where you are or what you're doing."

The younger sister quietly ate her lunch. She had quite a fan in Matt. Perhaps he'd start a club. She was flattered by his assessment, but she wasn't as sure as he was of her integrity, especially after she'd thrown Benji's keys down the sewer and told that girl to screw herself. That was sticking to her love-and-understanding principles?

"Do you know that guy?" Matt asked, pointing over Amanda's shoulder. She turned to look at a man leaning on the railing of the promenade just a few dozen feet away. She stood up when she recognized him. Paul McCartney saw her see him. Then he bolted.

"Paul, wait!" she called to him.

Matt sprang off the bench and went after Paul. Matt was wiry and quick enough to catch the Heights Cafe bartender before he'd gone far. Amanda ran after them. Matt grabbed Paul around the middle and threw him against the wrought-iron guardrail that ran along the edge of the promenade.

"Matt, take it easy!" said Amanda. To Paul: "You don't have to be afraid of me. I know how you feel. Your secret love for me. It's best to get this out in the open."

Paul looked at her as if she were insane. "Let go of me," he snapped at Matt. Matt looked to Amanda for instructions.

Amanda said, "I know everything, Paul. Sylvia told me that you've been secretly in love with me for years. Looking back, I can see the signs. I want you to know—

this might hurt—even if you were free, I don't think it could have worked between us, Paul. I think you should make another go at it with Sylvia. For the sake of the girls."

"What are you talking about?" Paul asked as he struggled with Matt. "I'm not in love with you."

"You didn't have a nervous collapse on Saturday morning when the *Post* came out with me on the cover? Your boss Todd Phearson and Sylvia both told me in person that you freaked out when you saw it."

Paul started to cough so hard that Amanda thought he might throw up. Matt said, "He's been watching you, Amanda. I saw him outside the store today, too."

"I haven't been following you!" Paul protested.

"So it's a coincidence," Matt said.

"I do live around here." Paul began sneezing uncontrollably. No one had a tissue. He wiped his nose on his sleeve. Amanda tried to touch his forehead to see if he had a temperature. He shooed her away and said, "Don't come near me!"

"Is my touch painful to you because of your secret love?" she asked, feeling a bit miffed that he was pretending not to have feelings for her.

Paul groaned. "Sylvia was lying. I don't love you. I hate you. I hate what you've done to my life. And I especially hate this . . . this . . . juvenile delinquent."

Matt, not liking the insult, said, "You'd better stop following us or I'll graffiti your house."

"You and this idiot are an 'us'?" Paul asked Amanda. "It's just one loser after another for you, isn't it?"

"You're the loser, dickwad," Matt defended himself artfully.

"I'm trying to help you, Paul," Amanda offered.

"You can choke on your help," he said, and, with a burst of energy, Paul knocked Matt on his keister and fled down the promenade. Amanda started after him, but stumbled on some flagstone. By the time she got back on her feet, he was gone.

Matt was right behind her. "He hasn't gone far. Let's go."

"No," she said, putting a hand on Matt's arm. "Leave him. I'll visit him at his home later." They went back to the bench to pack up their lunch. Her appetite was gone again.

Matt said, "Talk about mood killing."

"Do you think Paul meant it when he said he hated me? I know there's a thin line between love and hate. But he seemed so angry. And scared."

"I don't buy this secret love stuff," said Matt.

"Why not?"

"No guy could be secretly in love with you," he said. "A guy wouldn't be able to keep it in. He'd have to let you know how he felt." Suddenly—and awkwardly—Matt lunged at Amanda, taking her in his arms. She felt his breath on her ear. He was going to kiss her.

And then he let her go. Amanda reeled back a quick step. He was grinning, part guiltily, part sheepishly. The sun bounced off his winter white cheeks. She said, "I like you, Matt. You're passionate. You have ideas. But I don't want you to grab me like that ever again."

He said, "I'm getting to you. I can tell."

15

Evening. The sun had disappeared hours ago. Frank had been serving up the brew at Romancing the Bean all day, worrying. But instead of worrying about business, she could devote the tornado force of her anxiety to her personal life (dating Walter, offending Clarissa, reeling from Piper Zorn, weirded out by Matt and Amanda's lunch date). She supposed it was a good break from her usual daydreams of poverty and ruin. "But is this easier?" she asked herself.

"Pardon?" said the customer she was serving.

Frank scrutinized the woman. She was around forty years old in a wool overcoat and a skullcap, baby wrinkles bunched around her eyes and at the corners of her mouth. Her face was chubby but friendly. She smiled uncertainly at Frank and asked, "You were talking to yourself, right?"

Unsure what to say, Frank mumbled, "Here's your change." Amanda would have seen that friendly, sympathetic face and spilled the secrets of her soul. Frank had always marveled when people unloaded on strangers. Was a complicated personal life license to gather input from a wide pool of advice givers? Frank could almost see the conversation between herself and the crow's-footed customer unfolding. They'd sit down at one of the new Formica tables and discuss: Should Frank develop a new friendship, or try to embark on a risky relationship with a man she hardly knew, or stay safe and cozy in an emotional cave with no windows?

The woman said, "Have a nice day," took her cup, and left.

Another missed opportunity, thought Frank. The soul of discretion had to be pretty lonely indeed.

Amanda and Matt returned in the early afternoon, and the three of them worked steadily until evening. Business slowed around sixish.

"Clarissa should be coming in soon," said Amanda. "And Walter."

Frank detected a hint of teasing provocation in her "and Walter" remark. "What do you mean by that?" Frank asked.

Amanda said, "By what?"

"You know exactly what I mean," said Frank, avoiding eye contact by furiously scraping grinds out of a gold coffee filter.

"You're jumpy," said Amanda, fishing.

"I couldn't be more relaxed and confident."

Amanda smiled at Frank in an annoyingly coy way. "You Capricorns," she said. "Such surefooted goats. Sometimes even you slip on the climb. I can help, you know."

"With what? My footing?" asked Frank.

"Yes, actually."

Frank turned around to face Amanda, and for a hair of a second, she thought she saw a fuzzy blue haze around her sister's head. Was that an aura? Frank said, "Your all-seeing, all-knowing third eye is getting quite a workout today."

"Every day," said Amanda.

What does she *know?* wondered Frank. She'd never divulged a word to Amanda about Walter, his vague interest, her confusion, anything. Could Amanda really pluck clues out of the ether? Frank said, "Okay. I do need help. But I'm not sure you're the person to ask."

"Who'd be better?" said Amanda. "Not Clarissa. I think there's a conflict of interest."

On cue, Clarissa jingled in, the fur collar of her coat nestled high on her neck, tickling her chin and cheeks. Her hair was swept up in a wide bun, blond spiky bangs grazing her forehead. Frank had to smile at the sight of Clarissa and the way she swept into the store—into anywhere she went, probably—as if she deserved a round of applause.

Amanda rushed to join her at the door. They exchanged a few whispers, giggles. Frank felt hot and cold at the same time, like the quiet girl in the school cafeteria jealously watching the cool table. This repeat of adolescence had to end. Popularity? Frank had adult concerns— money, childlessness—to worry about. She wouldn't be cowed by the in crowd. Frank walked over to Clarissa and Amanda, a welcoming smile plastered on her face.

Clarissa greeted her. "Francesca, how can you look so serious when business is booming?"

More self-consciousness. Just what she needed. Frank

said, "I look serious?" For some reason, this made
Amanda and Clarissa giggle.

Amanda said, "Clarissa, you don't mind if Frank and
I disappear for a few minutes?"

Clarissa asked, "Where are you going?"

"We need to go over some accounts. We'll only be
upstairs for a few minutes. Matt can handle the counter.
Just hang out."

Frank let Amanda lead her outside and upstairs to
their place. Once Frank closed the apartment door behind
her, she said, "When you and Clarissa put your heads
together and laugh like that, what are you talking about?"

Amanda took Frank by the wrist and led her back to
the younger sister's frilly pink bedroom. "I told her she
looked lethal. She told me I was full of shit," said Amanda.

"That made you laugh?"

"It's not what was said, but the spirit of it."

"The spirit of what?"

"Of mutual appreciation and understanding," said
Amanda.

"You get that from 'you're full of shit'?" Frank would
never understand. No wonder she was emotionally stuck
in junior high.

Amanda said, "Walter should be here soon. We have
to get you ready."

Frank sat down on Amanda's ruffly bed and watched
her sister throw open the double doors of her closet. "Just
stop for a second," said Frank. "How do you know—"

"I can't explain how I know," said Amanda. "I've seen
you and Walter talking. I've watched you look at him."
The younger sister began rummaging. "I think one of the

reasons you went to confront Piper Zorn today was to test yourself. Zorn was a substitute. You really wanted to see if you could challenge Clarissa. For Walter."

Frank said, "I went to see Zorn to get him to stop defaming us in the newspaper."

Amanda said, "If I had to bet, I'd say Walter likes ankles. Half-calf to above-the-knee hemlines. And, as you know, your ankles are perfect. So let's start with this." She pulled a red sleeveless cocktail dress off a hanger and said, "Put it on."

Frank stripped. Despite the fact that the sisters had bathed together in a tub until they were eight and twelve, Frank hated to undress in front of Amanda. Frank was a bony stretch of desert highway compared to her sister's tropical lushness. Amanda sensed Frank's modesty and busied herself in the closet while Frank tried on the size-ten dress.

It hung on Frank like a sack. She examined herself in Amanda's full-length mirror and said, "I look like I'm playing dress-up."

Amanda appeared behind her. She cinched the waist of the dress and fastened it with alligator clips. "Not for you," said Amanda. "I might have to dig to find some of my skinny clothes."

"Don't bother. I appreciate what you're trying to do. But this isn't me. Dresses. Makeup. I can't do it."

Amanda stopped rummaging in her closet and sat down next to Frank on the bed. "A tube of lipstick can't hurt you, Frank," she said. "I thought you weren't afraid of anything."

Completely incorrect. Frank was full of fears. Among

them: disease, death, violence, drunk drivers, microwave poisoning, small places, large places, tainted food, aneurysms, emotional attachment, being laughed at by children, being barked at by dogs, senility, loneliness, being locked in a room with the .001 percent of the population who'd tested higher than she had on IQ and SAT tests, and being locked in a room with the 99.999 percent of the population who had scored lower than she had. The idea of dating a man mushed several of her fears into a solid ball of fret: While eating dinner (tainted food) in a cozy restaurant (small place), she might start to like the man (emotional attachment). Then, as they walked back to her place late at night (threat of violence), he could reject her (loneliness), leaving her blood pressure to skyrocket (aneurysm) which could make her die (death).

Frank said, "It's torture, really."

"What?" asked Amanda.

"Self-awareness."

Amanda said, "Someday a man is going to surprise you."

"How do you know?" demanded the older sister.

"You have to ask?" Amanda responded, tapping her mystical third eye.

Frank tried on another dress, a gunmetal gray silk sheath with spaghetti straps. Frank felt naked in it. She said, "Why do women who buy into this fashion and beauty obsession believe that women who don't are afraid of men? That's just the most abhorrent assumption. It spits in the face of individuality, morality. Honesty. Makeup is really a grand deception."

"Let's try a game," Amanda said.

"What are you talking about?"

"Just listen. Close your eyes. Visualize you and Walter on a date. At dinner. You're talking, drinking some wine." Amanda looked at her smirking sister on the bed. "Come on, Frank."

"This is getting more and more surreal."

"I'm trying to change your frame of mind," said Amanda.

"Tell me your flirting secrets," Frank said, embarrassing herself for wanting to know.

Amanda said, "What works for me won't necessarily work for you."

"Are you saying I'm flat chested?" asked Frank.

"Is that what you think works for me?"

"Are the hills alive with the sound of music?"

Amanda laughed. "Walter doesn't strike me as the big-jugs type."

"Well, that's a relief," Frank said. "Give me that blue dress."

"This?" Amanda grabbed a long-sleeved navy empire-waisted rayon dress off the rack. "It's too cutesy for you."

"Let me try it." Frank slipped on the dress. It was big, but that was okay. She did a spin. The dress lifted on air. She liked the sensation. The mirror was kind. Frank thought the dress was casual enough to be something she threw on. She didn't want Walter to think she'd gussied herself up for his benefit.

Amanda nodded at Frank. "I never would have thought to put you in that dress, but I've got to say: you look adorable."

Bang. The broom handle pounded the apartment floor/

café ceiling. Matt needed help. Amanda said, "Two minutes to put on makeup and then we go."

She smeared Frank's face with foundation, blush, mas-
cara, eye shadow, and lipstick in mere seconds. The rest
was fine-tuning. Amanda arranged Frank's straight hair
into a French twist with some strands hanging down
around her face. The bobby pins dug into her scalp. Frank
slipped on black tights and Dr. Martens. Amanda suggested heels, but Frank shook her head. Heels would be
too much. She was worried enough that the change in
hairstyle was a screaming advertisement for Trying Too
Hard. The sisters threw on their coats and ran downstairs.

Romancing the Bean was crowded again. Amanda immediately went to help Matt behind the counter. Frank
entered the café and took off her coat slowly, awkward in
her pretty-girl costume. She saw Clarissa holding court by
the condiment island, several women transfixed by her
retelling of what'd happened the night before, the fireworks, the police. There was another, larger cluster of
customers in the rear of the café. Frank wandered toward
them and heard his voice. Walter's.

She edged her way to the front of the group of a dozen-
odd women surrounding a table. Walter was sitting at it,
his flannel-trousered legs crossed, his long fingers encircling a coffee mug. Frank picked up the string of his mono-
logue: "So there I was, on the beach in Bermuda in the
middle of January, wearing nothing more than madras
shorts and Teva sandals. The girls were all wearing biki-
nis, you know, those Lycra cotton separates from J.Crew,
the pink tops and orange bottoms? Very sexy." As he
waxed vacuously, Walter's eyes traveled up and down

Frank's outfit, appraising her and moving on. He seemed neither pleased nor disappointed. He didn't recognize her.

Frank shrank away from the table, her breath stuck under her sternum. She couldn't believe she'd let her hopes float for that man back there. She felt deflated, mortified, like she wanted to tear off her dress and scrape off the makeup. As she backed away, not seeing where she was going, she bumped into someone.

Frank spun around to apologize. Clarissa stood before her, a beaming grin on her face. She said, "Well, Francesca. Look at you! I can't believe my eyes. What's the occasion? Big date?" As each word exited Clarissa's bowlike mouth, Frank felt more like a fool. She thought she might throw up.

Instead, she blew up. "You know what, Clarissa? You can have him. He's all yours. The two of you will be very happy together in your plastic lives." Her voice cracked.

Clarissa batted her eyelids. "Where did that come from?" she asked.

Frank wasn't sure why she'd insulted Clarissa. Not the best way to win her friendship. "We could never be friends," Frank heard herself say. "We have nothing in common. Not a thing. There isn't one single tiny thing we could ever do together or talk about."

The blonde was cool. "Calm down, Francesca," said Clarissa. There wasn't a degree of warmth in her voice. Not half a degree.

"I'm beginning to wonder if you have Romancing the Bean's best interests at heart," said Frank.

Amanda was at her sister's side in a flash. She whispered in Frank's ear, "Deep breath, in, out. In, out."

"Shut up, Amanda."

"Don't talk to her like that," barked Clarissa.

"Please don't bark at my sister," said Amanda to Clarissa. "She can say whatever she wants to me."

"Francesca?" It was Walter. The argument broke up the crowd in back.

Frank heard the voice behind her. She couldn't turn around or flee. The weight of her disappointment immobilized her. She'd have to stand there and take her mortification like a woman.

"Francesca," he said again, now in her line of vision. "I hardly recognized you."

"Obviously."

"You look great!"

"Drop dead."

"What's wrong?" he asked.

Afraid she would cry, Frank just shook her head.

"Can I have a moment alone with Francesca?" Walter asked Clarissa and Amanda. The two women backed away. Frank knew the customers were watching this scene of her own making. She closed her eyes and tried Amanda's trick of visualization. She pictured herself, upstairs, alone, under her covers.

Walter leaned close and spoke softly. "Clarissa knows I'm interested in you, Francesca. She's just a friend." He smelled like soap and sandalwood.

"I could never be interested in you," she said.

"Why?"

She wasn't sure. She'd felt an attack—that was the word for it—of disgust only a few minutes earlier, and now she couldn't seem to remember what had turned her off.

"You probably think I'm arrogant and vain," he said. "Frivolous, too. Right?"

She nodded. Yes, that was it.

Walter mirrored her nod. "But despite all that, you're still attracted to me." He put his hand on her shoulder. The contact sent blood gushing to her cheeks. He asked, "So are your doubts and fears really about me, or about you?"

Usually defensive, Frank felt herself reacting to his question, ready to reject it out of hand. But she stopped herself. She didn't know if it was because of the dress, her hair, the stress of the last week, the last year. It could be Amanda's influence to be more open, less aggressive. Frank found herself thinking first before putting up her dukes. She allowed for the possibility that Walter was on to something.

After a minute, Frank said, "I think I scared myself." When Walter hadn't recognized her, Frank's stab of insecurity had been breathtaking. What had come bubbling up from the wound was a flash of déjà vu: she'd been walloped by Eric when he'd swiftly dismissed her and their three-year relationship. That morning Eric had looked at Frank as if he'd never seen her before, too.

Walter's hand rested on her shoulder. The contact felt painful: a part of her had been asleep for so long and, as if on pins and needles, her passion hurt waking up.

She looked at him, his sideburns and pug nose, and said, "Would you like to get some dinner?"

Walter said, "You bet," and put on his wool overcoat.

Frank put on her puffy down coat and together they walked outside, ignoring Amanda and Clarissa as they watched from the cookie display. Frank knew she'd have a mess to clean up later, having insulted both women. But she pushed her guilt aside. Walter suggested the Heights Cafe for dinner. Frank agreed. She took hold of his arm. He patted her hand reassuringly, like the suitor of a Victorian virgin. What had Amanda told her a while back? If you didn't have sex for an entire year, you were, theoretically, a virgin again.

As they walked past the Bossert Hotel, the national headquarters of the Jehovah's Witnesses, Frank tugged on Walter's coat sleeve. He looked down the six inches of space separating the tip of his nose and the tip of hers. With bravery unparalleled, Frank said, "I'd like to make out."

Walter surrendered the six inches of air between them in a flash, brushing his lips against Frank's with cool softness. Then he cupped her cranium with his hands and fed off her lips and mouth as if he were a starving island castaway. Frank's legs turned to string and Walter gripped her around the waist to steady her. He pulled her hair out of the twist and fanned it over the puffy shoulder of her coat. He said, "There's the girl I want." Moisture collected in Frank's panties. A pack of Jehovah's came out of the hotel and said in unison, "Get a room."

With superhuman strength, Frank detached her lips from Walter's. His eyes were glowing. She said, "To be continued." He smiled. They linked arms and walked on.

As soon as they crossed the threshold into the Heights Cafe, Frank felt colder than she had outside. The waiters and waitresses didn't return her smile. Walter led Frank to the reservation stand. Todd Phearson was standing as tall as he could. Frank nodded politely at him. She said, "Hello, Todd. Business is good."

"Francesca," he said with frost on his tongue. "I'm sorry, but we don't have any tables." He seemed irritated.

"There are two empty tables right there," Walter said, pointing.

Todd shrugged. "I'm sorry, sir. Why don't you try coming back in a few hours? I might have something then."

"Like a conscience?" Frank asked.

Todd said, "Francesca, don't start."

"Like you might have a conscience when we get back? How many years have I known you? You cried at my parents' funeral. And now that Amanda and I are having some trouble, you won't give me the worst table in the house?"

"This isn't the time," he hissed, eyeing the backup of people behind them. He leaned close to Frank. "Blame your sister for dragging my restaurant into her sordid life."

"You selfish, tiny prick," Frank said loudly. "I demand a table, and I also demand a complimentary dinner and bottle of champagne."

She could have demanded the moon. Two burly waiters threw them out. Walter was handsome and sexy, but he wasn't brawny. It must have been embarrassing for him to be manhandled like that in front of his date. Feeling responsible, Frank said, "Let's go up to my place. I'll make you some linguine."

He said, "With meat sauce?"

"And garlic bread."

Hand in hand, they strolled back to her apartment. They made a game of sneaking past the Romancing the Bean storefront window so Amanda and Clarissa wouldn't see them. Once upstairs, they went to the kitchen. Walter sat down at the table and watched Frank take out a large pot to fill with water.

"You and your sister live here alone?" he asked.

Frank put a bottle of red wine on the table and handed him a corkscrew and a glass. "We inherited the place from my parents. They died almost a year ago."

He said, "I'm so sorry."

"Yeah, it was pretty awful."

"Did they die in an accident?" Walter asked.

Frank nodded. Most people assumed that if two relatively young people (they were in their late fifties) died together, it was in a car wreck. She said, "A train wreck of sorts." She watched him pour wine slowly and carefully into his glass. Walter put it to his lips. He didn't swish the wine in the glass to check the balance. He didn't sniff the vintage or gargle the wine in his mouth. He just drank. After a swallow, he smiled and took another sip. This was a nonpretentious, honest man, Frank thought. She hardly ever talked about her parents, but he could be trusted.

"They died right here," she said. "In this room. They'd put on a pot of water to boil, just like this one—I think it was this one—but the pilot light didn't ignite. They got distracted somehow—Amanda thinks they had sex—and forgot to check the pot. I don't really understand how anyone could put on a pot of water and forget about it. I was supposed to come over for dinner that night—a Friday. I canceled out of tiredness. Not even a good excuse. But I promised to come the next night to make up for it. That's when I found them sitting together in these chairs, tax forms and receipts piled on the table between them. It looked like a normal family scene, except for the overwhelming smell of gas and the way their heads hung. They'd been dead for a day by then. If I hadn't canceled the night before, I'd have saved them. No, no. Don't start. It's a fact. I'm to blame. I've had a year to get used to it."

Walter got up from his chair. He took Frank in his arms and said, "I'm so sorry, Francesca." Her name sounded sad and soulful when he said it. She hugged him back, and let herself fade into his body. He started kissing her. They progressed to the bedroom before Frank had a chance to turn on the stove.

And then it was over.

Before it was over, the couple toppled onto Frank's bed. Still fully dressed, they groped and ground. Frank shocked herself by acting like an animal. He rolled off her and said, "Strip."

Frank nearly died of self-consciousness. "I can't."

"I want you to." Could he be a control freak? "But if you don't feel comfortable, forget it."

She was no expert, but taking the dress off first would be a mistake. He'd see the stretched elastic waistband of her tights—a sight no man should see. Frank sat on the edge of the bed and peeled off her stockings, showing her skinny legs as much as possible in that awkward position. Thank God she was shaved and was wearing nice underwear—an ordinary cotton bikini, but pink. Impressed with her own confidence, she stood up, faced Walter, and lifted the hem of her dress. Her arms got caught a bit as she pulled the frock over her head. While she was blinded by her dress, Walter reached out and clasped her waist with his long fingers. He drew her toward him—the shift still tangled in Frank's elbows—and started kissing and licking her belly.

Frank freed herself and flung the dress across the room. Goose bumps covered her body. She let Walter pull her down on top of him. His belt buckle dug into her hip.

Frank said, "Ouch."

Walter breathed an apology and squirmed out of his clothes. His back and chest were covered in light, fine hair. Frank liked that. He wore boxers. They kissed in their skivvies for what seemed like hours, finally removing those last garments when they reached a point of keen frustration. Frank buried her nose in his chest, inhaling his flavor, his smell, his skin. For the first time in her sexual life, she'd become a tiny woodland animal, driven by hunger, searching for a warm place to rest.

They did it, like, five times. As her new sexual self, the Squirrel, Frank worked through her storage of orgasms for the winter. Afterward, she slept a hard sleep.

16

Amanda heard the knocking, but pretended she didn't. Who could possibly be banging on their door at 6:00 A.M.? Matt would answer. He was sleeping on the living room couch, ten feet from the front door.

The banging didn't stop, so Amanda got out of bed, slipped her feet into fuzzy slippers, and dragged herself down the hallway. Matt was sitting up on the couch, examining his nails.

"You can't open the door?" Amanda asked testily.

"I'm just a guest," he said.

"You're an employee," she snapped. "Oh, God. I'm sorry I said that." It happened again, she thought. How could she let stinging comments fly from her mouth like bees?

"Don't be sorry," he said. "I like this side of you."

"What side is that?" she asked, reaching for the doorknob.

"The one with an edge," said Matt.

Amanda didn't like the implication: In her normal

state, she was soft and shapeless? She pulled open the front door.

Clarissa stood on the other side, clutching a copy of the *New York Post*. She looked divine as always in a chocolate brown twin set, black jeans, stiletto heels, and a fur-lined overcoat. Amanda searched her face for signs that she'd forgiven Frank. Amanda had spent a good part of the night before soothing Clarissa's prickly feelings. When Frank had mentioned Clarissa's "plastic life," she'd been right on target.

"Your life isn't plastic," Amanda told Clarissa after Frank and Walter had left the night before.

"She thinks I'm a Barbie doll," said Clarissa.

"No, she doesn't. She really wants to be your friend."

"She doesn't want to be *my* friend. She wants any friend. Just because she's had more problems in her life doesn't mean her feelings count more than mine. How could she say I don't care about Romancing the Bean? I care. I care a lot. I care about a lot of things, profoundly."

Amanda said, "I think you care."

"That's good to hear," said Clarissa. "Because I do. And even if I didn't, does that make me a bad person? I'm doing a job here. For you and for me. The last thing I need is to be insulted by Francesca, who I could insult right back."

"I'm sure you could." Amanda didn't like where the conversation was going.

"Her fashion sense is absolutely nowhere."

"Clarissa . . ."

"And she's pathetic with men. She can barely talk to them. She can barely talk to women. She's just plain strange. And paranoid. And she's not as smart as she thinks she is."

Amanda didn't want to hear this. She said, "You know, Clarissa, Frank doesn't have a lot of control over her emotions. She fights to suppress them but she can't, and when they erupt, everyone nearby gets splattered. If you could try to understand her for a minute, I'm sure you'd be able to forgive her and forget everything she said."

The blond woman looked at Amanda, her lips pursed slightly. Then she smiled, as if she'd made a decision. "You're really so nice, Amanda. Sticking up for your sister, trying to make me feel better. I'm glad we met. It's nearly impossible to start up a new, close friendship with someone as an adult, don't you think?"

"Completely," said Amanda. Especially if your new best friend is someone you've known for your entire life, thought the younger sister.

"Amanda? Hello? Anyone in there?" asked Matt from his perch on the couch.

Amanda looked up to see that she'd been holding the door open to Clarissa without inviting her in or making room for her to enter. She said, "I must have drifted back to sleep. Come in."

Clarissa stepped inside and Amanda gestured for her to sit down on the couch. Clarissa looked at the spot next to Matt and remained standing. Amanda said, "Can I take your coat?"

"Look at this." Clarissa handed Amanda her copy of the *Post*. Under a not-so-flattering photo of Frank read the

headline: BORGIA SISTER BLAMES HERSELF FOR PARENTS'
DEATHS.

Amanda felt her stomach flip. "No," she whispered.

Clarissa quickly said, "I had nothing to do with placing
this story."

"Who's to blame for it isn't my main concern," said
Amanda. When Frank saw this she'd freak. The invasion
was full-scale. This wasn't a questionable publicity stunt.
This was cruel.

"I don't think it's worse than the *Post* alleging you
killed Chick," said Clarissa.

Amanda felt tears spring to her eyes. "It's much, much
worse, Clarissa," she said. Frank had told Amanda once,
the day of the funeral, that if she'd come home earlier she
might have been able to save their parents. The police
didn't agree, but Frank refused to believe them. Frank
hadn't said anything to Amanda—or anyone, as far as she
knew—about her misplaced guilt since that day.

Clarissa took a deep breath (in), and said, "There's
something else, Amanda. Piper Zorn didn't write this
one."

"Then who did?" Amanda asked, flipping the pages to
find the story. "Walter!" She gasped. The byline in ten-
point type: *Walter Robbins*.

The floorboards in the hallway creaked. Frank walked
into the living room, sleepy and content, rubbing her eyes
like a child. "What about Walter?" she asked. "Good
morning, by the way." Frank smiled nervously at Clarissa.
Amanda tried to hide the paper by sitting on it, but Frank
caught a glimpse of the headline.

"What have the Borgia sisters done this time?" she

asked, gesturing to Amanda to surrender the paper. The younger sister hesitated.

"Give it to her," said Matt.

Amanda passed the inky tabloid to Frank. Matt, Clarissa, and Amanda watched in silence as she read the pages in stony silence. Frank's eyes read down the length of one column and back to the top of the next. She showed nothing as she read, not even a flinch. Finally Frank said, "Excuse me." Then she went back into her bedroom and quietly closed the door.

Amanda stage-whispered to Matt and Clarissa, "She took it worse than I thought she would."

Clarissa sat on the edge of the coffee table. "How could you tell?" she asked.

"How could you not?" asked Matt. "That wasn't a normal reaction. She's crossed into no-man's land."

Amanda kicked Matt's legs off the edge of the coffee table. "Don't say that!" she demanded, frightened that he was right.

Clarissa said, "I can't believe this has gotten so out of control."

"Are you sorry?" asked Amanda.

"Of course I'm sorry," said Clarissa. "I'm not a monster. If I had an idea that Walter would write something so personal, I never would have agreed to this."

Amanda couldn't have heard right. "Agreed to what?"

"Everyone's guilty of something," said Matt.

"I need coffee," said Amanda. "Matt, would you mind? There's a Venezuelan blend in the freezer. Use the French press." It wasn't that she wanted Matt out of the room, but Amanda knew something was coming—something big—between Clarissa and herself. Matt's little comments wouldn't help.

Once Matt had left the living room, Amanda said, "Tell me again, Clarissa. How do you know Walter?"

The blonde tried to hold it together, but then she lost her poise, slumping over and staring at her ankle boots. "I met Walter through Piper."

"And how did you meet Piper?"

"At my print-media class last year," said Clarissa. "I introduced myself and we had dinner a few times."

Amanda assumed from the look on her face that they'd slept together. Clarissa confirmed it by saying, "My future livelihood depends on having contacts in the media."

"Walter?" asked Amanda.

"I'm getting there," snapped Clarissa, her eyes flashing.

Amanda said, "Don't snap at me when you're really angry at yourself."

Clarissa nearly snorted. "I could walk out of here right now and never look back."

"Could you?" asked Amanda pointedly. "I doubt that."

Clarissa's eyes softened. "Amanda, I feel terrible about this cover." She touched the *Post* on the table. "I met Walter when I showed up at the paper to talk to Piper about the Mr. Coffee competition. I told him all about you guys, the shop, the concept. He loved the David and Goliath aspect to the story; he wanted to get Walter Robbins, his protégé at the paper, selected as Mr. Coffee. Walter would do a first-person account of the Moonburst rivalry from the inside."

Amanda remembered how Clarissa had pushed for

Walter to be a finalist. "Why didn't you tell us about this?" she asked.

"Piper and Walter didn't think that was a good idea."

"Was part of the charade that you had a crush on Walter?" Amanda flashed back to her chatty conversation about double-dating with Clarissa.

"That solved a problem—having to explain why we were spending so much time together," she said. "You can't deny the fact that we got an avalanche of press from the *Post*. And that the press brought in tons of new business."

Amanda said, "That day you came in with all those copies of the paper. I thought you bought them."

"Walter gave them to me."

"Claude the designer and Mabel the painter?"

"Piper gave me their names."

"Not students, are they?" asked Amanda.

Clarissa shook her head. "I don't think so."

By now Amanda had concluded a few things: Clarissa was a pathological liar. Anything she'd said about their personal connection was meaningless. What was more, she'd purposely encouraged competition between the sisters so she could navigate a clear path between them.

Amanda said, "What I don't understand is why you've done this."

Clarissa's mouth formed a thin, straight line. "I just wanted to do my project for school."

"From the moment you jingled in our door, you acted a bit too pushy. You set us up from the beginning." Amanda made the accusation, not knowing for sure if it was true. "Are you really a grad student?"

"Of course I'm a grad student! Okay, the truth is that Piper asked me to come to your store and offer my services. I thought he was being generous. He said he knew Francesca from when she was a magazine editor, that he'd been keeping track of her and wanted to help her. I thought he was trying to do her an anonymous favor."

"You must have realized that was the opposite of his plan," said Amanda.

"I wanted to believe him. He promised me a job at the paper after graduation. For what it's worth, my ideas and efforts to save the café were genuine. I love the pink walls. I really do." The blonde stared at her boots again. "I'm a victim, too."

"Bullshit," said Matt. He was carrying a tray of mugs and a pot of coffee. He deposited his load on the table. "I know what you are," he said to Clarissa. "And *victim* isn't the word for it."

"At this point it doesn't matter what you think," said Clarissa. "What's done is done. Whether you believe me or not isn't going to change that."

On that somber note, Matt poured the coffee. He asked, "What do you think she's doing in there?" He tilted his head in the direction of Frank's room.

Amanda was wondering the same thing. They hadn't heard a peep. She got off the couch and started down the hallway. Just as she put her hand around the knob, Frank's door swung open. Her sister had gotten dressed in her usual non-body-conscious clothes—baggy jeans, a long-sleeved T-shirt, and sneakers. Her face gave away nothing. The blankness was bad enough. It was the flatness of her eyes that terrified Amanda.

Matt said, "Frank, fresh brew?"

"I heard Clarissa's whole story through the door," Frank said as she walked into the living room and picked up one of the three untouched mugs of coffee. "Venezuelan with"—she inhaled deeply—"Mexican and"—she sipped—"a touch of Brazilian." Of course, she was right. Amanda didn't know how Frank would leave coffee behind if the store closed down. Amanda might be sensitive, but Frank had a sense of coffee.

"I've made a decision," Frank announced.

Everyone looked at her. Amanda said, "Whatever it is, we support you."

"Don't be so quick to support me, Amanda," Frank warned.

"Whatever you want, I'll agree to it," Amanda assured her.

Frank nodded absently and sat down next to her sister on the couch. As she spoke, she searched her mug, as if God were about to appear on the surface of her coffee. "If Clarissa hadn't come into Barney Greenfield's two weeks ago, we would have filed for bankruptcy. I have no regrets about the contest. I think it was worth a shot. I liked the idea of getting people together, that the café would become a place for strangers to feel less lonely in their lives. Unfortunately, we'll never know if the original idea would have panned out because of all these . . . circumstances.

"And now our café has become a freak show. We've become freaks," she said, and sipped some coffee. "No one is ever going to forget what's happened. We're stigmatized, Amanda. Everyone in the neighborhood hates us." She paused. Her stone face was starting to crumble.

"I've decided to close the shop," she said. "I'm not going to fight anymore. I'm giving up. I've already placed a call to our rep at Citibank to see what our options are. But this is it. We're back where we were two weeks ago. At least we have all this humiliation and betrayal to show for it."

Then Frank started to cry, quaking with sobs. Her face was pinched unrecognizably. Amanda couldn't remember seeing her look that way—ever. She scootched closer to her shuddering sister and put her hand on Frank's shoulder, tentatively. Amanda could feel Frank's collarbone under her thin skin. Frank was so slight, so completely unprotected by a layer of thickness. Amanda pulled her sister into her arms. Frank sank into the plushness of her chest, making Amanda feel like a pigeon. Amanda smoothed Frank's hair and held her tight. Amanda wondered if Frank had ever let their mother comfort her like this.

Amanda said, "It's not like you to be so pessimistic, Frank." Still sobbing, Frank shook her head against her sister's bosom. Amanda continued, "Come on. I always count on you to look on the bright side of life."

Frank blubbered, "Forget it, Amanda. It's over."

The younger sister looked at Matt. He held up his hands to say, "What now?" Amanda smiled at him warmly. He sincerely wanted to help. Clarissa drank her coffee. She looked unlined and clear of conscience. Amanda suspected her regret had gone underground until she could face it.

After another minute of crying, Frank lifted her head

and wiped her eyes. She said, "I guess I'll make some calls."

Amanda said, "One toss."

"What?" asked Frank.

"One toss. That's all I ask. To see how our energy's flowing. If there's any change, I want another day before you bail. Give me one toss, and if that looks good, one day."

Frank said, "Dreaming, as always."

"Anything wrong with that?" Amanda had no idea what she'd do with the day, but she had to think of some way to stall Frank. Her older sister might feel differently in a few hours.

Frank wiped her cheeks with her sleeve and said, "Throw your pennies."

Amanda dug into her pocket and came up with six copper coins. She offered them to Frank. "I want you to do it, Frank," Amanda prompted. "It's important to me that you make this toss."

"Just throw the fucking pennies," Frank said.

Amanda threw the fucking pennies. They spun and fell. Amanda arranged them top to bottom in a line on the coffee table and examined the coins. She made some *hmmm, ohhh, ahhh* sounds.

Frank said, "Well? What's it mean?"

Amanda said, "It doesn't mean anything. Don't you know? The I Ching is a load of bullshit."

Frank actually laughed. "Okay," she said. "One more day."

17

After showering, dressing, and having a third cup of Brazilian blend, Frank was positively perky. She knew her sister didn't have a specific plan of action. Amanda wouldn't know where to start. Frank had a few ideas, though. She was glad Amanda had convinced her to try again.

The double whammy of Walter's and Clarissa's betrayal was brutal, but not as devastating as some losses Frank had dealt with in the past. If anything, she felt a bit of pride because surrendering to Walter's and Clarissa's charms meant only that she had socialized enough to care. Zorn must have hatched his revenge plot a year ago, when her review panned his book. His timing was perfect for maximum devastation. How could he have known that Frank had been on the brink when Clarissa walked in their door? There was one glitch in his plan, thought Frank: exposing the guilt she had about her parents was actually relieving it. When she'd mentioned it to Walter, her guilt had been eased. With the whole city reading about it, she felt lighter by the moment.

But there had been the initial shock to get over. The crying. Worst of all, Frank felt stupid. Matt had been right all along: her catering to Clarissa had blinded her to the obvious. To think, she'd been worried about dating Walter because it might hurt Clarissa. Somewhere in the back of her mind, she'd never trusted the blonde.

Walter had fooled her completely. He'd been so compassionate. She couldn't imagine why he had had sex with her. She'd given him grist for his story before then. Was it lust? Was it some kind of sick power trip? Frank had fallen asleep in his arms (when had he sneaked out?), believing that it would be the first night of many with him.

Of course, Walter would have to be killed. Frank wondered if Matt would take him out for a fee. As Frank and Matt finished the pot in the living room of the Greenfield apartment, she asked, "You ever killed a man?"

"You're not serious?"

"Forget it." It was a nice fantasy, but probably a bad long-term scheme.

Matt said, "Just for the record, I have never killed a man. I'm a pacifist. If you'd like me to vandalize someone's home or place of business, I'd be honored."

Frank said, "Maybe."

"I can see it now, in big red letters: 'Walter Robbins voted for Perot.' Something like that."

"You'd do that for me?" asked Frank.

"For the cost of supplies," said Matt.

Amanda was out of the shower and dressed. Just finishing some "touch-ups," she said, which included half an hour of blow-drying her hair. (Clarissa was in the kitchen making a series of phone calls.) Frank was frustrated by her sister's leisurely approach to the day. Maybe she was stalling, trying to come up with an idea of what to do next. It was already 10:00 A.M.

Amanda finally emerged from her room, fluffed and polished, ready to begin the day. She sat down on the couch. "Your turn in the shower, Matt," she said.

"If you want me to leave the room, just say so," he replied.

"It's not that I want you to leave the room," said Amanda. "I want you to take a shower." Matt got up, walked to the bathroom, and slammed the door.

Frank laughed. "You're blunt today."

Her sister said, "I have you to thank, Frank."

"And poetic."

"I think your directness is beginning to rub off on me. And I'm beginning to rub off on you."

Frank weighed Amanda's theory. There was no denying that she'd opened herself up to the world of emotions, the place Amanda called home.

Amanda continued, "It's just like the yinyang symbol. Your pinpoint of yin is spreading on your field of yang. And my yang circle is growing on my field of yin."

"If you say so." Frank pictured a white circle spreading like a drop of paint on a black canvas. White rivulets stretched out from the splotch like spokes.

"The image of a zebra just popped into my brain," said Amanda. "I wonder where that came from."

Clarissa called out to the sisters from the kitchen. "Amanda! You've got call-waiting."

"Who is it?" she asked.

"Benji Morton," Clarissa said. "Do you want to call him back?"

"She doesn't want to get off the phone—at *our* house. Who's she talking to anyway?" whispered Frank to Amanda. "Take the call."

Amanda yelled, "Coming."

The sisters walked into the kitchen. Frank immediately zeroed in on the wineglass on the table—a reminder of her night with Walter. She recoiled from the body blow of memory and breathed deeply in and out, as Amanda habitually prescribed. Frank had to admit, it helped. She continued to breathe in and out while Amanda took her call.

"Benji?" asked Amanda into the phone. "Are you calling me from jail? Oh, great. I'm happy to . . . I know, I'm sorry about that. I was reacting to . . . Yes, a moment of haste."

"What?" asked Frank.

Amanda waved her off. "I called Bert Tierney on your office phone. Yes. Yes. I know. You should ask yourself why you feel you have to lie about your . . . Because you know a lie doesn't . . . Okay, okay. We'll be right over."

She hung up the phone. Clarissa and Frank waited for her to speak. "We've been invited to Benji's apartment for coffee and scones," she said.

"Me?" asked Clarissa.

"Just Frank and me."

Frank said, "Why would Morton want to see us?"

"He needs our help," said Amanda.

"And he expects us to give it to him?" asked Frank.

"Remember your yin," said Amanda.

Frank might need Benji if they were forced to rent their space to Moonburst. It could be the only way to hang on to the apartment. She said, "Okay, let's go."

Clarissa asked, "What about me?"

Frank said, "You weren't invited."

The blonde said, "What should I do?" Without her evil puppeteers pulling the strings, Clarissa was aimless. A trifle.

Frank said, "Don't you have homework?"

Amanda said, "Clarissa, please stay here and take any calls. And tell Matt we stepped out for a few minutes."

The blonde nodded. Frank marveled at her sister's generosity. The two sisters put on their coats and left the apartment. Outside, they noticed that Moonburst was still closed. The line for coffee at the bagel place next door to Romancing the Bean was around the block.

When they'd reached Benji's brownstone on Joralemon Street, Amanda pointed out that the police tape was gone. That had to mean the police had finished the forensics and crime-scene analysis. Frank pushed Benji's buzzer—apartment two. He popped the front door without even asking who it was. The sisters went upstairs. Benji opened his apartment door wearing gray sweatpants and a stretched-out Moonburst T-shirt, no shoes.

"Don't get dressed on our account," said Frank.

"They released me an hour ago," said Benji. "I'm free on a hundred-thousand-dollar bond."

In the day since his arrest, Benji seemed to have dropped ten pounds. His usually ruddy face was as gray as his sweats. He invited them to sit on a red velvet love seat with tassels on the cushions. Frank wondered if he had bought it at a bordello rummage sale. All of his furniture seemed to be plucked from different, equally gaudy sets from a porn movie. Nothing matched, but there was a harmony of tackiness to the odd collection of pieces.

Benji took a seat on a big black leather captain's chair facing them. "I can't believe this is happening to me." Raking back his red hair, he continued, "I always thought, maybe one day I'll get cancer. Or I'll get mugged and cut with a knife. Or I'll be hit by a bus. No one ever thinks that he'll be falsely accused of murder."

Amanda said, "You poor thing! What can I do?"

Benji said, "Would you mind getting the coffee? It's in the kitchen. Around the corner." He pointed toward the back of the apartment. Amanda sprang off the couch, energized by a purpose.

Frank sat quietly. Benji looked at her, and then stared at his hairy toes. Embarrassed for him, Frank broke the silence. "There's a witness?" she asked.

Benji nodded. "Yeah, some woman. I don't know who she is. She was walking her dog when saw me and Chick arguing in front of the building. And we were. He buzzed me at two in the morning, wanting to spend the night. I told him to get lost, so he leaned on the buzzer for five solid minutes. I came down, told him off, and came back up here. The next thing I know, an ambulance siren is blaring in my window. I look outside and EMS guys are loading Chick's body onto a stretcher."

Frank asked, "Why was a woman walking her dog at two in the morning?"

"I have no idea," Benji whined. "Maybe the dog ate some Ex-Lax."

Frank raised her eyebrows. Benji said, "If this were happening to you, you'd be coming up with some weird theories, too. Whoever she was, whatever she was doing, she told the cops she saw me hit Chick over the head with a garbage can. She showed them a dent. There were fifty dents in each one of those cans. My fingerprints were on the handle. I live here, for Christ's sake! This is surreal. It's ridiculous. It's simply inconceivable that I'd kill a man, in plain view of all my neighbors, and then leave him on my own stoop. These cops don't seem to care if the story makes sense. They just want an arrest. Why would this woman lie?"

Frank said, "The police must have a motive."

"They don't need one if they have an eyewitness," he claimed. "She picked me out of a lineup."

Amanda returned with the coffeepot and three Moonburst mugs. She poured, served, and sat. Once they'd all had a bit to drink, Frank said, "It's impossible to taste where this coffee came from. It's burned beyond recognition."

Benji said, "I'm not up for a coffee debate, Francesca."

Amanda put her mug on the oversize ottoman/table. "I feel terrible for everything that's happened to you, Benji, but I'm not sure what Frank and I can do to help your case."

"The only way to get me off is to find the person who did it," he said.

"And you think we know who killed Chick?" asked Frank.

"I'm not implying that you're involved," he said. "The last thing I want to do is make you angry. I can't believe you agreed to come over here, considering how we've treated each other over the last year. I'm sorry, Francesca. I'm truly, deeply sorry about what Moonburst has done to your store. I know this isn't the time to get into it, but I've always felt that our jobs have kept us from having a personal relationship."

Was he talking to me? Frank wondered. "You see Moonburst as a job, but Barney Greenfield's—Romancing the Bean—is my legacy," she said.

Amanda said, "Frank, I think Benji is trying to tell you that he has feelings for you."

"I don't know how to respond to that."

Benji looked nervous. "I don't expect you to. Being arrested has made me realize a few things, and I wanted to say what I had to say. Think about it. If you want to date me, I'm interested."

"How romantic," whispered Frank to her sister. Frank was so uninterested, she wasn't even flattered. But it did go to prove to her that if you chose to ignore an entire area, you'd miss a lot.

Amanda said to Benji, "I'm still not sure why we're here."

"You were friends with Chick. I spent some time with him. If we put our heads together, we might be able to figure this out."

Frank said, "This does present a fact-finding opportunity for you, Amanda."

The younger sister nodded. To Benji, she said, "The truth is, I don't know Chick at all. I want to know more about him, out of respect, out of love. I'm not sure. I'd like to hear about how you know him."

Benji said, "You want me to just talk?"

"Please," urged Amanda.

The Moonburst manager fidgeted uncertainly with the leathery arm of his chair. "Well, the story starts before I ever met Chick Peterson. So should I start with Chick or give you the whole back story?"

"It's all relevant, don't you think?" said Amanda gently, drawing him out.

Benji nodded. "It starts in college. Bert Tierney and I went to school together—he's the man you spoke to in Vietnam, Amanda. We had a competitive friendship. After graduation, he went to Harvard Business School. I went to Fordham."

"Fordham is an excellent school," said Amanda.

He brushed off the compliment like lint. "It isn't Harvard. After we both got our M.B.A.s, he went off to seek his fortune in the world. I did, too, and I got as far as my backyard. Six years out of school, I'm the manager of a Brooklyn café.

"A few weeks ago," Benji continued, "Tierney called me at home. Totally out of the blue. He said he was in Vietnam, launching a resort hotel on some beach. The Vietnamese government is desperate to get tourism trade going, and they were helping the American from Harvard in whatever way they could. He'd already sunk millions of private investors' money into his resort in Buon Mathot— somewhere down south. He said the country's other resorts were run by locals who didn't know the first thing about what Western tourists wanted. He was going to make his resort a huge success, and then sit back and watch the money roll in. I listened to him brag, pretended to be excited for him, but I was burning with jealousy.

"So I blurted out that I was the vice president of global sales for Moonburst," said Benji. "I thought that sounded international enough to impress him. He wanted to know why I wasn't in Seattle. I told him that the organization had made me their man in New York. I told him I spend most of my time traveling, brokering deals for coffee with plantation owners all over the world. And Tierney believed me! Not only that, he wanted to do business. He knew about a coffee plantation nearby. The locals who harvested the coffee had to give eighty percent of their crop and profits to the government, but he said he'd use his ties to help me get a deal for the remaining twenty percent.

"That was when I started to freak," Benji said. "I made some noncommittal noises. Tierney said he knew an American who'd been working with the montagnards—the native hill tribesmen—to create a hybrid robusta/liberica tree that yielded beans with twice the natural caffeine of Indonesian plants. Tierney thought the beans would be a huge hit in America."

Tierney was right, Frank thought. How many Americans drank coffee for the caffeine alone?

Benji continued, "I told him that I couldn't buy any coffee until I'd sampled it. He said I should come to Vietnam. Now I was stuck. I'd just said that I flew all over the world for Moonburst. So I told him we were locked into contracts until at least March. He let it drop. But then he hit me up for some investment capital—the real reason he'd called. I found out later he'd called everyone in his address book looking for money. I told him I'd send a thousand dollars. We hung up. I hoped I'd never hear from him again."

Frank was sure Benji would have sent the thousand dollars just to keep the charade alive. "Chick—the American botanist—showed up at my store a week later," Benji said. "In about five seconds he'd figured out that I had no power in the Moonburst operation. I was prepared to admit to every lie, but then Chick said, 'Since I'm here anyway and I've got a pound of beans, let's make a go of it.' I did have some contact with a regional retail director in Seattle. I found myself getting excited. To toast our new pact, Chick and I brewed a pot from the pound of roasted beans he smuggled in—he also brought some raw beans, which, he said, were for his personal consumption—and we sat down to discuss strategy. I took one sip of the brew and nearly fainted. My heart raced, my blood was pumping from the caffeine, and the flavor was dreadful. There was no way Moonburst would sell coffee that tasted that bad."

"I beg to differ," said Frank.

"You haven't tasted this coffee," said Benji. "I told Chick the coffee venture was a bust. I felt guilty about the whole thing, so I offered him a place to stay. He was a polite guest, but after a few days I wanted my space back. He was getting on my nerves, too, hanging around Moonburst, talking to my customers about his miracle beans. He kept coming behind the counter, taking samples of coffee and pastry. My patience ran out and I told him he had to leave. He landed, apparently, on your doorstep."

"Where's the pound of roasted beans?" Frank asked.

Chick must have finished off the raw stash himself (minus the beans Matt gave Frank), overdosing in the process.

"Chick kept most of it. He gave me about a quarter-pound sample to hold on to, just in case I changed my mind. It's locked in the store safe. He never asked for it back. I assume it's still there."

"Can we get it?" Frank asked. She was curious to taste the brew.

"Unfortunately, the keys to the safe are now some-where in the New York City sewage system," said Benji.

Amanda giggled. "Sorry about that."

Frank had no idea what they were talking about. But she didn't really care. "We can always break the safe," she said to herself out loud.

Amanda asked, "Tell me more about Chick. When he stayed with you, did he sleep late? Jump up at the break of dawn? Did he cook for himself or eat cereal out of the box? Did he read before bed? Clean up after himself?"

Benji said, "I don't know."

"How can you not know? He lived here for a few days."

"Yes, but I hardly saw him here. I leave by six to open the store, and he wasn't up then. He did eat my food—leftover pasta and chicken, fruit, cereal, eggs—but I don't know if he ate it out of the container or on a plate. He usually cleaned up after himself. I'm not sure if he read before he went to sleep. I hit the sack at ten."

"You slept in your room?"

"In front. I'd say I was turning in, close my door, and that was it for the night."

"Where did Chick sleep?" asked Amanda.

"On the couch."

"On this couch?" she asked. "This is more like a love seat. How did he do it? He was well over six feet tall."

"I don't know," said Benji. "I never thought about it."

Amanda said, "First he slept on a very uncomfortable couch, and then on the basement floor at our place. His last few nights must have been tortured and restless. He grabbed food where he could, hungry, desperate, craving human contact. Chasing his dreams that would never come true."

Frank said, "You're romanticizing him."

"Why do you say that?"

"I'm getting a different picture of Chick."

"Such as?"

"He was a freeloading operator."

Amanda gasped. "He was a botanist!"

Frank bit her lip. She could have gone into detail about Chick's pattern of using someone until a door closed. If Amanda hadn't humiliated him on their date, Frank was sure she would have had to deal with Chick sleeping at their place until she had to throw him out, too. In fact, it occurred to Frank, Chick's intention was to seduce Amanda into opening her home to him. Maybe that was part of the reason he ran out of the Heights Cafe, so that Amanda would look for him the next day and beg him to stay with her. Could this be possible? Was Chick a manipulative user? Frank kept her theory to herself. The last thing she wanted to do was upset Amanda. Frank was surprised by how much she liked the idea of their complementing each other, that they'd not only opened up to each other, but a part of each had opened up inside the other. Frank didn't want to spoil all that by popping Amanda's Chick bubble.

Frank said, "You're right. Chick was just down on his luck."

Benji said, "Which brings me back to the murder. Does any of this trigger something for you, Amanda? Are you getting any of your messages?"

"It helps put Chick in context, but nothing is coming up," she said. "Let me percolate for a few hours. Something may rise to the surface."

"All I can ask is that you try," said Benji.

Frank brushed off her jeans and stood, too. "Let's go, Amanda."

The sisters thanked Benji, wished him luck, and left. Out on the street, chilled by the air and by Benji's plight, Amanda said, "All the time and energy we've spent building up Benji to be a ruthless adversary seems wasted. He's just a desperate schmo."

"Like the rest of us?" Frank asked as they walked.

"You don't believe that for a second," Amanda countered, "You think you're damn smart. Admit it."

"And you think you're damn pretty."

"Well, I do hate false modesty," she said, batting her long lashes.

Frank said, "Matt might know where the rest of the coffee is."

"We can ask him," said Amanda.

"I'm curious about those beans." Frank agreed that highly caffeinated beans would be attractive to consumers. Of course, if they caffeinated you to death, that was a problem. But this was only the first generation of the hybrid. Mixing robusta and liberica with arabica plants might make for greater caffeine content plus better taste. A refined hybrid could be worth a fortune.

Instead of turning on Montague Street to go home, Frank said to Amanda, "I have an idea. Take a walk with me."

"Where are we going?" asked Amanda.

"Just come."

Amanda shrugged, bundled her coat tighter, and followed Frank. They continued down Hicks Street all the way past the promenade, into the North Heights. Frank made a left onto Middaugh Street. It was one of those tucked-away single-block streets that felt out of place with the rest of Brooklyn Heights' upscale Victorian style. Many of the houses on the block were made of wood, not brownstone. All of them were dilapidated, slouching with neglect, with withered shingles and paint-stripped front doors. This was the slum stretch of Brooklyn Heights, which was probably the equivalent of the ritziest street on the Lower East Side of Manhattan. They walked the length of the block, stopping on the corner of Clinton Street. Frank looked up at a sagging gray house. She checked the number on the door and said, "We're here."

She began knocking on the dirty gray door. The street-level windows were soaped white, but Frank could see heavy curtains hanging inside. She kept banging even though no one answered after a few minutes.

"I don't think anyone's home," said Amanda.

"He's sleeping," Frank surmised. "He sleeps during the day."

"Are we interviewing a vampire?" asked Amanda.

"A baker."

At that moment a giant marshmallow answered the door. Patsie Strombo was wearing pink-striped pajamas that reminded Frank of Piglet from Winnie the Pooh, only about five thousand times the size. His brown hair was curled. And it was just that—a single hair wrapped around and around his head. His scalp looked like a cinnamon swirl.

"Whazzis," he asked, more exhausted than angry.

Frank said, "Patsie Strombo, hi. I'm Francesca Greenfield. I send you a check each month." Frank hadn't laid eyes on him since high school. In the year of running the business, she and Patsie had corresponded with notes and phone messages, never face-to-face. "It's been a while. You haven't changed," Frank noticed. He hadn't. Maybe the hair was longer.

Patsie smiled, showing dingy teeth. "Francesca Greenfield. You look more and more like your father."

"How's your head, Patsie? I hope it's okay," said Amanda.

He smiled sleepily at her and said, "And you look just like your mother. My head is fine. I owe you an apology for frightening you like that."

If Amanda lopped off his head, this guy would apologize for squirting too much blood, thought Frank. "May we come in?" she asked. It was cold on the street.

Once inside, Frank scanned the four hundred square feet. Against one wall loomed a double-size Sub-Zero fridge. Next to that, a massive Viking stove. Upon a huge table with a steel counter sat a five-gallon Cuisinart. In the back corner Frank spied a cot—a king-size cot, mind you—and an armoire. A door near the bed must have led to a utility bathroom with a stall shower.

"My work is my life," said Patsie, as if to explain his living conditions.

Amanda said, "I really admire a man who isn't obsessed with acquisition. Material objects can't supply you with love or even peace of mind, and they certainly don't get you one step closer to any kind of spiritual enlightenment."

Patsie nodded. "At times, when I'm alone at midnight, making cookies, I can almost hear the sound of the earth spinning."

"Zen and the art of dough baking?" asked Frank. Under the cot, she saw an ashtray and a small red bong.

Patsie shifted uncomfortably on his tiny feet, suddenly self-conscious. "What can I do for you?" he asked. "Is there any problem with the breadstuffs?"

Frank said, "No problem at all. But I was wondering if you happened to have found half a pound of coffee beans in our basement on one of your deliveries."

"Half a pound of coffee?"

"I assume it was in a bag."

"You never store coffee in the basement," he said. He was right. Frank bought small amounts so the beans would stay fresh and kept it all upstairs.

"Maybe someone gave it to you? Or sold it to you?" Frank had a theory, the magic-beans theory. Chick was living in the basement, and he needed some cash quick to court Amanda. So he sold some magic beans to the giant. They must have crossed paths at some point in the basement. Frank wasn't sure what Chick'd said about the beans to Patsie, but the baker wasn't too swift.

"I smell something," said Frank. Her bloodhound nose led her toward a baker's rack near the stove. Each shelf held a different ambrosial treat: scones, cakes, muffins, pies, biscotti, little pots of crème brûlée. She couldn't distinguish the coffee scent from goodie to goodie. Frank said, "It's in here, right? The coffee is here."

Patsie sighed wetly and nodded. "The brûlée took me hours. Double broilers. Ramekins. But they're worth the effort. The recipe called for powdered coffee, so I had to grind the beans and then pulverize them by hand. And I love how the Coffee L'Orange Scones worked out. Two heaping tablespoons of fresh-ground coffee per dozen. I've already eaten a tray of those myself. Maybe that's why I've been having trouble sleeping." When he spoke, Patsie's chin was nearly indistinguishable from his neck.

"What's this?" Frank asked, lifting a pastry in a tiny tin dish.

"Good choice," he said. "That is a Chiffon Caffe Mini Pie. Graham-cracker crust. Egg yolks. A cup of double-strength, extra-strong brewed coffee. Squeeze of fresh lemon juice—and a sprinkle of zest. Eat. Enjoy."

Frank stripped the pie of its metal skirt and nibbled the crust. She took a bigger bite. "Ahh," she cooed. It was incredible. Frank ate the whole thing. "I just destroyed evidence."

Amanda said, "I'm confused. That's the Vietnamese coffee? Baked into pastry?"

Patsie said, "Vietnamese? Matt said that the beans were specially grown in Singapore for baking."

Matt? Matt sold him the beans? Well, Frank's magic-beans theory was off, but only slightly. "You're talking about Matt, the scruffy guy. The one who hit you on the head with the cappuccino machine?" asked Frank.

Patsie nodded, his chin disappearing. "Yes, him."

"Thanks for your help," said Frank. She'd have to find out how the beans had passed from Chick to Matt. No problem there. She'd just ask him. "Promise me one thing?" she said to Patsie. "Don't eat or sell this stuff. Freeze it." However terrible the beans were for brewing, they were fantastic for cooking. These Vietnamese jumping beans might have commercial potential after all. A caffeinated snack. Would Americans buy that?

Patsie agreed to freeze the coffee treats. The sisters thanked him, and they headed out. Patsie called after them. "Wait! Should I invoice you or Mr. Phearson for January? I can just send your bill to the Heights Cafe."

"What does Todd Phearson have to do with our bakery bill?" Frank asked.

Patsie seemed confused. "Tomorrow is January fifteenth."

"So?"

"You don't know about the deal?"

Frank felt a chill, but not from the cold. "What deal?" she asked.

He shook his head. "You girls had better have a talk with Mr. Phearson."

"I have nothing to say to him."

"I'm sure he'll have something to say to you," said Patsie as he closed his weatherworn door.

18

Amanda feared the new setback would push Frank over the edge. She wasn't having a problem herself. In fact, now that she'd found the edge to her personality, Amanda quite liked it. She could actually envision a crystalline sharpness forming in her brain, and wondered if her cheekbones would soon appear chiseled. There was much to be said for embracing the edge: just look at Frank, razor thin, a rapier intellect, a cutting sarcasm. But at that moment, Frank's hard line was blurred by her hopping rage.

Amanda said, "Calm down."

Frank said, "I'll calm down when I'm dead."

"I'm sure of that, Frank. But I wish you'd try to relax in the meantime."

"Shut up, Amanda."

The sisters watched as their nemesis-come-lately, Todd Phearson, taped a sign on Romancing the Bean's metal gate. It read: *Property of the Phearson Restaurant Group.* He stood on his tiptoes to tape the top corners.

Todd finished his dirty work and hung the role of

electrical tape around his wrist. He said, "Frankly, I'm surprised you girls didn't know this was coming. Your parents never discussed their finances with you?"

Frank said, "We had an appointment with them to do just that, but they blew it off by dying."

Todd said, "They should have explained this to you."

Amanda said, "Why don't you explain it to us?"

He looked up at Amanda and rolled his eyes, as if the exertion of talking was too much to contemplate. Then he said, "You know the ownership history, right?"

Frank said, "Our grandfather had a long-term lease, and Mom and Dad bought the building from your grandfather's landlord about twenty-five years ago."

Todd nodded. "Right. They got a thirty-year fixed-rate mortgage in the mid-seventies, when interest rates were sky-high. And they never refinanced after rates dropped! Your parents were never very good with money. Anyway, a little over a year ago, when Barney Greenfield's started to falter, your parents wanted to take out a loan. But Citibank thought your folks were a bad risk, considering how they hovered on the verge of bankruptcy. So your folks came to me. I gave them a loan of fifty thousand dollars, plus ten percent interest, payable in just over a year's time—that would be today, at five o'clock. If your parents—or their heirs—couldn't make the payment, the title on the building would be turned over to me."

Frank said, "That's the stupidest deal I've ever heard. They had only a few years left on the mortgage. This building is worth at least eight hundred thousand dollars."

Her sister was right, thought Amanda. Sure, it was small and run-down, but a Montague Street storefront with an upstairs apartment, in this real estate boom? Had to be worth a ton. It was their nest egg, the reason Amanda didn't think she'd ever have to worry about retirement savings.

Todd said, "Go get yourself a buyer who will give you fifty-five thousand dollars in cash by five o'clock. I don't care if you sell; I just want my money."

"You'd rather have the building and you know it," said Frank. "You intentionally kept this arrangement a secret from us so that we'd have no recourse. I want proof that this deal even exists."

Todd removed a sheet of paper from his wool coat pocket. He handed it to Frank, and the sisters read it. The official-looking agreement was signed and notarized two days before their parents' deaths. Amanda noticed that Bernie Zigler, their parent's lawyer, had signed off on it. Why hadn't he told them about this deal at the funeral? Had he forgotten to mention it in the melee?

"See the date? They probably planned on telling us, but they never got a chance to," said Amanda.

Frank nodded. "We should have investigated any claims."

"I just assumed all we had to do was pay the mortgage every month," said Amanda.

"How could Mom and Dad have made this deal?" Frank asked. Amanda had wondered that, too. Their desperation was written all over that piece of paper. They must have been terrified of losing the store, but optimistic that a loan could revive business. Amanda was glad her parents didn't have to see the man they thought of as a friend cut the sisters off at their knees.

Frank said, "I'm calling our lawyer."

"Do," said Todd.

The way he said it, Amanda suspected that Zigler, their parents' trusted lawyer, was somehow involved in keeping this deal a secret. But she didn't say anything. There was nothing to say.

Frank said to Todd, "No wonder you've been so hostile to us. When you said we were hurting your business, you didn't mean the Heights Cafe; you meant Romancing the Bean." Frank held the contract at Todd's nose level and ripped it in half. The pieces fluttered in the wind and blew down the street.

"That's a copy, Francesca. The original is locked in my desk at home."

"It's a fake," she protested.

"Call Bernie Zigler. I'm sure he has your parents' original in a vault. Perhaps in the confusion after Flo and Marv's deaths, you overlooked it?" Now Amanda was sure the lawyer was in cahoots with Todd. She closed her eyes to the ugliness, but could still see it on the underside of her lids.

"And if we don't come up with the money by the end of the day?" asked Frank. It was around 1:30 P.M.

"I'll come over with a locksmith and change the locks."

"You'll have to go through me first," Frank said, plastering her body across the metal gate.

"So be it."

"How are we supposed to get fifty-five thousand dollars in a few hours?" Amanda asked. "It's impossible."

Todd said, "I'd be happy to claim the store now."

"Fuck you and a half," Frank said to him.

Todd laughed as he headed back to the Heights Cafe. Amanda turned to Frank, hoping to hug. But Amanda could see that the softening of Frank had ceased. She was withdrawn again.

"I'm finding a major glitch in my overall life philosophy," said Amanda. "I keep expecting the best, and getting the worst."

"Even if you expected the worst, it'd still hurt when you got it, believe me," said Frank.

"Can we go inside?" Amanda asked. "It's freezing out here."

They went upstairs to confer at home. Clarissa and Matt surprised them with a beautifully clean apartment. They'd scrubbed from top to bottom. They must have worked hard—this was the first time Amanda had seen a sheen of sweat on Clarissa's brow (and it looked good on her, too). Matt was mopey as he held a broom. Amanda hugged both of them in thanks.

Clarissa said, "We couldn't help overhearing your conversation on the street."

"Not with our heads out the front window," added Matt.

The sisters were led by Matt into the kitchen (sparkling, shiny, and smelling of bleach) and they sat down at the nicely loaded table (hot tomato soup and grilled cheese sandwiches). Amanda wanted to ask Matt about selling the coffee to Patsie. But she'd been so battered already. And why should she expect anything but lies from him? After a lifetime of trusting strangers, friends, lovers, anyone who seemed kind, Amanda realized that the only person she could really count on was her sister. Instead of loneliness at the thought, Amanda felt a reassuring calm. Funneling her trust into one person—her family—had more kick than the diffuse, free-floating goodwill she'd spread around the cosmos. Focus fortified her. If she'd been searching for direction, she now had it: her new life goal, one notch above finding a soul mate, was Frank's happiness and stability.

While Frank went into her bedroom to call Bernie Zigler, Amanda enjoyed some lunch. She said to Matt and Clarissa, "Thanks for cleaning up. I wish I could believe you had honorable intentions, but it's more likely both of you acted out of guilt, not kindness."

Frank came into the kitchen. Her face told the story of her phone call. "We have bigger sharks to skewer, Amanda," said Frank. "I think Zigler is in on this deal. He was so unctuous in his apology. 'How could I forget to discuss this with you?' he said. I hate him. And, of course, Todd will have to be killed."

"I'll have to dig up my arsenic and old lace," said Amanda.

"I'm serious."

"You don't have to kill him." The sisters turned to face Matt, still holding his broom. "You just have to pay him," he said. A fine assessment of the obvious-yet-impossible, thought Amanda.

"You stole from us," Frank said.

Matt put a finger to his chest. "Me?"

"You sold Patsie the baker some coffee beans you found in our basement," she explained. "If that bag was in our basement, it was our property."

"Chick left the beans in the basement. I sold them to Patsie before I knew you had any interest in them."

"You could have said something."

"You didn't ask," he responded.

Frank pursed her lips. "If you knew Patsie already, why did you bash him on the head when Amanda came down the basement steps?"

Matt stammered. "He grabbed her."

"So?" Frank asked.

"Just because you've done business with a guy doesn't mean he's not a rapist. He grabbed Amanda; she was screaming. I picked up the first heavy object I could get my hands on and clobbered him. I worked on instinct, Francesca. I let my natural urges guide me."

Frank stared at him blankly. Amanda was a bit flattered that Matt was so protective of her, even if she hadn't been in any real danger.

He plucked the rubber gloves off his fingers. "Amanda, let's take a walk. I know when I'm not appreciated." He glared at Frank. She scrunched her eyebrows at him.

Amanda wanted to stay with her sister, but Frank said, "Go ahead. If Matt's instinctive natural urges are guiding him outside, who am I to stand in his way?"

"I'm surprised you can be so flip at a time like this, Francesca," said Clarissa, leaning against the fridge. "You're about to lose everything. Your store. Your self-respect."

"Yes, I've lost a lot. Only my virginity and my sense of humor left," said Frank.

Clarissa gasped. "You're a virgin?"

"So much for my sense of humor."

The phone rang. Amanda reached to pick up the receiver, but Frank waved her off, saying, "Let the machine get it."

The answering machine picked up after the third ring. The four people in the kitchen waited patiently. Finally a voice came over the speaker: "Francesca, it's Walter." Someone gasped. Amanda assumed it was her, but she wasn't sure. Frank stared at the wall inscrutably. The message continued: "If you're there, please pick up. Okay, I don't blame you for screening. And you'll probably never speak to me again. But you have to know the truth. I didn't write that story. Piper Zorn wrote it and put my name on it. He badgered me into telling him about our date. I admit that I went out with you for information, but after we . . . after I got to talk to you, I knew I couldn't stay on the story. Zorn threatened to fire me if I didn't tell him what we talked about. So I told him. I assumed he knew. He seemed to know everything else about you. I can't tell you how sorry I am. I'm humble and groveling. I'm sure you never want to talk to me again. But please reconsider. I really care about you, Francesca. I had a great time last night. I want to see you. You've got to give me another chance. I'll call back later. I'll call back every day if I have to." *Click.*

Amanda studied Frank carefully. She tried to pick up on her sister's vibe. What would she do? Amanda suspected Frank would blow him off. That was probably a good idea: he was tainted. Frank must have felt the six eyes on her. This moment, suspended almost, was heavy, palpable.

"How's it feel to be a player?" Clarissa asked Frank.

Amanda thought that was an astute question. Frank was usually an observer, a witness, in life. But this moment was all about her. She was the main character in a romantic drama. And from all appearances—she wasn't wet eyed or flushed or jittery—Frank was coping.

Frank said, "To forgive is to let go. So I think I'll hate him forever. That way I get to keep him."

Amanda said, "Forgiving gradually might be wiser."

"You and Matt were going to take a walk?" asked Frank.

When they got outside, Matt asked Amanda, "You think she'll call him?"

Amanda hoped she wouldn't. "I have no intention of discussing personal matters with a deceiver like you."

"Oh, come on, Amanda. I totally forgot about those coffee beans. I don't like it that you don't trust me. I want you to have faith in me."

She said, "How much did you get for the bag of beans?"

"Ten bucks."

"You could have gotten more," she said.

"I don't need more," he said. They were walking across Montague Street as they talked. Once they'd stepped up on the curb, Matt said, "Here we are."

"The Olive Vine?" asked Amanda. "You crave olives?" They stood in front of the tiny specialty store that fulfilled Brooklyn Heights' olive, olive oil, and olive paste needs. There was also a Western Union wire in back.

The owner, Mrs. Vitz, couldn't be a fan of the *Post*. Amanda accepted her warm greeting, her fat, dangly upper arms encircling Amanda's neck, cutting off the precious flow of oxygen to her brain. Amanda loved physical affection. She was practically the Queen of Hug. But when Mrs. Vitz enveloped her with her olive smell, Amanda cringed. "Hello, Mrs. Vitz," she said warmly. "How are you today?"

"It's Monday," she griped. "How should I feel?"

"Happy?" Amanda tried.

"Happy? Feh!"

"I bet you could tell me stories."

"Don't get me started."

Matt said, "What the hell is that?" He was pointing at a twenty-gallon vat, filled to the top with olive oil and giant green olives the size of plums.

"Harvested by hundred-year-old farmers in a remote island—not bigger than a square mile—off the coast of Greece," said Mrs. Vitz. "So luscious, so tasty, after you have one, you can never go back."

"How much?" he asked.

"Thirty dollars a pound."

Matt whistled. "That's outrageous."

Amanda explained, "If you love olives, price is no object."

Mrs. Vitz pinched her cheek. "Sweetie," she said, and then squeezed the stuffing out of Amanda again. "Such a pretty face."

Matt said, "I'm expecting a telegram from Texas. For a Matthew Schemerhorn."

Mrs. Vitz examined Matt anew. "Do you have verification, young man?" she asked. Matt took out his wallet. The two of them pored over his identification material,

and Amanda drifted toward the back of the store to look
at the calamatas. She popped a black Italian olive in her
mouth. Her tongue depitted the black fruit. She spit the
stone into her hand and put it in the pocket of her pea
coat. When she turned back toward Mrs. Vitz, the olive
lady was handing a yellow telegram to Matt. He said to
Amanda, "We're done here."

The puzzled younger sister said good-bye to Mrs. Vitz
and submitted to another rib-crushing hug. Once outside
she said, "So, Mr. Schemerhorn. Telegram from the underground? Is it anarchy yet?"

"What would you say if I told you I come from a
Texas oil family that's got more money than God, but
has alienated me with their extravagance and Southern-
fried racism?"

"You don't have a Texas accent."

"I'm going to bail you out, Amanda," he said, glinty
eyed. "I'm going to save your sorry-ass store, perpetuate
your dream, and help you get revenge on the people
who've fucked with you. This telegram"—he waved the
yellow paper in the wind—"is confirmation that eighty
thousand dollars has been wired to your checking account
from my dad's bank in Dallas. I got your account number
from your checkbook last night. I couldn't sleep. Your sister is very loud when she has sex."

"You went through my purse?"

"I didn't find any birth control." He smiled sheepishly.
"Much to my disappointment."

"I cannot believe you!"

"I thought about giving you money last night, but after
I heard what that dwarf Phearson was up to, I called Dad

right away. First time we've spoken in months." Matt beamed at Amanda. "I'm going to be your savior. What do you say to that?"

Amanda said, "I'm still not over the invasion of privacy."

"It's not worth eighty thousand dollars?"

She considered this. "You're not *giving* us this money."

Matt said, "If I agreed to waive any kind of partnership, would you accept it?"

"No," said Amanda. "I wouldn't understand why you're doing it, and I'd feel awkward."

He said, "What if I told you I was doing it because I can?"

"I wouldn't believe you."

"Or that it's because I respect what you're trying to do?"

"I already know that's not true."

Amanda had to admit, the fact that he had money made him more interesting to her. She wondered if, in five years, Matt would be running the family oil business and laughing about his years as an anarchist graffiti artist. She liked the image. She found it sexy, even. Amanda had always liked Matt. She knew he was part of her destiny when he'd walked into the store for a job and fit the jeans. She said, "Just how much money does your family have?"

"Eight hundred million. At last count."

The sound of that amount was like Cupid's arrow to Amanda's heart. "Your money makes you sexy."

"I would hate to think you found me attractive for my money only. But I won't hate it too much."

"I still can't accept it," she said. Amanda didn't see how she could. She'd known Matt for only a couple of weeks. He could be tricking them, too, the way Todd had tricked her parents. Besides, the last week had saddled her with a moral debt to Chick and a financial debt to Todd. However attractive Matt seemed in his loadedness, Amanda didn't want to owe anyone anything for a while. At least until she'd cleaned her slate.

"I see how much you want to help," she said, "but I can't trade one debt for another. And yours would be bigger."

Matt said, "You want the truth? Fine. I do have a selfish motive in making this loan. I told my dad on the phone that I wanted the money to invest in a small business. He always wanted me to take over his company, and I told him that this smaller project would be a trial. He could see if I had the right stuff. If this business succeeds, I'll go home and work for him. If it flops, he'll agree that I'm not cut out for his world, sign over my trust fund, and let me pursue my own goals. I'm giving you this money so you'll fall on your ass within a year, and then my dad will cut me loose from his golden suspenders, and sign over the three point four million I've got coming to me from dear old dead Granny."

"And with that money you'll lead the revolution?" asked Amanda. He was just as greedy as the rest of them.

"I'd do something better than buy Porsches and herds of cattle for slaughter."

"And this money has absolutely nothing to do with how much you want me?" she asked.

He blushed. "I'm not trying to buy you."

Amanda believed him. "Did you love your grand-mother?" she asked.

He was confused by that, but admitted, "Yeah. I really did."

"Do I have to promise that we'll fail?"

"On that score, I won't need a verbal guarantee."

Amanda held out her hand. "Then I accept."

○○○○○○

19

Frank watched Clarissa fuss with her hair, her nails, her clothes. Being alone with Frank was making Clarissa uncomfortable. Guilt did mess with one's composure. Despite the fact that the blonde deserved a taste of emotional distress, Frank took little satisfaction in feeding it to her. Expose the most popular girl in the cafeteria—not as clever or as formidable as she seemed—and you're left with hair, nails, and clothes to pin on the paper doll.

Frank said, "I'm going to take a cue from Amanda and forgive you for everything. I don't hate you. If anything, I pity you."

"You pity *me?*" asked Clarissa.

Frank said, "I'm happy and relieved to say that I do."

Clarissa asked, "And why's that?"

How could Frank explain? Her attraction to Clarissa had been baseless. She'd believed Clarissa held powers she lacked, as if a friendship with this dazzling creature would fortify her drab self and fill her up with things she never had. A vain bit of foolishness, Frank knew. But how sad for Clarissa: Had anyone been genuinely interested in Clarissa for herself? Frank, in her own fumbling, awkward way, had tried to use Clarissa; she never really cared for or about her. No sense in lingering on her own bad behavior, though. Frank had paid her price. A high one. Clarissa didn't appear to mourn any loss at all. Not even of her own myth.

"Why do I pity you?" asked Frank. Because Clarissa had no apparent feelings besides guilt. Because she operated out of pure self-interest and therefore had to be lonely and disconnected—and she didn't seem to know it. Even after she'd been lied to repeatedly by Piper, she still thought he was her friend.

Clarissa said, "Yes. Tell me."

"I don't know."

The blonde tapped her nails on the kitchen table. Could she be impatient for a character assassination? Frank said, "I think it'd be a good idea for us to move on to a more productive topic."

"For instance?" she asked.

"Redemption."

"Redemption?"

"Yes," said Frank. "How you can make up for the harm you've done. Otherwise—and I'm not a Catholic, so you'll have to help me with the religious connotation— you're going to hell."

The older sister studied Clarissa's reaction. The only moving parts on her face were her poreless pink nostrils. Frank said, "You're not going to cry, are you?" Frank couldn't help marveling at the idea that her words could wound the stone princess.

Clarissa shook her head, "Of course not."

"Your nostrils are fluttering."

"This is very hard for me."

Frank was shocked. "I'm sorry if I upset you. I didn't mean to do that." Maybe Clarissa had remnants of a sympathetic heart after all.

"It's always difficult to talk about money," said Clarissa.

Had the conversation taken a turn? "Now I'm mystified," said Frank.

"You know all the renovations we did before the contest? And the ad in the paper? And the new sign and awning?"

"The ones you told us not to worry about paying for, yes. I remember them." Frank's head began to swell. After what she'd done, Clarissa wouldn't dare ask her for money. "What about redemption?" asked Frank.

Clarissa said, "This isn't funny, Francesca."

"I'm not laughing."

"I put out three thousand dollars."

"I guess you'll have to eat that expense."

The blonde's fluttering nostrils were flaring now like those of a mad cow. "I have no intention of losing that money," she said.

Frank couldn't believe . . . no, scratch that. At this point, she should have expected this from Clarissa. To think that she'd felt sorry for this bloodsucker. Frank said, "In the balance of our debts to each other, I think you're making out pretty well to lose just three thousand dollars."

"I want what's rightfully mine," said Clarissa. Now

that a job at the *Post* was probably remote, Clarissa must
have realized how desperately she needed the money. She
was a student, after all. And Armani didn't come cheap.
Frank sensed that if she were to get additional service
from Clarissa, she should strike now.

"You'll never see a penny," said Frank calmly.
"Unless . . . no, forget it."

"What?" Clarissa asked.

Frank shook her head. "You'd never go for it."

"I might."

Frank had to smile as she reeled in her piranha. "I'll
write you a check right now"—it would bounce from here
to Cleveland—"if you'll perform one last task as chief mar-
keter and head of public relations for Romancing the
Bean." Clarissa pursed her lips skeptically. Frank continued. "I want you to call Piper Zorn and ask him to dig a
bit on Todd Phearson. Titles, mortgages, arrests, blood
tests, DMV, pet registration, fishing license, tax returns,
whatever he can find." The *Post* had unlimited access to
City Hall, the Internet, the IRS. The researchers at the
paper could get information that might be damaging to
Todd. Frank wasn't above blackmail. It was grasping, but
if she didn't grasp, she'd sink.

Clarissa said, "You want me to lie to Piper?"

"As the wheel turns."

"You think this is some kind of soap opera?"

"No, I meant that he lied to you, and now you can lie
to him." Frank wondered again how she could have put
so much faith in Clarissa. She wasn't that smart at all, nor
savvy. Frank had wanted to believe in her so badly—for
the café's sake, as well as her own—that her brain had

edited out the flimsy parts of Clarissa's character, and dwelled on the impressive.

Clarissa said, "Instead of a check, I'd like cash."

"I can pay you fifteen hundred dollars today, the rest next week." Or next lifetime, as Amanda might say.

"Okay, I'll do it," she said, and picked up the kitchen phone to call the *Post*. Clarissa stared at Frank while she said, "Piper, it's Clarissa. Great story by Walter Robbins today. Uh-huh. Yeah. Listen, I have a favor to ask. I'm doing some business with a man out here in Brooklyn. He's been hitting on me. He says he's not married, but I want to be sure. Can you look into that for me? Uh-huh. Yes, he said he's rich, too. And that he has a big car. I know. I know. Uh-huh. Yeah. Yeah. I know. Can't you ask one of those computer guys to do a search on him? Todd Phearson." She spelled it. Correctly. "Lives in Brooklyn Heights. Owns the Heights Cafe. Yeah. Okay. Hold on one second. I have to sneeze."

She cupped the receiver in her palm. "What's our availability?"

Frank said, "We'll go to the bank to get some cash, and then come back. Half an hour. But don't have him call here. We'll call him."

Into the phone, Clarissa said, "I'll call you in half an hour for an update. No, I'm not near a fax. Or a phone. Battery's dead. I'll have to call you." She hung up. To Frank, she said, "He's going to do it. I suppose he feels guilty about playing me. He's really not such a bad guy."

Frank had to pinch her arm to keep from saying anything. She needed to keep Clarissa on somewhat friendly terms until she got the dirt on Todd. After that, Clarissa

would have to be banished. Frank looked at her watch. It
was two o'clock.

"Shall we?" asked Frank. The women put on their
coats and walked outside. The gate was still locked in
front. Frank fought back a sob sound as she thought of
the encounter with Todd earlier. Looking for blackmail
material was a desperate move, but she had to go through
the motions. Fighting a battle wasn't so awful when you
knew the outcome.

People rushed by on the street; the sun was dropping
like a basketball. Everything seemed to be speeding up as
Frank neared the finish of one part of her life. Even
though the end loomed bleakly, Frank couldn't wait to get
there. Amanda would probably call this optimism. Frank
wasn't ready to commit to that.

The two women walked silently all the way to the
Citibank on Montague Street, across from the Rite Aid.
Frank filled out a withdrawal slip and took her place in
the teller line behind a young married couple with a baby
girl in an umbrella stroller. Clarissa waited by the Christ-
mas tree that still stood in the corner of the cavernous
bank (actually, a converted mansion with giant marble columns and a glorious mosaic on the smooth-tiled floor).
The young couple were talking quietly about their plans—
could they afford to stay in the city with the baby? Could
they stand to leave? The unhurried conversation about
their future together disarmed Frank. When she was
twenty-three, Frank assumed she'd have a fantastic career
in publishing and a loving husband, kids by thirty. At
thirty-three, Frank was surprised by her reaction to this
young couple. Instead of envying them, she considered

them bland and ordinary, compromised by their child and each other.

"Next!" called the teller. The couple walked off, clutching their deposit slips and stroller handle.

To herself, Frank said, I wouldn't change places with them. She wouldn't change places with anyone. The pleasant surprise of self-acceptance had come suddenly. When a teller flashed her light and said, "Next!" Frank didn't hear her.

The man behind Frank tapped her on the shoulder. She snapped out of her epiphany-induced freeze and moved forward to take her turn. Frank handed the teller— an elderly black woman—her withdrawal slip and Citicard. The teller punched keys on her computer.

"How would you like this?" she asked.

Frank said, "Fifties and hundreds."

The teller handed Frank her cash and a receipt, saying, "If you'd like to talk to our investment services, you can make an appointment with the rep at the information booth."

"Pardon?" Frank couldn't see the need for investment advice about the six hundred dollars that remained in her account.

"You don't want to let seventy-nine thousand dollars just sit in a checking account, do you?" asked the teller.

Frank said, "There must be some mistake." She glanced at her receipt. Her eyes blinked twice: the remaining balance was $79,343.00.

The teller punched a few more keys. "There was a deposit of eighty thousand dollars made to your account earlier today."

"Oh, yes. I forgot." Frank had no idea what was going on, but if this was a bank error, she certainly didn't want it corrected.

"You forgot about eighty thousand dollars?"

"I'm on medication," Frank said. She leaned forward and whispered, "Prozac." The teller's eyes got wide. Then Frank said, "I'd like a money order for fifty-five thousand dollars, please."

The teller said, "I'll need a photo ID and another withdrawal slip. Also, I think I need to clear an amount that large with the bank manager."

She didn't have a driver's license, and her passport was back at the apartment. She said, "Clear what you need to clear. I'll be back in fifteen minutes with an ID."

"The bank closes in fifteen minutes."

"Shit," Frank said. "Where's a phone?"

○○○○○○

2○

The phone rang and rang in the Greenfield apartment. Amanda didn't hear one ring. She was busy arguing with Matt on the street below.

"I say we take this telegram and shove it up Todd Phearson's dwarf ass," said Matt.

Amanda cringed at the crassness. "I think he'll want a check. Besides, we have to find Frank and tell her about this first."

"So she can make all the important decisions in your life?" he asked. "Why don't you take charge, for once?"

"Frank doesn't make all the important decisions," said Amanda.

"Name one important decision you've made in the last year," he challenged her.

Amanda pulled her pea coat tightly around her body. "Why are we having this conversation in the middle of the street?"

"Trying to change the subject?" he asked. "There's nothing wrong with letting someone else be in change,

Amanda. If you're content to be a subordinate player in your own life. Of course, we're all pawns to the government. I mean on a personal level, between you and Frank."

"And you'd have me roll all over her?" Amanda asked.

"I don't mind the image, but I'm suggesting nothing of the kind. I have given you eighty thousand dollars, and your first instinct is to pass the responsibility off to someone else. When you ever get married, your husband will completely control you while you float about, happy and oblivious, sensing things."

Amanda almost said, "And what's wrong with happy and oblivious?" but she knew what was wrong with it. Look at what happy and oblivious had wrought so far. Matt's vision of Amanda's future—the same picture she'd painted for years, the one that had filled her heart with joy—now sounded tinny and childish. In the cold, visible breath of the moment, Matt had swapped her placid dreams with a void.

She said, "You hurt my feelings."

"I should be able to speak freely and honestly with a friend and business partner," he said. "Silent partner."

"This is silence?" Amanda asked.

"Well, what's your call?" he said. "Where do we go from here? And don't tease me by saying we go to bed."

"Maybe I should look for a husband who would rather be controlled than be controlling."

"I said, 'Don't tease me.' "

Amanda laughed. "To the Heights Cafe."

She wasn't sure she could handle a confrontation with Todd or—worse—Paul McCartney, the bartender. She hadn't seen him since the chase on the promenade. But the freezing air was turning her lips blue under red lipstick, making them look purple (a misery with her pale skin). She had to get out of the cold, and the Heights Cafe was close. Frank wouldn't hesitate when daunted. She even seemed to enjoy facing off with an enemy. Amanda had to admit that Matt was right. She'd passed off the dirty work to Frank consistently and without qualms. The time had come for Amanda to be brave.

As they approached the front door of the restaurant, Amanda breathed deeply—in, out—and willed herself to *be* Frank. What would her sister say? What would she do? Morphing into her sister, in certain situations, could serve her well. Maybe she could incorporate a bit of Frankishness into her very soul. Then she'd never be alone.

Amanda muttered to herself, "I am Frank. I am Frank."

Matt asked, "Are you schizing out on me?"

"Just channeling."

Amanda pushed open the door of the Heights Cafe. Every eye in the bar set upon her skin, lighting it on fire. That was a nice change from frozen, but after an instant Amanda had to take off her coat, fearing that she might spontaneously combust. Todd was nowhere in sight. Matt said, "Let's wait for him."

Amanda nodded and sat on one of the familiar bar stools, draping her coat across her lap. Matt excused himself for a moment. On his way to the bathroom, he directed Amanda's attention toward the kitchen.

Through the circular window of the "in" side of the kitchen's swinging doors, Amanda watched Paul McCartney. He was talking, laughing to someone; she couldn't see who. He pushed back into the bar and pretended not to see Amanda right away.

She said, "Hello, Paul."

He refused to make eye contact. She said more loudly, "How's it going, Paul?"

"You shouldn't be here," said the bartender.

Amanda studied the neon lights, bright and colorful even in the daytime. "I was sitting in this very bar stool. I can't believe it was only three nights ago. Are you going to scream that you hate me again and run away?"

"I'm working," he grunted.

"Then I'll have the usual," she said.

"Kir Royale?" he asked. "Now?"

"What's stopping me? It's not like I've got a store to open." As Paul fixed her cocktail, she said, "How's your wife? The girls?"

Paul put her drink in front of her on a napkin, leaned across the bar, and snagged her wrist in his fist. "Don't you talk about my wife," he said.

Amanda removed his hand, peeling back one finger at a time. She felt jittery, excited. Or was it fear? Did Frank respond this way when she instigated a confrontation? Did she like it? Amanda decided she wasn't sure if "like" was an appropriate assessment, although she could see how conflict could be useful in oxygenating one's skin (her heart was beating wildly). She was also forcing Paul to show another side of himself. In her conflict-free existence, Amanda wondered if she'd been seeing the whole world in just two dimensions (despite her third eye) all along.

"Why did you lie to that *Post* reporter about me?" she asked.

"I haven't lied to anyone," said Paul. "That reporter called me at home, said he was a cop and that if I didn't tell the truth, he was going to bring me in as an accessory to murder. I told him what I knew. He made up every quote of mine. And then I got in trouble with Todd. He didn't like his restaurant's name in the paper, and he was furious at me for talking to a reporter. Your bad date almost got me fired."

So he'd assigned the blame of his misfortune on me, Amanda thought. Of course, if they ever were, they could never be friends again. Her social circle shrank by the minute. At the rate she was going, Frank would be all she had. Maybe Frank *was* all she had.

"Did I miss anything?" asked Matt. Back from the bathroom, he stood at Amanda's side, a protective hand on her shoulder. Would Matt turn out to be a loose connection, too? At least they were bound by money. Bound. That didn't sound voluntary.

Matt looked at Paul (steam rose from the bartender's head at the sight of Matt), and asked, "How's the secret love?"

"Where did this secret love nonsense get started?" demanded Paul.

Amanda said, "Your wife told me."

"Sylvia?"

"Got another wife?" asked Matt.

"I'm so close to punching you," Paul threatened.

Matt laughed at him, but stepped back a bit.

Paul's head steamed a bit more (he could have cooked

an entire bunch of broccoli), but then he simmered off.
He actually sighed. Elbows on the bar, he said, "Sylvia
was upset. She doesn't like it when Todd gets angry at
me. I tried to defend myself, and I might have said that I
felt bad for you, Amanda. Sylvia said, 'You care more
about Amanda Greenfield than you do about Todd.' And—
this was my big mistake, I guess—I agreed. Well, she exploded at that. Ran off with the girls. She came back—I
guess that's when you saw her in our building, Amanda—
packed a suitcase for herself and the girls, and left. I was
supposed to meet her on the promenade to talk the next
day, and you showed up there, too."

"That's why you were trying to avoid me," Amanda
said. If Sylvia saw them together, it would reinforce her
wrong impression. "So you never had a secret love for me
at all?" She was a bit disappointed.

Paul softened. "If it ever crossed my mind, I had no
intention of acting on my attraction."

Matt's protective arm on her shoulder turned into a
steel beam. He said, "Keep it in your pants."

"You keep it in yours."

"Boys!"

To Matt, Paul said, "You have nothing to worry about,
junior. I'm not laying a hand on anyone until my wife
comes home—which should be soon. She's been staying
with her father. And he won't put up with the kids for
too long."

"Her dad lives in the neighborhood?" asked Amanda.

Paul seemed confused. "Of course." Paul twisted his
rag. "You don't know?"

"Know what?"

Paul said, "Why do I work so hard? Why do I put up with so much crap from Todd? Because I like it? I do it because I have to. I'm not going to be openly antagonistic to my father-in-law."

"Todd is Sylvia's father?" Amanda asked. She had no idea Todd had any family at all. Her parents always spoke about him as though he was a lonely, sad man who needed their company. She dredged up a vague memory of her parents discussing his divorce.

"Todd is her father. And I'm the son-in-law who's expected to take over when he retires," Paul said.

A business that would have doubled in size at 5:00 P.M. had Matt not come to the rescue. Amanda said, "Tell me you didn't know about the deal my parents made with Todd."

Paul put his palm on the bar as if it were a pulpit. He said, "I didn't have any idea until day before yesterday. I would have told you. Look, I realize I haven't been treating you well—I've been wrapped up in my own personal nightmare—but I'm sorry about Barney Greenfield's."

"Where is Todd now?" she asked.

Paul said, "I think he went home to shower before the dinner rush."

"Home is?"

"Two fifty-six Hicks." Amanda knew the building on the corner of Hicks and Joralemon. One and a half blocks from Paul's place on Grace Court Alley. And only half a block from Benji's place on Joralemon Street.

Matt helped Amanda put on her coat. Her Kir Royale sat untouched on the bar. She said to Paul, "Drink's on you. You owe me a lot more than that. You could have given me thirty hours' warning about Todd and my café, but you didn't. Why? Greed? Anger? Revenge? All of it makes me sick. We are no longer friends. We'll never be friends again. When I see you on the street, I'll look away. When you try to talk to me, I'll ignore you. I'm not going to forgive you. And I'm not going to forget, either."

Matt and Amanda left quickly. She was shaking from her speech. Matt hustled her along Montague Street, making the turn down Hicks toward Todd's home. Amanda, calmed by the cool air, was able to slow her pulse and deepen her breath. She'd never said such cruel words to anyone before. And she meant it all the way to the marrow of her bones. Despite her shaken limbs, Amanda felt as if she had wrested control. She had taken responsibility, done some dirty work. She felt righteous.

Matt said, "Man, I hope I never do anything to piss you off. It's scary when warm people freeze over."

"Scarier if they never do," Amanda said.

21

No one answered the phone. Frank stood at the pay phone in front of Rite Aid with a stack of withdrawal slips, filling them out one by one. Without the proper papers, Frank couldn't get a money order. The teller told her she could take out up to two thousand dollars in cash without having to produce an ID. That meant twenty-eight slips, which all had to be processed in the next ten minutes.

Clarissa, meanwhile, used the neighboring phone to call the *Post*. She was thrilled with Frank's news of the bank error.

"Does this mean I can have the other fifteen hundred today?" she asked Frank.

Frank nodded. "You can have it after you call Zorn for the information about Todd."

That established, the women left the bank and began their phoning. Frustrated, Frank left an urgent message on the answering machine at home: "Amanda! If you get this in the next ten minutes, get my passport in my night-table drawer and run to the Citibank at the corner of Montague and Clinton!" She slammed down the receiver and ran back to the bank, leaving Clarissa at the phone booth. There were about seven people ahead of her, and only three tellers were open. According to her watch, teller service should close in about five minutes. But since she was already in line, surely they wouldn't turn her away.

Wrong. At precisely three o'clock, the tellers quickly finished with the customers at their windows, and then a bulletproof screen slid down, closing up shop. The three people in front of Frank groaned in unison and walked away, leaving without a fight. Frank continued to stand in line, her twenty-eight slips in hand, and wondered what to do next. She banged on one of the bulletproof metal screens. "Open up! I have a banking emergency!"

Nothing. She ran into the main area of the bank. A security guard was helping the stragglers out. She avoided him and rushed over to the deserted information booth. "I need some service, Goddamn it!" she yelled, her voice bouncing off the marble columns. The bank personnel ignored her. Most of them were snapping their pocketbooks closed or disappearing behind an "employees only" door.

A security guard walked toward Frank. He said, "Ma'am, we're closing up now. You'll have to wait until tomorrow, or conduct your business at the ATM machines."

She said, "You don't understand! I was in line!"

"I'm sorry, but you'll have to leave now."

If she were arrested, she'd never get that money. Frank said, "How much can you withdraw from an ATM?"

"I couldn't say."

Frank ran toward the ATM vestibule. There were ten machines; nine were in use. Frank put her card in the free machine and punched in her PIN, 447463 ("I grind"). She pressed all the appropriate windows. English, get cash, from checking. When asked to specify an amount, Frank typed in $55,000. The machine hummed for a moment, and the screen flashed the message: "The amount is too large. Please enter a smaller amount." Frank tried entering $2,000. She dreaded the prospect of having to withdraw an even smaller amount—that would take forever. But the machine accepted the request, and Frank took her two thousand dollars in cash. The machine asked if she would like to conduct another transaction. She requested another cash withdrawal, same amount. She thought there was a limit, so the withdrawal surprised her.

By the time Clarissa came into the ATM vestibule, Frank had already withdrawn ten thousand dollars. She was running out of room in her pockets for the cash.

Frank said, "Give me your pocketbook."

Clarissa hugged her black nylon tote against her chest. "It's Kate Spade."

"Give me the bag!" Everyone in the vestibule turned to look at the deranged woman. She toned herself down. "I need it for just a few minutes. I'd greatly appreciate it if you'd hand over the fucking bag. Thank you."

Clarissa surrendered her Kate Spade. "There's something you should know, Francesca."

Frank barely heard her. She stuffed the money into the bag and resumed her furious punching. A message on the screen suddenly popped up: "This ATM is out of cash. Please try another."

"Fuck!" Again Frank won the attention of everyone in the vestibule. Frank ran to get in line for another ATM. She impatiently stamped her feet as though she had to use the bathroom.

Clarissa stood next to her. "Francesca, listen to me," she urged. "Piper Zorn has been arrested."

"Glad to hear it," said Frank.

"Don't you want to know why?"

"Why is this line so long?" Frank asked herself out loud. She noticed Clarissa's glare. "What did you get about Todd Phearson?" That would distract her from the wait.

Clarissa said, "You really don't care why Piper was arrested."

"Just give me the Todd Phearson notes, okay? I can only focus on one enemy at a time."

The blonde said, "I had to speak to an intern."

"What did she say?"

"He."

"What did he say?"

Clarissa raised some scribbled Post-it notes to eye level. "Todd Phearson, two fifty-six Hicks Street, Brooklyn; Social Security number 111-09-8444; driver's license number 235-111-222; registered owner of a Toyota Corolla; net income for 1997, sixty thousand dollars."

"Sixty thousand?" Frank said. "That's it? He must have a clever accountant."

Clarissa continued, "Pays alimony to Lucy Phearson of fifty-seven Pineapple Street, Brooklyn. No minor dependents, but he has a daughter named Sylvia McCartney of five Grace Court Alley, and two granddaughters, Tracy and Betina McCartney."

Frank said, "I think I knew he was divorced. Lucy Phearson?"

"Apparently she's a writer of sorts. The intern did an Internet search on her name. She'd posted a few religious poems at some Christian Web sites."

Lucy Phearson couldn't be Lucy the crone, the crazy, Bible-thumping family valuer. She was way too old to be Todd's ex-wife.

Frank stepped forward in line. "You can wait with me to get your money," she said to Clarissa.

The blonde shook her head. "I'll get it another time. I want to go see Piper. He's been taken to two thirty-three Adams Street. That's close to here, right?"

The Brooklyn municipal courts were only a couple blocks away. Frank said, "Make a right, walk to Court Street, and then go across that plaza to the courthouse." Her curiosity finally caught up. "Why did Zorn get arrested?"

"The intern wasn't completely clear on what happened, but allegedly he'd stolen some toxicology reports from Long Island College Hospital on Atlantic Avenue."

Frank's heart sputtered. That woman from the hospital morgue! Frank had completely forgotten the date she'd arranged for Piper when she took the call at his desk. She couldn't keep herself from laughing out loud.

Clarissa said, "I don't think this is very funny, Francesca." Then she removed her wallet and keys from the Kate Spade tote and left.

Frank edged forward in line. She finally got her turn at a different ATM machine, and cleared it out of twelve thousand dollars. She got back in line and repeated this interminable cycle until she'd squeezed fifty-five thousand dollars into Clarissa's bag. It was bulging with the load—Frank figured it weighed about twenty pounds (lots of fifties and twenties). She left the ATM vestibule, confident that no one had been watching her fill the bag with big bucks.

Despite the awkwardness of walking with the equivalent of a house down payment on her shoulder, Frank was awash with a new sense of calm. It was only three forty-five. She had over an hour to walk the few blocks to the Heights Cafe and save the day. She decided to stop in at her apartment first to put on a sweater (the afternoon had grown even colder while she was in the bank), and exchange the tote bag for a duffel.

As she neared her building, she couldn't help notice the police car parked out front. The lights weren't flashing—thank God—which would have made two highly public visits from the authorities in the last few days. She walked up to her apartment door and fumbled with her keys. Before she got a chance to open the door, one of the policemen, a tall, slim man with a mustache and a three-button wool suit and overcoat, approached her.

"Francesca Greenfield?"

"Yes?" she said, clutching the tote close to her body.

"My name is Det. Carlos Luigi. I met your sister the other day."

"When you arrested Benji."

He nodded kindly. "Are you familiar with a man named Piper Zorn?"

"Unfortunately," she said.

The detective said, "We brought him in because he's

been accused of illegally soliciting information about a police investigation from a hospital secretary. But he's confessed to a higher crime. We have reason to believe that you're involved. We'd like you to come with us for questioning."

Frank said, "The woman at the hospital . . . you mean about those reports? I don't know anything."

Detective Luigi blinked. "Zorn confessed to attempted murder."

The bag began to weigh on Frank's shoulder. She wanted to go inside and then get over to the Heights Cafe. She said, "When did this attempted murder take place? I was in my apartment all night. And I have two"—or three, depending on when Walter left—"witnesses who can verify my whereabouts."

The cop nodded. "That sounded very *Columbo*."

Frank smiled. "It's the truth."

"Don't you want to know who Zorn attempted to kill?"

Frank had assumed it was some girlfriend in a domestic disturbance. "I suppose."

"Walter Robbins. He's currently warming a hospital bed with three broken ribs, a broken leg, and a concussion. Zorn confessed to pushing him off a subway platform into an oncoming number 2 train. Mr. Robbins is lucky to be alive."

That couldn't be true. "He called me this morning."

"If he did, he called from Long Island College Hospital. Can you come with me, Ms. Greenfield? We'd like to talk to you about Mr. Robbins."

Frank looked at her watch. It was too close. She had only an hour. "I can't."

"This is a serious crime, Ms. Greenfield."

"I didn't do anything."

"Let's discuss it in my office," he said.

Frank hesitated. Politeness counts, she thought to herself. "I'm sorry, but something has come up. I just can't make it right now."

"I'm not asking you on a date," said the detective. "Get in the car. Now."

22

Two fifty-six Hicks Street was a typical Victorian brown-stone, built sometime at the turn of the century. Atypical of the neighborhood, however, were the heavy, dark curtains that covered all the windows on each floor.

"Maybe the people who live here are light-sensitive," Amanda suggested. "Photophobic."

Matt said, "You just made up that word."

"I did not." Actually, she wasn't sure.

"They're not light-sensitive," he said. "They don't want anyone knowing their business."

Amanda buzzed Todd Phearson's first-floor apartment. A woman's voice crackled over the intercom. "Hello?" It sounded like Sylvia, but Amanda wasn't sure. They'd spoken only briefly.

"Hello. It's Amanda Greenfield. I'm here to see Todd Phearson."

Static. It had to be Sylvia. She must hate me, thought Amanda. She wondered if Paul had called ahead to warn his wife and father-in-law. No matter. A warning wouldn't have done much good. Todd had to see Amanda. It was about money. As for Sylvia, it wasn't Amanda's responsibility to make her understand the truth about her friendship—now over—with Paul. Amanda buzzed again. The intercom said, "Amanda?" It was Todd. "This isn't the time and place to do business."

"I've got the money, Todd. All fifty-five thousand."

The door lock released. Matt pushed it open and stepped aside to let Amanda enter first. It was very gallant of him. Todd was standing inside his apartment, the door opened just a wedge. He nodded and said, "Amanda." She introduced Matt as her partner. Todd nodded at him.

"May we come in?" she asked, looking down at their reluctant host's scalp.

"This is very unseemly. I don't know this man. He could be dangerous," said Todd. To Matt, he asked, "Are you carrying a gun?"

Amanda said, "He's just glad to see you."

Matt said, "Why do you assume I'm dangerous? Because of the way I look? Too scruffy around the edges for a man of your distinction? Who'd have thought that someone who dresses like you would be a thief and an extortionist?"

"I resent—"

Amanda said, "Do you want your money or not?"

"Of course I want my money," he said.

"May we come in?" Amanda asked again.

Grudgingly he stepped back and let them enter. The decoration in Todd's apartment fit the era. He'd painted the walls pastel green. The couches (three in the front room of the huge parlor-level floor) were all covered with heavy brocade fabric. The legs of the couches had lion's paws, like a bathtub, as did the cedar coffee table. The Oriental rug on the floor was magnificent—hand-stitched, at least fifteen feet long and ten feet wide. The colors— burgundy, brown, dark green—were too somber for Amanda's taste, but it was undeniably authentic, must have cost him twenty thousand dollars. Amanda wondered if her parents had ever seen this place. She knew they'd have hated the overdone opulence. Matt seemed turned off, too.

Amanda said, "Sumptuous rug, Todd."

"It'd be a lot nicer if the dog hadn't peed on it." Suddenly a little Jack Russell terrier came bounding toward them from the back of the apartment. He ran right up to Amanda. Dogs loved her. Animals communed with her on a cosmic level.

She said, "Hello, lamb chop," and bent down to let the dog sniff her hand. He sniffed, flexed his lip muscles, and then snapped at her. Luckily Amanda's reflexes hadn't been frozen in the cold, and she yanked her hand away just in time.

"It's my daughter's dog," Todd said, as if that explained its actions. Amanda flashed to her run-in with Sylvia in her lobby. That's right: she knew she'd seen this dog before. Todd yelled, "Sylvia! Restrain your cur."

Skittish, dirty-blond Sylvia appeared instantly from the hallway, as if she'd been lurking there, eavesdropping. Amanda smiled brightly at her. She'd been as much a victim as anyone.

Amanda said, "It's nice to see you again."

Sylvia said, "Come on, Rover." Completely ignoring

Amanda's greeting, she snagged her pooch of the flying jowls by the collar and scurried back into the hall with him.

"Now," Todd said, sitting down on his plushest couch. His feet dangled off the edge. "The money?"

Amanda handed Todd the yellow telegram. He said, "What's this?" He read it. "That's very exciting. Congratulations, Amanda. You'll have something to fall back on. I told you I wanted cash. This slip of paper proves nothing."

"It's after banking hours," said Amanda. "I'll write you a check."

He shook his balding head. "Cash or nothing, Amanda." He slid off the couch onto his tiny feet. "You must think I'm a complete idiot. That you can come to my house, say you have the money, and offer to write a check? I don't believe this hoax. And I don't have time for nonsense. I'll be at the Heights Cafe in an hour. If you have the money, as you claim, bring it—in cash—to the restaurant. I'll even give you until five-thirty. And I'll bet free dinners for everyone in the neighborhood that you won't make it."

Amanda's stomach sank to her ankles. She breathed in, out, in, out, fighting to retain composure. She said, "Dinner for everyone in the neighborhood. You're on."

Matt and Amanda left. She had no idea what to do. It was well after 3:00 P.M.; the banks were closed. Would they have time to withdraw thousands and thousands of dollars at an ATM? Did ATMs have that much money in their slots? Matt said, "There're a Citibank and a Chase by the Rite Aid. In the two banks, there must be fifteen ATMs."

Amanda and Matt ran toward bank row on Montague Street. The air temperature must have dropped five degrees in the last fifteen minutes. Amanda's fingers stiffened in her coat. They arrived at the Chase branch at just after 3:45.

"We should go to the Citibank so I don't have to pay an additional fee of a dollar-fifty per transaction," said Amanda.

Matt said, "Just get in there."

After waiting about five minutes in line, Amanda took her turn at an ATM and frantically punched her PIN number, 424464 ("I Ching"). She requested a cash withdrawal of five hundred dollars.

Matt said, "What are you doing? Ask for five thousand."

Amanda added a zero to her request, and they waited. A message appeared on the screen, instructing them that they couldn't take out more than two thousand dollars at a time. Amanda altered her request, and the money came spilling out of the cash slot. She was dazzled to see so much green, all in crisp new hundred-dollar bills. She put the money in her pocket and tore out the receipt. She handed it to Matt and began punching numbers again.

Matt said, "Something's wrong."

"What?"

"This receipt says the balance is only nineteen thousand dollars!"

"That's impossible." Amanda punched the touch screen to get information. Sure enough, she saw the record of the day's transactions, from the wire of eighty thousand dollars, to the dozens of ATM withdrawals of two thousand dollars apiece.

"Frank's been here. She's got the money. We have to find her," said Amanda. "She must be on her way to see Todd." Had they passed Frank on the street? What was going on? How did Frank know about the deposit? This was an unorganized mess.

"Should I redeposit this money?" Amanda asked of the two thousand dollars in her pocket. She turned nervously to the half-dozen people standing in line in the maze of metal bars.

"Hold on it. We may need mad money," said Matt. "You think Frank's at the Heights Cafe?" His voice was shaky. For all his apparent disinterest, Matt was nervous about his money.

Amanda gave him a quick hug. "Don't worry. I'm sure Frank has the money. It's in safe hands. She's probably giving it to Todd right now."

"No, she's not," said a loud voice behind them. Amanda turned to see who was speaking, and was shocked to see Sylvia McCartney standing at the head of the ATM maze, holding a sharp, foot-long butcher knife in one hand, the dog's leash in the other. Rover, sensing the energy of the moment (or keeping up appearances), snarled.

The half-dozen people who'd been in line, and the three people currently using ATMs, assessed the situation, and decided it'd be prudent to vanish. Once they'd hustled themselves out of the vestibule, Sylvia jammed the bank door from the inside. The three of them—Amanda, Matt, and Sylvia, oh, make that four, counting Rover—were now alone.

Matt said, "Maybe we should have gone to Citibank."

23

With the Kate Spade bag bursting with greenbacks, Frank got in the police car and sped to the same Court Street precinct where she'd directed Clarissa not twenty minutes before.

Frank had been in the white-elephant municipal building before, when she'd been called for jury duty. Upon entering and passing through the metal detectors (Detective Luigi and his partner, a larger man with a spotty beard, set off beeps and whistles, which were ignored by the uniformed officer manning the station), Frank was led down a hall and into a small reception area. She was directed to sit at a wooden plank bench against a lime green wall, while the detectives walked through a large oak door marked NO ADMITTANCE.

To her delight (then quickly dismay), Clarissa O'Mac-Flanahagan was seated at the same bench, waiting for her audience with the attempted murderer, Piper Zorn. Frank thought she looked ludicrously out of place with her faux fur and perfectly disarranged hair.

Clarissa stood and gave Frank a tight embrace. "Francesca, I'm so glad you're here," she said. "They've refused to let me see Piper. And they've been making me sit out here for hours." More like thirty minutes. "I can't bear to suffer this kind of treatment."

"It's downright criminal."

"It is."

They sat. Frank clutched the Kate Spade tote against her chest. Clarissa asked, "Is the money inside there? All fifty-five thousand?"

Frank nodded. "I'm not very comfortable carrying this much cash with so many lawyers, jurors, and cops around, to say nothing of the indicted."

"Did you take out my fifteen hundred?"

Frank nodded. She'd taken out an additional two thousand dollars for emergencies. She reached into the bag and counted out Clarissa's remaining payment. She handed it to the comely blonde, satisfied that she was officially free of Clarissa.

"Thanks," said the blonde, folding the bills into a wad and stuffing them into her coat pocket. "That bag costs three hundred dollars."

Frank peeled off another three bills for Clarissa. "We're square now. I guess we have no reason to stay in contact." She was relieved to say it.

Clarissa tightened her frosty lips and said, "We don't. But do me one favor: tell Amanda I'll call her next week."

Frank would do nothing of the kind. She didn't think Clarissa would actually call anyway. And Amanda wouldn't dare make plans with her. "I'd be happy to pass on the message," she said to end the conversation.

The large oak door opened a crack. Detective Luigi's mustache, and then the rest of his face, peeked out of the wedge of space. "Ms. Greenfield. Please come in."

Frank stood and walked through the door. She was suddenly bombarded with noise. The level of activity and randomness reminded Frank of the *Post* offices, with men in and out of uniform talking, answering phones, waving files of papers all over the place. Blinking computers, gun holsters, and guns were everywhere. The detective asked her to sit at a large oak desk in the rear of the room. He asked her if she'd like some coffee. "What do you have?" she asked.

"Burned and not quite burned," he said.

"I'll try the latter," she answered.

The detective asked, "Why are you carrying around a pocketbook full of cash?"

"This looks a bit suspicious, doesn't it?"

"I'll let you think of an answer while I get your coffee."

Instead, while she waited, her thoughts turned to Walter. So he was in the hospital. He'd called her from his bed to beg forgiveness. Amanda, with this knowledge, would probably be at the hospital by now, soaking his sterile white sheets with her globular tears.

The detective returned with a full Styrofoam cup—porous and gritty, it was possibly the worst vessel for coffee. Frank dared to take a sip. Canned, of course, and unpalatable. A steady diet of this charred fluid would destroy anyone's taste for coffee. "As I mentioned on the street," said Frank, "I've done nothing wrong, and I have an urgent appointment at five o'clock."

"Making a drop?"

"Yes, actually."

He said, "Not even curious why Mr. Zorn tried to murder your lover?"

Frank leveled her brown eyes at him. "Walter Robbins is not my lover."

Detective Luigi picked up a sheet of yellow paper off his desk. It was covered with chicken scratch. Frank had been able to decipher some of it: she knew it was a signed confession from Piper Zorn. "May I read some of this to you?" he asked. Frank nodded. Whatever would speed this up. "You know what I think? You're a lot more interested than you're acting. You really do care about Walter Robbins—a lot—and you're pretending not to as self-preservation."

"A police detective and a psychologist," Frank said. "To be honest, I'm too distracted to let myself care right now. I'm a linear thinker—I'm not entirely sure my right-and left-brain hemispheres are connected neurologically at all—unusual for a woman, I know. I've got important business to attend to, as I've already said. Once that's concluded, I'll cry and cry and cry about Walter. So if you'll skip the analysis, we can get through what needs to be done here and I can go."

The detective said, "Would you verify some facts?"

Frank tapped her fingers on the Kate Spade bag. "My pleasure."

"Zorn claims to have met Robbins outside the Romancing the Bean coffee bar at two-thirty this morning," said the detective while consulting the sworn statement. "The purpose of the meeting was for Robbins to divulge any and all information he'd learned about you, Ms. Greenfield, to use in a newspaper article. Zorn wanted bank records, diary entries. The plan was for Robbins to steal documents from your apartment. Zorn would photograph the papers, and then Robbins would return the documents as soon as he could so you'd never miss them. Robbins met Zorn as planned, but instead of bringing materials, he told Zorn he was out. He didn't want to do the story anymore. He'd quit his job if he had to. Zorn pressed Robbins for information and some was exchanged, but not enough. Zorn was furious. Robbins walked toward the subway. Zorn followed him. They argued onto the subway platform. Robbins threatened to discuss Zorn's inappropriate methods with the paper's managing editor. Zorn was so enraged that he pushed Robbins off the platform. He said he didn't realize the train was coming. The train conductor saw him and pulled the emergency break. That's why Robbins is alive."

Walter wanted to quit his job for me? thought Frank. "Could Piper get the death penalty for this?" she asked.

"Not for attempted murder," said the detective. "And Zorn seems contrite. I've never seen a grown man bawl so hard."

"I'm sorry, but I can't verify the time Walter left our apartment. He did tell Zorn some things I'd told him in confidence, but I doubt Walter stole anything. You have the article from the *Post* this morning?" Detective Luigi nodded. "The byline is Walter's, but Zorn wrote it."

"We know that already. Robbins was in no condition to write anything this morning." The detective rubbed under his mustache for a few seconds while Frank sat motionlessly. He said, "You're a peculiar woman, Ms. Greenfield."

"May I go now?"

Detective Luigi said, "I have to admit that I was hoping you'd want to press charges against Mr. Zorn for slander."

"Is that option closed if I leave now?"

"No," he said. "Zorn had it out for you. I'd like to know why."

"Have you asked him?"

"Not yet."

"He'd know better than I would," she said and stood. She checked her watch: 4:45. "I really have to leave."

The detective nodded slowly, stroking his mustache. "We'll be in touch. And be careful with all that money."

Frank ran out of the building, passing Clarissa on the way without saying a word, and rushed up Montague Street toward the Heights Cafe. As she ran, frosty air filled her lungs.

Walter cared, she thought. He genuinely cared.

24

Amanda reached out to clasp Matt's hand. It was warm, but not clammy. "You're remarkably dry," she whispered to him.

She couldn't say the same for herself. A flop sweat caused a string of beads to sprout across her forehead. The knife in Sylvia's hand gleamed, as if she'd scrubbed it clean with a steel-wool pad before coming after them. Amanda assumed she'd gotten the restaurant-quality knife at the Heights Cafe—it was too large and sharp for home use. If Sylvia had picked up that knife at the restaurant on her way over here, she would have seen Frank. Where was her sister? Amanda wondered. Where was the money?

Matt whispered, "I can take her."

Amanda wasn't so sure. Matt might be scrappy, but Sylvia had the glimmer of desperation and dementia in her gray eyes. The restrained terrier, Rover, tugged menacingly against his leash. For a medium-size woman and a small dog, they were an intimidating, even gruesome twosome.

"Sylvia, deep in your heart you know Paul doesn't really love me. You're the mother of his children," Amanda said.

"Yeah, think of the children," added Matt.

Sylvia walked through the maze toward the cowering couple. She said, "I'm going to think of myself for once."

"But Paul doesn't love me!" repeated Amanda. "He might be attracted to me in a base, hormonal way, but his heart is all yours."

The blond knife-wielder asked, "You think this is about my husband?"

Amanda nodded. "What else?"

"I can't let you pay back my father. I've been waiting patiently for over a year now. I want that store. It belongs to me. I deserve it, and no one is going to keep me from getting it."

Her father was giving her the store? Amanda was surprised. She'd naturally assumed Todd would sell the place and make a mountain of profit for his fifty-thousand-dollar investment. "A café of your own?" Amanda asked.

"I couldn't care less about coffee. As of five-thirty tonight, I'll be the owner of Sylvia's Jewelry Nook, located on the former site of Barney Greenfield's coffee bar."

"You're a designer?" asked Amanda, trying to soothe her.

Didn't work. Sylvia waved the massive knife as though she were testing the thickness of the air. She said, "Nobody moves for another forty-five minutes. Both of you! Sit!"

No one sat, except Rover. If Amanda were to be a woman of action, this was the time. How could she extricate herself? *Throw something.* The two thousand dollars in her pocket? Amanda closed her eyes and tried to clear her brain to let the ideas come.

Matt said, "Not a good time for a nap, Amanda."

Sylvia leaned against the metal bar of the ATM maze. She said, "It's the perfect time."

Suddenly Matt sprang as if on hind legs and lunged at Sylvia. She flicked her slender wrist. The overhead lighting reflected on the knife blade, momentarily blinding Amanda. When she could see, Matt was on the floor, a seam of blood coloring his cheek red. He touched the wound as he scrambled to his feet. His lunge had accomplished one thing: he was now closer to the door. He fumbled, trying to unlock it. Sylvia was on him in a flash, jabbing him in the leg. He crumpled to the floor.

"Don't push me!" yelled Sylvia. "I've killed one man already, and I'll kill you, too, if you blow this for me."

"I think you've blown things for yourself," said Amanda. "Matt may be seriously hurt. We have to get him to a hospital."

Matt was pale, but he wasn't bleeding too heavily. A woman outside climbed the ramp to the ATM vestibule entrance, found the door locked, and left. Amanda remembered that the doors were tinted on the outside like a two-way mirror. They could see out, but no one could see in. So much for the Good Samaritan escape plan.

"I'm okay, Amanda," said Matt, trying to sit up. "She didn't hit a vein." Dark blood seeped through his jeans. "Or maybe she did." Matt shuddered a bit and then fainted, his head hitting the floor with a thud.

Amanda breathed rapidly in and out. She had to get

Sylvia to drop the knife. *Talk*. Amanda was a good talker. She scrambled for words. "You've killed one man already?" she asked. Not the least inflammatory choice.

"Chick. The Coffee King guy," said Sylvia.

The woman who'd identified Benji in the police lineup said she'd been walking her dog. Sylvia had killed Chick and tried to frame Benji. Just so she could assume ownership of the café? It hardly seemed reward enough. She and Frank had been willing to live and die for the store, but they wouldn't have killed for it. "Chick was harmless," Amanda said, feeling tears in her eyes.

"He was rich. He could have helped you."

"He wasn't rich."

"Everyone in the neighborhood knew about the man with the golden beans."

Quite a turn of events. She'd killed Chick, believing his yarns, only to find out this late in the game that another man had come through with the cash. "Aren't there other storefronts you could rent?" asked Amanda, one eye on Matt to see if she could detect breathing.

"It's not any store; it's *your* store. You Greenfield girls have goaded me my entire life. And now it's my turn to win."

"I don't even know you!" They were close in age, but Amanda was sure no Sylvia Phearson went to the Packer Collegiate Institute, the sisters' private school on Joralemon Street.

Sylvia said, "Every time my dad would come home from an evening at your parents' apartment, I'd get an earful of 'Francesca Greenfield was valedictorian at Packer'; 'Amanda Greenfield makes her own clothes';

'Francesca Greenfield got into Dartmouth'; 'Amanda Greenfield is modeling at Bloomingdale's.' I'd never done anything except graduate public high school and get married to Paul. And Dad doesn't even like Paul."

Her parents had bragged about her to Todd? Bragged about Frank? That was so beautiful it hurt. Amanda couldn't remember her parents telling a single story about Todd's daughter. "You have two beautiful children," said Amanda. She noticed that Matt's head rolled from side to side as she spoke.

"My accomplishments are my kids?" asked Sylvia. "Do you know how insulting that is? You went to college. You had a job in the city. After your parents died, you got to run a store. I've had nothing for myself. Nothing. Not even my husband. I'm a slave to those kids. They own me. I want something to own."

Matt was fully conscious now, inching toward the door. He was behind Sylvia. She wouldn't notice him as long as she was talking to Amanda. "I wish I'd gotten married and had kids," she said.

"No, you don't."

"I do."

"Someone like you could never handle the responsibility."

"I happen to be very responsible." Starting to be, anyway. "As God is my witness," she said. "I will never be flighty again."

Sylvia said, "My mother was right about you Greenfield girls. She knew you were godless creatures."

"I believe in God," said Amanda.

"Mom couldn't stand hearing about you two from Dad either. And I swear, the strain of his expectations of me destroyed their marriage. The fact that she spends more time in your café than she does with her own grandchildren hasn't endeared me to you, either."

"Do I know your mother?"

"You don't even know who she is, do you?"

Matt was inches from the door now. If he could just get a bit closer, a bit higher, he could reach the lock and call for help.

"Who is your mom?" asked Amanda.

"Her name's Lucy Phearson."

Lucy? The crabby old editorial-page writer? Lucy of the light Brazilian roast? Couldn't be. But it was. Sylvia nodded as she watched Amanda. "That's right," said Sylvia. "My daughters think she's a nutcase." The acorn hadn't fallen far from the nutcase tree, thought Amanda.

Rover, who'd been sitting and panting at Sylvia's feet, started barking loudly. He was barking at Matt, now on his knees, struggling again with the door lock. Sylvia screamed and darted toward Matt, but not before he'd swung open the bank door and screamed, "Help! We're being held hostage by a vengeful housewife!"

Matt's body was lying half-in, half-out of the bank door, making it impossible for Sylvia to shut it while holding both the knife and the dog's leash. She dropped the lead and started tugging at Matt's belt to yank him back inside. He grabbed at her knife hand and struggled with her. "Help!" he yelled again. "Manic domestic run amuck!"

Amanda raced to the door to help Matt, but Rover leaped at her leg, sinking his teeth into her pants. She wasn't sure if he'd broken her skin—the adrenaline kept her from feeling pain. She tried to shake off the dog, but had to kick at him with her free foot, yelling, "Off! Off! Get off me, you stupid dog!"

"What is going on here?"

Amanda, Matt, Sylvia, and Rover looked up. It was Frank, holding the bank door wide open, a large black tote bag on her shoulder. Amanda yelled, "Frank, she's got a knife!"

Frank instantly swung her bag at Sylvia. It had to weigh a lot: Sylvia was thrown backward on impact, the knife clattering to the floor at Amanda's feet. She picked it up and bopped the dog on the head with it—he let go and ran whimpering to his fallen human companion.

Matt stood up, favoring the nonstabbed leg, and leaned against the wall. Amanda ran to her sister and enveloped her in a tight hug. Frank asked, "Who's she?" She pointed at Sylvia, who sat on the floor in shock.

Amanda said, "Matt's family is rich and he gave us enough money to save the store. That's Sylvia—Todd's daughter, Paul's wife. She tried to kill Matt and me so she could have the store for herself. And she killed Chick, too, because she thought he had money. But he didn't at all. And Mom and Dad were very proud of us!"

Frank said, "Piper tried to kill Walter. But he's alive and in love with me!"

Amanda said, "That's wonderful!" They hugged. Matt, wanting in on the action, encircled the two women, making it, officially, a group hug. An orgy of hugs. Amanda felt tears welling.

Frank looked at Sylvia and her dog. "I'm not entirely clear who you are. But we have an appointment. You'll have to excuse us. Amanda. Matt. We're off."

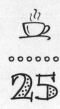

25

Sisters Amanda and Francesca Greenfield sat next to each other on vinyl-covered chairs inside their co-owned Brooklyn Heights café, sipping their coffee and staring at the busy city street. That each sister was pretty would be plainly obvious to any stranger, though both women seemed to share a certain sharpness around their eyes—a curious complement to their smiles.

"What about that one?" asked Amanda, pointing at a man on the street. "Tall, scruffy, yet affable. The beat-up jeans and tattered coat signs of purposefully hidden extreme wealth. Husband potential?"

Frank laughed. "Father material?"

The man in question walked into the Romancing the Bean coffee bar, shivering slightly from the February cold. He approached the sisters at their Formica-topped window table. "Is this how you run a business? Sitting here like lumps? There's work to be done. Get up. I'm serious. Let's move!"

Amanda said, "Shall we snap to?"

Matt Schemerhorn sighed. "I don't know what's happened to me. I've become everything I hate. In two weeks
I've gone from apathetic to apoplectic."

"I liked apathetic better," said Frank. "But since
you're so motivated, why don't you walk the dog?"

Rover, the first official Romancing the Bean mascot,
ran in circles at Frank's feet. When Sylvia had been arrested, the dog became an orphan. Apparently Sylvia's two
daughters and Paul had always hated Rover. Lucy, who
was moving in with her granddaughters (much to Paul's
dismay—karma coming home to roost, Amanda said), had
no intention of cleaning up after the mutt. Todd Phearson
would have been delighted to euthanize the little carpet-
defiler, but Amanda couldn't stand the idea of being the
indirect cause of the animal's death, even though Rover's
bite had left a scar on her leg. So Frank suggested adopting
him. Amanda was shocked by her generosity. Frank
thought it'd be nice to bring another personality into their
lives (what was one more orphan in the household?).
Matt, who'd moved in semipermanently, welcomed the additional male presence, what with both sisters spending so
much time in the bathroom lately, forever experimenting
with that blow dryer.

"Walk the dog?" Matt threw up his hands. "Why do
I have to do everything around here?"

The sisters couldn't help laughing at his distress.
Amanda said, "You're so cute when you're angry." She
stood up and gave Matt a big, tight squeeze and a sloppy
kiss on the lips for good measure. "I'll take Rover for a
walk. A pet is a big responsibility, and, as you both know,
I'm the queen of responsible."

Amanda walked to the back of the store to find the leash. Matt, still recovering from the kiss from his beloved, followed after her as if she had a leash around *his* neck. Frank noticed that Matt's limp improved each day. Rover bounced along at Amanda's heel. Watching the three of them—her freshly expanded family—Frank caught a small sob from escaping her lips.

She'd been crying sporadically over the last couple of weeks, since the horrible day with Sylvia at the bank. The only bright spot of that mad, scrambling Monday was dropping the bundle of cash on Todd's lap, and then informing him that his daughter was a murderer. Frank had been careful to ask for a receipt.

To Frank and Amanda's horror, Todd seemed happier to have his money than he was upset to learn the truth about Sylvia. He insisted that he had no intention of ever giving Sylvia that retail space. He'd just made that promise to shut up her repeated requests.

Todd did make good on his bet to serve the entire neighborhood free dinner that night. As the sisters stuffed their faces, trying to eat Todd out of business, Amanda said, "It's no wonder Sylvia hated her father and herself."

Frank nodded as she scarfed lobster tails (the most expensive item on the menu). "We have to find a new lawyer."

Matt, with a mouthful of meat loaf, said, "My father can give us a referral."

And he did. Pam Schneiderman was a godsend. She came into their lives like a human mop and cleaned up the mess. She dealt with Todd, and she acted as liaison with the police in the as-yet-unresolved Piper Zorn slander

suit (Pam assured the sisters that they could expect a significant punitive settlement with the *Post*). She also brok-
ered a deal with entrepreneur/coffee grower Bert Tierney
in Vietnam and Patsie Strombo to create a line of super-
caffeinated coffee cakes and snacks (final papers still pend-
ing). The samples were still on ice in Patsie's bedroom
freezer. The fledgling partnership/company would go by
the name Chick.

Matt's father, such a nice man, was so taken with
Amanda (what a few phone calls will do—Frank was convinced that her sister could transmit prettiness over phone
lines) that he paid off their remaining mortgage. The sisters now owned the building outright (with a hefty tax
bill to pay next April). Their bag-lady fears were put to
rest—scratch that one off Frank's mental list of anxieties—
and the new relaxed attitude made Romancing the Bean
the café of choice in the neighborhood (Moonburst, under
new management, managed to stay afloat, unfortunately).

Frank wasn't exactly sure when Matt and Amanda
had hooked up. She assumed it was sometime between his
dad paying off their mortgage and Amanda deciding to
take control of her life instead of being swatted about by
external forces. Amanda hadn't mentioned Chick Peterson's name in days. Frank assumed her sister had resolved those issues, and that stirring the pot by bringing
him up would be counterproductive.

For her part, Frank was struggling to regain control
of her wildly leapfrogging feelings. The events of the past
month had served to unplug her emotional cork. The ensu-
ing overflow kept Frank from making even the smallest
decision without being knocked over by a wave of tears,

of joy and pain. She'd had to delegate a lot to Matt. He was understanding. Frank knew this period of loose-cannonness was temporary, that in time she'd be able to feel like a normal person without being bowled over by gladness, sadness, anger or fear. But until then she had to tread lightly or she could make crucial mistakes. Mistakes were not to be tolerated.

"Watch it, Frank. It's that kind of rigidity that got you stuck in your brain in the first place," said Amanda as she walked toward her sister with the dog on a leash. Amanda was wearing Frank's puffy down jacket.

"Reading my thoughts again?" asked Frank. "Why, I oughta—"

"Look at that one," said Amanda, pointing out the window again. "Sculpted cheekbones, sign of obvious intensity and intelligence. Long sideburns show he's a nonconformist, a breaker of rules. The crutches and leg cast—a sign of true dedication to style."

The older sister said, "You don't have to sell me. I know what he is." Frank had to suppress another sob. This was so embarrassing, she thought.

Amanda grinned. "I like you so much better this way. Let's hug."

"Will you leave now?" asked Frank. Matt appeared, all bundled.

"Leaving," said Amanda. She took Matt's hand and they left with Rover. As they exited the café, the handsome man with the long sideburns came in. He smiled at Frank and kissed the top of her head.

"Who do you have to sleep with to get a cup of coffee around here?" he asked.

"How's the leg?" she asked, rising to help him sit.

Walter Robbins sat down in the chair and propped his crutches against the table. "Unemployed."

"Don't you get grumpy on me."

Walter had to laugh. "This coming from the mildly discontented woman I fell in love with?"

"I'll break your other leg," she said as she walked behind the counter and fixed him a cup of hearty Costa Rican. She brought the coffee to Walter. He drank too quickly and burned his tongue.

He said, "Valentine's Day is coming up."

Frank blushed furiously. She realized that this would be the first Valentine's Day in years that she would spend with a man she loved passionately. The thought made her cry—again.

He reached out and rubbed her shoulders. "I'm supposed to ignore that, right?"

"If you don't mind."

"Francesca?" a customer called from across the café. "Should I leave my money on the counter?" She was a regular, the forty-year-old woman with a kind, open face. Frank had had a few chats with her over the last couple weeks, and they were just starting to share some intimate details of their lives. Frank dared to think of it as a blossoming friendship.

"Sure. Thanks."

"I've left you two dollars for the cup," said the customer.

"It's only a dollar fifty," said Frank.

The customer smiled and waved her hands. "Why don't you keep the change?"

Frank said, "I'll do my best."

VALERIE FRANKEL

is a contributing editor to *Mademoiselle*. In her nine years at the magazine, she's written monthly advice columns on love, friendship, and currently, sex. Ms. Frankel has contributed to many other national magazines, written four mystery novels and co-authored three nonfiction books including *The Heartbreak Handbook*. She lives in Brooklyn with her husband and two daughters.